This book is dedicated to my wife, Kathleen,
who has always accepted me "as is."

Acknowledgements

Thanks to all the dealers, collectors and pack rats who make the flea market at Brimfield one of the truly great visceral experiences one can encounter—rich soil in which to plant a multitude of stories, including my own. While I've taken care to depict Brimfield factually, I did take some liberties in the details—length of shows, etc. I hope the colorful environment will ring true to those who have attended in the past, as well as serve as an incentive to those who have never been there, to put on a pair of comfortable shoes and head for the next show at Brimfield.

I also wish to thank the many people who provided support and encouragement including Paul Stevens, Peg Mavilia, Sandi Fossa, John Kiehl, Biff Martin, Richard Emerson, Janet Morris, Ray Rivas, Jeanne Lombardi, Russ Veduccio, Lance Jensen and Jim Reilly. A special thanks to my agent, David Replogle, a strong advocate of this book, as well as my other ongoing writing projects.

"You Know What I'm Saying?" by Irving Feldman, © 1996. First appeared in POETRY and is reprinted by permission of the Editor of POETRY.

We do not live in a world of things
but among benedictions given
and—do you know what I'm saying?—received.

—from *"You Know What I'm Saying?"* by Irving Feldman, © 1996

BRIMFIELD

1

Zoe was not a collector of stuff until her husband died. She had never been one to obsessively amass novelty salt and pepper shakers, woven splint baskets, whale oil lamps, painted pantry boxes, ceramic flower frogs or pine country crickets. To Zoe, vintage clothing was just that, garments of an era gone by. And old china, glass and stemware, chipped or otherwise, were merely objects of a grandmother's dining room cupboard. No, Zoe had always grounded herself in her husband, and possessing each other and the life they shared had always been enough. Memories, merchandise of the heart, were what they had sought together, and they had spent whatever spare time and money they had roaming the surfaces of the earth, both foreign and domestic.

Richard's fifty-six year journey came to end while they were in Rome. It was early in the afternoon and along with a small crowd of fanny-packed tourists, they were quietly admiring Michelangelo's Pietà. Like the millions who had gazed at the statue before him, Richard's heart went out to the sorrowful Virgin holding her dead child in her lap. His pity, like that of all the others, only added to the human power of the two static figures.

While he meditated on her maternal pain, he was interrupted by a familiar shooting sting to his chest and left arm. With the warning of two previous heart attacks he knew what was about to occur, but his knowledge of it could in no way prevent it. Like a pilgrim over-come with emotion, he collapsed in his wife's arms. The weight of the full-figured man forced Zoe to her knees, his head tilting in her lap. As if witnessing a real life Passion Play, the onlookers turned their attention to the two on the floor. Stunned by the full animation of pain, all the viewers could do was watch as Zoe cradled him.

She would never forget how heavy he felt as he lay there as motionless and public as the stone Jesus. Her arms ached with death. Her tears bounced off his marble gray face like raindrops—some of them running down from his own still eyes as if he were crying for her and the void that would be her future. That was two years ago, almost to the day. And although her heart had since scabbed over, the smallest remembrance of Richard could make it bleed again.

—————

"Do you want to bring your cemetery angels? One of them's missing most of a wing, you know." Melissa ran her finger along the weathered break of the marble cherub.

"It doesn't matter," said Zoe. "I'm sure someone there will want them. God knows, angels are hot, broken or not."

Melissa was packing the rust-eaten van with the more fragile contents of their antique shop and as always, she obsessed over what to include. This would be their first trip to Brimfield, the grand dame of outdoor flea markets in the United States, and according to some, the largest in the world. Both of them desperately wanted to do it right and avoid looking like amateurs in the dusty fields of the pros. In fact, financially, they had to do it right. In spite of all the record multi-million-dollar prices being brought for art and antiques at major auction houses, the real antiques business is as drab and secondhand as the average yard sale. There are very few Picassos or Renoirs sitting on the damp, early-morning front lawns of middle America. And neither Melissa nor Zoe had ever found one as they searched through interminable cardboard boxes full of chipped Pyrex baking dishes and oversized, decorative salad forks and spoons. They, like so many dealers, were bottom feeders, hoping to find items old enough to have earned some value, and buy them cheaply enough to make a few dollars in the process. Brimfield offered them the opportunity to do that in bulk.

In the year and a half since they had opened under the name of One Piece Antiques, they had never done a major show. Instead they had focused most of their attention on their shop, located in a small but workable building on Church Street in Noble's Cove. Like any retail establishment, they had their share of good days and bad days. Although the negatives usually outnumbered the positives, they made enough to cover their overhead and take a little home for themselves. When they did exhibit at antique shows, they set up at ladies' clubs and local fund-raisers' shows to display their rather average wares. It was nothing too stressful, and quite gentile. It wasn't too profitable either. Sometimes they barely covered the cost of the booth.

Brimfield, on the other hand, happens three times a year, and is a free-for-all of the desire and chase that characterizes the antiques and collectibles market. For one week in May, July and September, over five thousand dealers set up everything from fine antiques to kitsch collectibles on the open fields in Brimfield, Massachusetts. They turn the cozy, New England white-steepled town into a Walmart of hand-me-downs and attic treasures. During the course of the week, over one hundred thousand people wait anxiously in line to be the first to touch, purchase, and give the artifacts new life, sometimes after centuries of dormancy.

Zoe was just as nervous as Melissa about their first major league show but tried not to show it. While Melissa painstakingly bubble-wrapped virtually everything breakable, Zoe casually loaded the larger pieces—the less-than-perfect country chairs and tables in old paint, objects that could survive another nick without losing any value. With almost disrespect, she placed them in the van. Her haphazard packing did not go unnoticed.

"Zoe," she yelled, "be careful with my hanging cupboard. It's mid-eighteen hundreds."

"I know when it was made," she answered, feigning academic authority, "and it won't look a day younger when we get there."

"I just don't want you to wreck it, that's all. You know how I am about surface."

"I know, Ms. Lipton. That's why you wear so much make-up, right?" she teased.

"Don't be an asshole," she laughed. "My wrinkles have nothing to do with this. Furniture may get more beautiful with age, but people just get old and ugly. So I have to compensate for it, that's all."

"I don't know about that," she said. "Your ex-husband may come to have a new appreciation for you, now that you have some patina."

"Patina?" she said incredulously.

Zoe pushed the robin's egg blue dry sink into the van, scraping it along the side wall as she did. "He might like you better a little rough around the edges. Like this piece of furniture, raw age makes you look a little more sexy. Closer to God, you know?"

Melissa managed a diminutive smile at her remarks, knowing full well that Zoe meant no ill. She just loved to tease her about her on-again, off-again relationship with her ex-husband, Brad. Better known as "Backhoe" Lipton because of the one piece of heavy equipment he owned, he had, through his infidelity, put their marriage into a deep hole five years earlier. The two of them were still trying to find a way to climb out of it and move on again a second time as man and wife. Unfortunately, it seemed that each time they were close to reuniting, an afternoon of boiler makers at the Jack Tar House would get the best of Backhoe, and he would conspicuously park his safety-yellow Caterpillar in front of Sheila Corcoran's beachfront cottage on Sand Eel Road. Because the road itself was as narrow as the sexual views of the residents, his visits never went unnoticed. Melissa's so-called friends were always more than happy to let her know about her ex-husband's trysts.

In spite of his prodigal nature, she wanted him back. Brad was her high school sweetheart and she had no other experience with men. Flawed though he was, she at least felt comfortable with him. That's where her makeup came in. Melissa concluded that men who dig in the dirt all day want to come home to a woman who looks like she didn't, so face paint had become an important facet in her reconciliation strategy.

Aside from the lightest of blush, Zoe very rarely wore much makeup herself, particularly since the loss of her husband. At fifty, she felt no need to make facial excuses and that demeanor alone gave her a natural radiance that belied her years. At five foot ten, she towered over Melissa, and Zoe's body was well toned from the most rudimentary of exercise gadgets. Nothing tightens the thighs, chest and arms like the weight of a country cupboard or mahogany sideboard. Being the larger and more athletic of the two, Zoe always took the heavy end and her body benefited greatly by it. On occasion, she would pick up something so heavy that it reminded her of Italy. Only then would her arms weaken and tremble with the memory of her loss.

By five o'clock the van was full, and a murky Brimfield sky was moving over them towards the west, where they would head at four the next morning.

"We're screwed if it rains," observed Melissa. "We should have rented a tent."

"We'll be okay. Anyway, we can rent one up there in the morning if we need to."

"What if they're out of them?"

"Stop worrying, will you?" said Zoe, imagining the two of them standing mop-headed in the rain. "We'll be fine."

Before they could continue the conversation, their attention turned to a white van pulling into the parking lot next to the shop. Zoe recognized the vehicle immediately by the jagged rusty dent to the right front fender. In the business, it is called a "deductible dent," damage large enough to be noticed but minimal enough that it isn't covered by the insurance deductible. Since most antique dealers learn to live from hand-to-mouth, they also learn to live with their dents.

"It's Elliot Baker," Zoe said with anticipation. "Maybe he's got something for us."

"Something for you is more like it," remarked Melissa. "He's got such a crush on you."

"He's just a lonely guy, that's all." Zoe smiled. "Harmless enough."

The tall, slightly overweight man got out of his van in the same manner as he always did—slowly. While most antique dealers and pickers move quickly and opportunistically, always trying to be first to pick up the obvious item of value, Elliot Baker had always relied on the speed of his eye to spot the less apparent but equally valuable object d' art. In his youth, he had been without peer. But as the years passed, the information readily available in antique price, style and source books made experience virtually obsolete. His competition grew to include almost anyone with an obsession for objects. Too often he would come in second, a mere vulture picking at what little the lions had left.

"Hi ladies," he smiled politely, walking toward them. He combed back his shoulder-length, thick black hair with his left hand, a sign that even though he was over fifty, he still viewed himself as quite virile.

"Hey, Elliot," said Melissa.

The wind at Elliot's back carried the scent of Old Spice toward Zoe while he was still a couple of feet away. His zealous application of it startled her sense of smell. Since her late husband had been allergic to all fragrances, being around men who reeked of men's cologne was unfamiliar and sometimes uncomfortable for her.

Zoe rubbed her nostrils with the top of her forefinger. "Nice to see you, Elliot."

Elliot grinned, and pushed his hair back again. "My pleasure."

Since they had opened their shop, Elliot would stop by every few days to either sell them something he had picked up, or to buy something there that still had "money in it," and could be turned over to some other dealer for a profit.

Zoe eyed the brown lunch bag in his hand, wondering if he had picked up something. "Anything for us today?"

"Just a few pieces of sterling you might like," he answered, lifting the bag slightly toward them. "Nothing special."

Elliot was one of the nomads of the business, a dealer without a shop. He was what they call a "picker," and he was as migratory as those who followed grapes or lettuce. Each morning he would get into his van and drive—some days just around the corner to a local Massachusetts dealer who may have gotten fresh merchandise out of a house. But more often he would head to Maine, New Hampshire and Vermont, to scour the antique shops along the main country routes of the less populated New England states. Because he had no physical place to display his inventory other than his tiny rented house and his van, after a buying trip he would ride from shop to shop to offer what he had found. And because his livelihood depended on turning over the merchandise quickly, his prices always left some margin for the resellers.

Zoe took the rumpled bag from him and removed three unmatched, but boldly embossed, sterling silver serving spoons. Although they were covered with years of tarnish, she knew they would clean up well. "These are wonderful, Elliot," she said, handing them one by one to Melissa for inspection. "Victorian?" she asked tentatively.

"About eighteen-sixty, I'd say," he answered. "Thirty dollars for the three, if you're interested."

Zoe looked over at her partner who nodded with approval. "We'll take them," she said. "I'll polish them tonight, and we'll bring 'em to Brimfield with us tomorrow."

Elliot smiled. "That's right. It's your first Brimfield. Well, you're in for a surprise."

In spite of her solid cosmetic foundation, a pale of apprehension swept across Melissa's face. "What do you mean?"

Remembering Melissa's ability to misconstrue almost anything, Elliot laughed and rephrased his remarks. "What I mean is that it's going to be a wonderful experience for you. It's like no other place in the world."

"Oh." Melissa was relieved.

Elliot looked up at the sky like an antique weatherman and then turned his attention back to the two Brimfield novices. "Did you rent a tent?"

Melissa shot a glance at Zoe. "I told you we should have rented one."

Without acknowledging her scolding, Zoe answered Elliot's question. "No, but I thought we could rent one tomorrow." She hesitated. "Can we?"

"Maybe...but normally you have to rent one in advance."

"Great," Melissa said sarcastically.

"Don't worry about it, Melissa," he said. "Listen, I'm going to be set up on the same field that you're on and I've already rented one. I've got one at home that I can bring up tomorrow in case you get stuck. It's not perfect," he said apologetically, "but it will keep most of your stuff dry."

"That's really nice of you," said Zoe. "Do you want me to pick it up tonight?"

Elliot imagined Zoe coming to his lonely rented house where they would have to sit on the same corduroy couch, the only piece of furniture that wasn't part of his inventory in the two room cottage. His heart beat with anticipation at the thought of the two of them in that vaguely lit room, sipping wine and talking about the business. As he undressed her in his mind, he was suddenly shocked to his senses. The unspeakable pleasure, even the idea of being with Zoe overwhelmed him. "She would never..." he told himself.

Once composed, Elliot turned his attention to their over-crowded van. "You don't have room in there for it," he surmised, wiping off the small beads of sweat breaking out on his fore-head. "I'll just bring it with me."

"Thanks, Elliot." Melissa looked at Zoe. "Next time, we'll be sure to rent one."

"You should," he said, with the wisdom of twenty years of Brimfield under his size forty-two belt. "You can almost always count on rain up there."

"We'll learn," smiled Zoe. "C'mon in the shop and I'll pay you for the spoons."

The three of them went into the compact, freestanding building. Except for a few large pieces of pine furniture and a couple of wicker chairs, the space was empty.

Elliot looked around. "You didn't leave much behind, did you?"

"Only what we couldn't fit," laughed Zoe. "Do you have time for a glass of wine?" she asked, taking three ten dollar bills out of the cash box.

Elliot looked at his watch and thought of his couch. "Just one," he answered.

"Good," she said. "I'd like to pick your brain a little about what we should expect at Brimfield. Neither of us really knows what we're getting into," she blushed with newcomer's embarrassment.

"That's for sure," said Melissa. "I didn't even want to do Brimfield, but she talked me into it."

"You'll be glad she did, Melissa," smiled Elliot. "You'll love it."

One glass of white wine became three as Elliot poured out the story of Brimfield. He gave them a history of the event, describing how it had grown from a casual flea market on a single field to an almost week-long event—a country mile of fields along Route 20, attracting people from all over the United States, Canada, and even Europe. As his imagination grew large from the wine, so did the stories of his exploits and his finds there. He told them of a Grueby Arts and Crafts vase that he had purchased from a Florida dealer for forty dollars and then resold to a dealer from New York an hour later for twenty-two hundred dollars. Then there was the Georgian silver tea tray that he scooped for twelve hundred dollars from a woman from Philadelphia, and resold minutes later for thirty-five hundred.

Real or apocryphal, the stories held the two women spellbound with thoughts of their own windfalls on their first trip to Brimfield.

"However," he warned, "Brimfield is also the easiest place in the world to get burned."

"What do you mean?" asked Melissa.

"The fakes, the forgeries, the misrepresentations," he said with great respect. "They're everywhere. And unfortunately I've bought my share of them and didn't realize it until I got home when it was too late to do anything about it. Once Brimfield is over," he said with finality, "it's over. After that, it's just a bunch of empty fields again. Only the mistakes last."

He proceeded to tell them of the signed Tiffany lamp he bought that turned out to be bogus, and the oil paintings by well-listed artists he had purchased, only to learn later that the signatures were forged. In category after category, he confessed to his own blindness, confessed to the cataracts of greed that make even the wisest, most prudent dealers and collectors throw caution to the wind, even though they know that the treasures they're buying from someone else are probably not what they profess to be. "Brimfield is a one-night stand," he announced, tilting his wine glass as he spoke. "The ultimate one-night stand. Be careful what you fall in love with. It might not be what you think it is."

"I can't believe someone put something over on you," said an astonished Melissa. "You know so much about the business. How could that happen?"

"You'll see for yourself tomorrow," he said. "It's a very seductive place that makes it too easy to think you've found what you're looking for."

Zoe offered the two more wine. Both declined, but she decided on another for herself anyway. "I don't think we have to worry about getting ripped off," she said. "Hopefully, we'll be concentrating on selling what we've got. I don't want to come back with this stuff," she said, staring out the window at the overflowing van. "In fact," she laughed, "I never want to see it again."

"That's exactly how everyone else feels," said Elliot. "They're there to unload, and they never let their scruples get in the way. It's like playing Old Maid...they never let on that you're about to pick just the object they want you to. Once you get it and realize that it's not right, you turn around and try to unload it on someone else. It's endless," he laughed.

For the next few minutes they sat and continued talking until Zoe finished her wine. As if her last sip were his cue, Elliot excused himself, telling them he had to go home and finish packing. He planned to leave by three-thirty in the morning and he wanted to get a good night's sleep so he would be reasonably well rested.

"I'll see you there," he said as he slowly walked out the door and back to his van.

"Thanks for all your advice," said Zoe. "And I'm really glad we'll at least know someone when we get there."

"I'm sure you'll recognize a lot of faces," he promised. "Everyone's going to be there."

"Good night," said Melissa. "And please," she begged, "don't forget the tent."

"I won't." He smiled and looked affectionately at Zoe. "I wouldn't want two of my favorite dealers to get rained out on their maiden voyage to Brimfield."

"Thanks," said Zoe, being careful not to encourage his regard for her. "See you tomorrow."

Zoe drove the short distance from her shop in the center of Noble's Cove to her converted summer cottage, located on a thin peninsula sandwiched by the harbor on one side and the Atlantic on the other. In spite of its opulent views, the house itself, like so many others in Noble's Cove, had begun as nothing more than a makeshift summer place for the lobster-in-the-rough crowd.

In the 1930s, while the wealthy beach enthusiasts from Boston built substantial part-time homes in the towns to the north and south, the tradesmen contingent, those who could do the manual labor themselves, discovered the equally democratic views of Noble's Cove. Like any good squatters, they began with tents. Then came the one room shacks followed by additions and more permanent creature comforts like plumbing and electricity. By the 1950s, Noble's Cove was covered with seasonal homes sporting every zoning violation one could think of. The town fathers, a tolerant group with heavy investments in local waterfront property, merely looked the other way. Over the years many of the architectural aberrations of summer had been winterized and converted to quarters for year-round living.

Zoe and Richard Madden had bought their four room home just four years ago, the same year that their daughter Joanna had graduated from college. Free of children and the financial responsibilities that come with them, they saw no good reason to stay in the more permanent four bedroom cape on a child-safe street on the west side of Noble's Cove, where they had lived for almost twenty years. If Joanna could fly free after graduation, they'd argued to themselves, why shouldn't they? Without hesitation and to the slight consternation of their only child whose bedroom would now be relegated to the living room couch when she returned home for an occasional visit, the couple bought the humble seaside residence even before they sold their own home.

Their first spring and summer there were almost hypnotic with a sense of beginning. The sound of the constant waves, punctuated by gulls, filled Zoe and Richard with hope for the future and a sensuality for the moment. The closeness to the elements brought them even closer to each other, and they made love as often and as spontaneously as newlyweds. They nested like newlyweds as well, playing house with their newfound space. They painted both inside and out, and aside from the naturally stained shingles, everything else was white, light-house white. At the time, Zoe laughed at the confidence of her husband, so sure that the paint they were using would hold up for the ten years guaranteed on the side of can. Little did she know then that the paint on the exterior trim would outlive Richard.

When Zoe got into the house, dusk had almost played itself out. The barely illuminated moon, somehow managing to peek through the keyhole in the clouds, had begun to creep smoothly along the living room floor. Breaking its fluid motion was the blinking red of the "message waiting" beacon on her phone. Ignoring its flashing immediacy, she made her way through the maze of inventory she couldn't fit into the shop. Odd tables, trunks and architectural fragments were scattered along the walls of the living room, and she gingerly avoided them, making her way to the light switch.

As she flipped the switch, her eyes instinctively focused on the far wall of the room where a grouping of twelve, framed letter-size watercolor pictures hung with an almost obsessive precision. They were opaque Italian watercolors, or gouaches, and all of them were scenes of Italy. Some were of festive and everyday street scenes. Others captured the romance and commerce of the canal systems. The most dramatic were those of Vesuvius, some in full eruption.

Italian gouaches first became commercially popular in the last half of the nineteenth century, and many were painted specifically for the tourist trade. For Europeans and Americans alike, they were an inexpensive way to take home an artistic glimpse of Italy. Zoe began collecting them shortly after she returned alone from Italy, and in spite of the pain that surfaced while viewing them, they had an upside as well. Italy had always been her husband's favorite destination. Although he had in no way been a patron of the arts, he had always been in awe of Italy and the spiritual and architectural monuments that were at its very foundation. Luckily, for the most part, Italian gouaches were not in great demand by either dealers or collectors, and she had been able to buy most of them for under a hundred dollars apiece. Although she knew that those purchases verged on extravagance for a widow, she was always looking for more, as if an impossible-to-obtain, complete collection would somehow bring her husband back.

The entranceway to the kitchen was partially blocked by a stack of three cardboard liquor boxes of newspaper-wrapped china and pottery destined for her shop. As she walked by, her knee caught the top box, tumbling it to the floor. Although the crumpled newspapers muffled the breakage like a silencer on a pistol, the damage was still done.

"Shit," she said, picking up six pieces of a McCoy vase. "There goes thirty bucks."

Rather than try to fix it, she threw it unceremoniously into the trash bucket in the kitchen. Then she poured herself a glass of white wine from the refrigerator. "I never liked McCoy anyway," she said out loud as she filled the glass.

As a widow, Zoe often spoke aloud in the house, just to keep the silence from overgrowing her life like some inaudible weed. She also conversed often with the spirit of her deceased husband, and these conversations were as real as if he were sitting in the room with her.

Without giving the broken pottery another thought, she opened the cabinet below the sink and took out a jar of silver polish. Then she carefully removed the three silver serving spoons that she had bought from Elliot and placed them on the kitchen table. She studied each of them and wondered what kind of families they came from, wondered what kind of dinner conversations they had been privy to over the last hundred and thirty years. She began to clean each one, gently stroking the shafts with a soft damp cloth containing a small amount of polish, until the tarnish gave way to the shiny soul underneath. Unlike pottery, Zoe had a fondness for anything silver. Not because of the precious metal that it was, but because she had the godlike power to bring it back to life. Sterling silver is a very forgiving substance and with just a small amount of effort and love, she could make it whole, pure and new again.

Zoe was in the middle of cleaning the grape leaf design of the second spoon when the shrill sound of the phone fractured her thoughtful atmosphere. Perturbed by the interruption, she hastily wiped her stained hands on the thighs of her jeans and picked up the phone by the third ring. "Hello?"

"Didn't you get my message?"

"Oh, hi Jo." Zoe looked at the red button on the phone. "I didn't realize that was you. I didn't bother checking the machine when I got home."

"That's why it's there," scolded her daughter, Joanna. "I need to talk to you."

Zoe knew better than to be alarmed by the urgency in her voice. Everything with Joanna was always an emergency, issues that needed to be dealt with at once, if not sooner.

"What is it?" the mother asked patiently.

"It's that Spanish son of a bitch."

Zoe smiled. "You mean, Ramon, the man you're engaged to?"

"Yeah," she answered disparagingly, "that son of a bitch."

"What is it this time?" laughed Zoe.

"It's not funny, Mom," Joanna said, annoyed by the tone of her mother's voice. Then she hesitated for a moment and spoke quietly and painfully. "I think he's seeing someone else."

Zoe sensed the genuine anguish in her voice and felt badly that she had taken her daughter's initial words so lightly. She picked up the spoon she had been cleaning and rubbed it with the thumb and index finger of her left hand. The natural oils of her skin seemed to work even better than the cloth she had been using, and the gloss began to show through the remaining darkness of the spoon. "What makes you say that, Jo?" she asked sincerely.

"He's been working late almost every night for the last month," she said, as if she had chalked the number of times on the wall of her heart.

"That in itself isn't proof," offered Zoe.

"I know that, Mom. But he's as distant as he is late. So I know something's going on."

"Have you talked to him about it?"

"Of course I have. And of course he denies it. Listen," she continued, "I've got to talk to you about this. Can we have dinner tomorrow night after I get out of work?"

In the midst of her maternal empathy, Zoe was about to agree. Then she remembered her own date with the country's largest flea market. "I can't do it tomorrow night, honey. I'm leaving for Brimfield at four in the morning."

"You mean the big flea market?" She sounded astonished. "You're going to set up at that?"

Zoe knew exactly what her daughter meant. Joanna had often teased her about being nothing more than a junk dealer, reselling items she'd bought at local yard sales. "Yes," she laughed, "Melissa and I are going to leap into the business feet first. Hopefully, we'll come out alive."

Although Joanna had never been to Brimfield herself, she had seen news clips of it on television. All she could think about were the thousands upon thousands of people there, running around like maniacs with no regard for human safety. For a moment, she put aside her own personal concerns while she imagined her mother being trampled in the process. "Be careful, okay? I don't want anything to happen to you."

"I'll be fine...but thanks for thinking of me." Zoe paused for a moment. "How about dinner on Friday night? We'll do it here in town."

"That would be great. Ramon is going out with some friends anyway. Or at least that's what he told me."

"Don't worry about it, okay? We'll figure it out."

"I'll try not to Mom."

After Zoe hung up, she finished the three spoons. She put them in a fresh paper bag and tucked them into the inside pocket of the oversized, beige canvas tote that served as both pocketbook and shopping bag for small antique treasures. It was a gift from her daughter when she opened One Piece Antiques. Joanna, who was never without a briefcase herself, insisted that her mother needed an antique dealer's version of the classic leather millstone of business. The woven casualness of the canvas seemed to fit the occupation perfectly.

Too preoccupied to make time for even the smallest of dinners, Zoe spent the next hour packing backup clothing in a separate, small canvas bag. She wanted to be as prepared for Brimfield as possible—an extra pair of jeans, two sweatshirts, two pairs of wool socks and of course, extra panties, would be in order, she felt. She also decided to pack three bottles of spring water, a pocket-size price book on antique art, and a small magnifying glass for examining signatures. Finally, for good measure, she included an unopened bottle of white wine. Following her husband's death, drinking had become even more important to her than it had been in her marriage. In the midst of all the unknowns of widowhood, knowing where her next bottle of wine would come from became important to Zoe.

By nine-thirty, she had zipped up the bag and was ready for the morning. By then, the clouds had also zipped up the moon and by the looks of it, would keep the sun equally sequestered the next day. Zoe undressed, got into bed, and set the alarm for three-fifteen. As she did, it seemed to set off an alarm in her head. She spent the next two hours imagining Brimfield and the events in her life that would bring her there.

Selling antiques to subsidize her late husband's less-than-adequate estate was the last thing she'd expected to be doing at fifty. Richard had been just four years away from early retirement but, like most men, many years away from true financial security. They had confidently, almost arrogantly, planned to jet around the world after he got his gold watch, just as they had done in the past—to Rome, Tuscany, Paris, Dublin, the Islands.

Brimfield, on the other hand, had never even been a side stop on their itinerary. But with Richard's death came Zoe's need for reminders of their life together. In her constant search for Italian gouaches, she had begun to shop as actively as most collectors and dealers. Ironically, on many of her excursions to yard sales and flea markets, she would bump into Melissa, who was scouring the same territory for sterling silver or silver-plated baby cups. Their shared sense of obsession had led to their partnership in One Piece Antiques.

Staring at a spider crossing the ceiling above her, Zoe thought of how she had become some sort of traveling salesperson. She was headed for Brimfield, as if it had become her territory. She too would show her wares, hoping for enough sales to put food on the table. Then, like so many solitary men and women of the road, she would come home to an empty house.

Just before midnight, she finally felt weary from her mental travels. Like objects in a rear view mirror, her last thoughts of Richard faded behind her half-opened eyes, allowing her lids to close and giving her permission to fall asleep in the arms of their unfinished dreams.

2

The windshield wipers whizzed back and forth like tennis rackets, whacking the balls of rain from the glass almost as fast as the wind could serve them. Melissa, designated driver for the trip to Brimfield, was sandwiched on both sides by get-out-of-my-way tractor trailers. She squirmed in her seat as if she were looking for a sweet spot that would relieve her skittishness.

"I hate these trucks," she said emphatically. "We'll be lucky to make it there alive."

"Just relax," Zoe said, between sips of her black coffee. "They'll be past us in a minute."

Almost on cue both trucks pulled past the van, and their rear wheels rooster-tailed a car-wash size spray on the windshield making it impossible to see.

"Jesus!" Melissa yelled, gripping the steering wheel as hard as she could.

"Just slow down," Zoe said anxiously. "Back off."

Melissa followed the instructions of her copilot, and within seconds the trucks were far enough ahead of them that her visibility returned. As it did, she relaxed her grip and let out a large, long sigh.

"Do you want me to drive? I don't want you to have a nervous breakdown before we get there."

"No, I'm okay now, Zoe. Those trucks just scare the shit out of me. They drive like they own the turnpike."

"Just consider them part of our adventure," smiled Zoe.

Melissa turned the windshield wipers on high. "I wish you hadn't talked me into this. I don't think this rain is going to let up, and I bet you any amount of money Elliot will forget to bring his tent."

Zoe laughed. "No he won't. And stop complaining, will you? I want this to be fun. I think we're going to sell a lot of stuff...I'm looking forward to doing a little buying too." She took another sip of her coffee. "I wouldn't mind finding a couple of nice Italian gouaches to add to my collection," she said wistfully.

For the first time since she got onto the Massachusetts Turnpike, Melissa took her heavily, plum-shadowed eyes off the road and turned her head directly toward her partner and friend. "You know, Zoe," she said thoughtfully, "you've got to let go of Richard and get on with your life."

"What do you mean?" Zoe asked defensively.

"You're carrying this Italy thing too far. Pictures of Mount Vesuvius aren't going to bring him back, no matter how many of them you buy."

"Oh...and what about your little dented baby cups?"

"I haven't bought one in over a year, Zoe. Anyway," she continued, "I think it's time you started thinking about other men. Live men," she added.

"I've had a few dates," Zoe protested. "You know that."

"Those weren't dates," argued Melissa. "Those were dinners with friends. I'm talking about the kind of date where you take someone home with you after dinner."

"Melissa!"

"Don't 'Melissa' me," she laughed. "It wouldn't kill you to unbutton your blouse for someone else, you know? Do you think Richard expected you to become a nun after he died? I don't think so."

The conversation was making Zoe uneasy. She turned her head away and looked out the passenger side window, trying to find something in the bland, turnpike landscape to focus on. "I know what you're saying, Melissa. And I'm not a nun. I just haven't found anyone that I'm interested in, that's all."

"I don't think you're trying hard enough," she said sincerely.

Zoe turned her head back to Melissa. "And what about you? How much longer are you going to wait before Brad zips up his pants and comes home to you?"

"That's different," said Melissa. "I'm divorced," she said. "And don't take this the wrong way, Zoe," she cautioned, "but you're a widow. We still have a chance to get back together, and I'm sure that once he finishes sowing his wild oats he'll come back."

Zoe wished her own situation could be just as hopeful. In spite of the pain, there is always a thread of promise in infidelity, just a hint of possibility. She knew exactly why Melissa waited with patience for her ex-husband's return.

"He probably will come back, Melissa," she said with resignation. "I wish I could say the same about Richard."

Melissa looked away from the highway again and took a dangerously long gaze at the sad woman next to her. "Zoe," she said softly, "I know what it means to love someone. And I know how much you loved Richard, but it's time to move on. I don't want to see you spend the rest of your life alone."

Tears began to well in Zoe's eyes, but before she could respond, the air horn of a truck screamed at them as the van slowly drifted into the passing lane that was monopolized by the tractor trailer.

"Melissa," yelled Zoe, "watch out!"

Melissa jerked her head back to where it was supposed to be and pulled the wheel to the right. As she did, the truck pulled up next to them. The angry driver leaned over as far as he could to the passenger side of the cab and mouthed what looked like obscenities at the two women. As if they had been together in that scenario before, they both defiantly lifted a free hand and gave the man the finger. Realizing his own vileness was outnumbered, the truck driver returned the discourtesy and gunned his rig, leaving them howling in laughter behind a blinding deluge of water kicked up from belligerent tires as the truck pulled away in front of them.

By six o'clock, Melissa and Zoe were on the last lap of their journey. They had already made it through the bottleneck exit on the Mass Pike. It was bumper-to-bumper vans and rented trucks, many of them wearing furniture on their roofs like hats, some covered over with bright blue tarps to protect the antiques from the rain. They had already passed the many opportunists along Route 20 who schedule their own yard sales during Brimfield week. They wondered why anyone would stop and pick through such ordinary goods when the country's largest flea market was only a few miles ahead. Finally, about a mile from the event, traffic came to a stop. With a moving-size U-Haul truck in front of them, and their not knowing Brimfield, they were in the dark as to whether they had arrived, or were simply in some early morning traffic jam.

"Are we there yet?" asked Melissa with childlike curiosity.

"How do I know?" laughed Zoe, hanging out the window like a dog, trying to see around the truck in front of them. "I've never been here before, either."

"I can't believe that there's this much traffic in the middle of the woods. My God," said Melissa, "this is really weird."

"This is going to be great," Zoe said with enthusiasm.

Their van continued to crawl along with the line in front of them. As it did, they began to notice some activity that indicated they were close. Both sides of the road were peppered with orange flags being waved enticingly by young men and women.

"Parking," said Zoe, reading a homemade sign next to the waver closest to them. "We must be there."

"But where's our field?" asked Melissa. "What's the name of it, again?"

"We're going to May's. I know it's on the right-hand side, but that's about all I know."

"But where is it?" Melissa asked nervously.

"Melissa," Zoe said kindly, "I'll find out, okay?"

Zoe opened her door and got out of the van. Her sudden departure startled Melissa.

"Where are you going? Are you going to leave me here alone?"

Zoe stuck her head in the open door. "I'm going to ask the truck in front of us. Anything that big must know where May's is."

"Okay," said Melissa tentatively. "Just don't leave me here for long."

"Would you relax, please? I'll be right back."

Since traffic was almost at a standstill, it only took Zoe about a minute to get the information she needed, and to Melissa's relief, get back in the van.

"It's about half a mile up on the right," she said, pointing in the same direction.

"Good," said Melissa, holding her crotch with her left hand, "because I've got to take a wicked pee."

"Well, hang on," smiled Zoe, "we're almost there."

The caravan continued to move at a brake-pedal pace, and

it was not until they passed the bend in the road that they could finally get their first look at what was creating all the traffic. Ahead of them on the right was the white spire of the Congregational Church. Hundreds of cars were parked on the green knoll in front of it, an amount surely never witnessed at a typical Sunday service. Thousands of pedestrians enthusiastically walked west along Route 20, and teenagers with orange flags waved madly in the morning rain. People, flags, and wedding-size colorful tents stretched as far as the eye could see.

"Jesus," Melissa said in awe, "this is unbelievable!"

Zoe tilted her head back and inhaled the unmistakable aroma of barbecuing chicken. She looked at her watch, smiling at the early hour. "This, Melissa," she said, "is Brimfield."

The Brimfield Flea Market rises like Oz from the miles of underused pastures along Route 20. The desires and aspirations of those who exhibit and buy there rise as well. In their own secret and unstated ways, each devotee who travels there is in search of a new heart or brain, some metaphoric organ that will make them feel more alive, more connected or reconnected— something that will transform them home, wherever that Kansas may be. For Zoe, it was Italian watercolors. For others, it was china, precious metals, Popeye collectibles, Art Deco cocktail shakers, Pez containers, or any of the other millions of objects on the field that could act as talismans capable of lifting the human spirit. It is that way three times a year in Brimfield. The rest of the time, it is merely bucolic country landscape, void of human form and flat, deflated of topographical anticipation almost to despair.

By the time they turned into May's and found their chalked off exhibition space, it was almost seven-thirty. As soon as they were settled, Zoe went to the administration office to check on a tent. Even though she knew that Elliot had one for them, she hoped she could still rent one, just to keep Melissa from proving her wrong. To her chagrin, they were all out. She asked for the space number of Elliot Baker and went off into the crowd of dealers looking for the man who would keep them dry for the day.

After a few minutes, she figured out the numerical system of the aisles and she found him. Completely oblivious to the activity around him, Elliot sat peacefully in his van totally engrossed in the *Boston Herald*.

"Hi, Elliot."

Hearing his name, he looked up from the paper. The sight of Zoe so early on a gray, cold morning in May cheered him immediately. "Zoe," he said enthusiastically, "it's good to see you."

"It's good to see you," she said, breathing a sigh of relief. "They're out of tents, of course."

"No problem," he said, getting out of his van. "I've been waiting for you to show up so I could give you my spare."

"I really appreciate it."

"My pleasure."

Elliot walked to the back of his van and opened both doors, revealing the royal blue of the plastic tent. "You grab the poles," he said, pointing to them on the right side of the van. "I'll get the top and we'll get you set up."

"I'm sure Melissa and I can figure it out," offered Zoe. "You don't have to help."

Happy for an excuse to participate, he responded. "No, this tent gets a little tricky sometimes."

"Are you sure?"

"I'll have it up for you in no time," he promised.

The two of them walked diagonally across the field until they came to the rusty red van with "One Piece Antiques" neatly painted on the side. Elliot greeted Melissa and got right to work, using the two woman as minor assistants in the process.

Within fifteen minutes, the blue plastic was stretched along the top of the poles, revealing two problematic rips that would work like small open skylights to the rain.

"I usually tape plastic garbage bags over them," he said. "Do you have any?"

Embarrassed by their lack of preparedness, Zoe answered. "I'm afraid not."

Reaching into the large pocket of his yellow slicker, Elliot removed two green trash bags as well as a roll of masking tape. "I figured you wouldn't," he smiled. "So I brought these for you."

"Thanks," said Melissa.

As Elliot was about to patch the ceiling, Zoe hastily took both bags and the tape from him. "We're not going to have you do that, too. We'll take care of it."

"Okay," he said, without protesting. "Then I'm going picking for a while. You might want to do the same. You know," he advised them, "you can't set up your stuff here until nine."

"You can't?" Melissa responded in disbelief.

"Nope...so you might as well hit some of the other fields that opened at daybreak."

Melissa seemed confused. "But the show opens at nine."

"Right," said Elliot. "But in the past all the dealers would pick over the other dealers' stuff before the show opened. The people paying admission complained. So now you can't even unpack until the gates open."

"That must be an absolute zoo," said Melissa, imagining the worst. "Every other show we've done, we've always been able to set up before it opens."

"Not at Brimfield," smiled Elliot. "And it's worse than a zoo. But you'll sell a lot in the first hour because of it. Just pull the stuff out of your van as fast as you can."

"Thanks for the advice," said Zoe.

"You're welcome. Now," he said turning toward the direction

of the front gate, "I'm off to find that needle in a haystack."

"Good luck," smiled Zoe.

"I'll check on you two later," he promised. Then he disappeared into the swarm of humanity, in search of that elusive object that might just make him a wealthy man, or at the very least would make his trip to Brimfield in the rain financially worthwhile.

The scene was reminiscent of the clawing, riotous footage so often shown of emergency food and rations being distributed from the back of a truck in some godforsaken, Third World nation. But unlike the pleading, bony malnourished arms reaching up at the tailgate to get a meager cup of rice to feed their families, the dealers and collectors behind One Piece Antiques' van looked to be very well fed. The only malnutrition they suffered from was the insatiable hunger to possess those treasures closest to their hearts.

At exactly nine o'clock, May's had opened its floodgates to the crowd, and the buyers ran through the field like children in an Easter Egg hunt. At the same time, the six hundred or so dealers began unloading their wares. Like the rest of them, Zoe and Melissa pulled their inventory out of their van as fast as they could. Around the van were about twenty people, some pointing, some screaming, "I'll take it!" Two aggressive women tore at the arms of a Victorian baby doll until Zoe, like King Solomon in all his wisdom, pulled it back to her chest and awarded it to the woman who seemed to have a greater respect for its fragile fabric antiquity.

Fists of money flew out of the fat wallets, and it almost didn't seem to matter what people bought as long as they could purchase it immediately. There was no thought or consideration given. They grabbed piece after piece of country furniture, china, collectibles, and the three shiny spoons that Zoe had polished just the night before. Table lamps, some broken, were paid for even before a close inspection could be made. Virtually everything was touched, grabbed or fondled, and most of it sold within the first forty minutes. When the crowd receded, Zoe and Melissa knew that they had witnessed impulse buying in its most raw and archaic form.

"Could you believe that buying frenzy?" Zoe giggled with delight. She lit a cigarette in celebration of the moment.

"That was scary," shuddered Melissa. Then she looked at her watch "Elliot was right. It hasn't even been an hour, and we hardly have anything left. Amazing."

With the cigarette hanging from her mouth, Zoe diligently counted the money they had taken in so far. Although there were a couple of small checks, the bulk of it was in cash, the preferred form of payment throughout Brimfield. When she finished, she stuck the wad of money in the front right pocket of her jeans, turned and smiled at Melissa. "Over forty-two hundred dollars," she said. "Is that something or what?"

"It's unbelievable," said Melissa, shaking her head in shock. "Unbelievable."

"Well," said Zoe, crushing her cigarette with the heel of her boot, "I can't wait to spend some of it. One of us is going to have to go look for some stuff to restock the shop. Do you want to go...or stay here and watch the booth?"

Melissa didn't even hesitate with her answer. Although she was pleased with their success, she knew wandering around in such an enormous crowd of people would make her quite anxious. She felt much more at home at yard sales and local consignment shops. "I'll watch the booth," she said. "Just let me go to the bathroom before you go."

"You must really like those portable toilets," teased Zoe. "This will be your fourth time this morning."

"They're unbelievably gross, aren't they? Just the thought

of sitting on it makes me cringe," she said, tightening every muscle in her body.

"Just don't drink too much coffee," advised Zoe.

Melissa nodded. "I'll be right back. And if I'm not," she joked, "call an ambulance. I'll be the one passed out with my jeans down around my ankles. Overcome with fumes, you know?"

Zoe squeezed her nose with her thumb and index finger. "Just go like this," she wheezed.

Melissa reciprocated by squeezing hers. "Okay," she answered in an equally squeaky tone. Then she bravely walked toward the bay of festive, green and blue modern-day outhouses, one of the least favorite, yet absolutely necessary stops at Brimfield.

Zoe's enthusiasm to shop Brimfield was quickly replaced by confusion. After walking past the first forty or so dealers, sensory overload set in, making it difficult for her to focus on any one thing. In her two years of experience, she had never seen such a sheer mass of objects. It was the Noah's Ark of flea markets, with the entire world of antiques and collectibles present. Unfortunately, the orderly notion of only two per species standing side by side did not apply. If she saw one cottage pine bureau, twenty others would follow. The fact that they were all in different booths made comparison almost impossible.

Soon she temporarily abandoned the notion of buying for the shop. In spite of the truth of Melissa's remarks earlier in the day, she decided to look for Italian watercolors. After an hour and a half of walking, she had not found even one painting, and was about ready to head back to her booth and check on Melissa. Then her eye caught an unmistakable patch of Mediterranean blue at a booth some twenty feet away. It was a many-fathomed, deep bright blue, almost the color of her borrowed tent. Without taking her eyes off it, she went directly to the booth. She climbed over two, six-board blanket chests to reach where it was leaning against the side wall, just inside the white tent. It was a picture of a quaint Italian harbor, and the colors were brilliant, almost loud. Unlike the normal wash of watercolors, there is nothing subtle about Italian gouaches. They have the straightforward density of finger paints and a finish just as outspoken.

Like many items displayed at Brimfield, the unframed painting carried no price tag, allowing the price to be set by the level of interest of the person looking at it. Zoe picked up the picture and immediately fell in love. By then she had completely dismissed Melissa's concerns, and turned to find the owner. Seated in an antique leather club chair in the corner, he was reading *Maine Antique Digest*, a thick monthly newspaper dedicated to the trade. He was a striking man who appeared to be in his mid-thirties. Brimfield is not known for either the beauty or youth of its exhibitors, two characteristics that the man in front of her obviously possessed.

"How much for this?" Zoe held the painting at arm's length so she could get a good look at it.

The dealer looked up and smiled. "That's a good one," he said, baiting the excitement in her voice. "I can let you have it for twelve hundred."

Zoe was in sticker shock. "Twelve hundred? Isn't that a lot for an Italian watercolor?"

"Not for that one," he said, pointing to the lower right of the painting. "Look at the signature."

Zoe followed his finger until she came to the name in the lower right. "G. Ventura?" she said. "I don't know the artist."

"Giuseppe Ventura. He was one of the best tourist picture painters. That one was done around eighteen-seventy."

"Well, I've got some at home that are almost as nice, and I only paid around a hundred dollars apiece. Can you do any better?"

The dealer nodded his head. "He has real strong auction listings," he said. "I can't let it go any lower than that. I'm sorry."

Zoe knew that she could not afford twelve hundred dollars and carefully put the painting back in its place. As she surrendered it, a wave of depression came over her. Perhaps the expensive painting was a sign that it was time to let go—that she could no longer afford to obsessively hold on to the memory of her husband.

"Do you like Italian art?" the dealer asked.

"What?" Zoe was lost in thought about the paintings on her living room wall, and wondered if she should sell her collection and move on with her life.

"I said, do you like Italian art?"

Zoe turned her attention to the handsome young man, who looked Italian himself. He had tightly-curled short black hair and a five o'clock shadow that was five hours early. But there was nothing Neapolitan about his height. He was well over six feet tall. Overall he looked more like someone you would expect to see strolling the city in an Armani suit, rather than tramping through the muddy fields of Brimfield in jeans and a sweatshirt.

"Yes, I do," she answered, her pendulum swinging back without compunction to her husband again.

"I have something you might like," he said, reaching down to the ground next to his chair. "I've been holding it for a guy...he was due back here an hour ago to pick it up. So it's available if you're interested."

As he lifted the object from the damp ground, Zoe almost fell to her knees. She immediately became weak, and she felt Richard's presence all around her. In his hands, the dealer was holding a snapshot of death and the memories that linger each time you look at it. He was holding a cat-size, cast bronze replica of Michelangelo's Pietà.

"Stunning, isn't it?" he said, admiringly. "It was done in the late eighteen hundreds by a sculptor named Bellini, then cast by a well known foundry in Florence."

Zoe, too dumbstruck to say anything, just stared straight ahead at the form which held her in deep arrest.

"Are you all right?" The dealer couldn't help noticing the pallor that had come over her.

Without answering his question, she asked him the price.

"Three grand," he said.

She reached out her hands and took it from him, feeling its dead weight in her arms just as she had felt her husband's only two years before. She examined it closely and was amazed at how well it captured, not only the work of art that it was modeled after, but also the very essence of her husband. Then she carefully handed it back to the dealer and pulled the wad of money out of her pocket, making sure that he could see the thickness of it.

"I'll give you two thousand for it...in cash," she said in a business tone that strained her vocal chords.

The dealer hesitated for a moment "Okay...two thousand in cash."

Zoe wet her thumb with her tongue and carefully counted out two thousand dollars from the layers of bills in her hand, never once considering the consequences of such an expensive purchase. The Italian watercolor, she thought, had merely been God's little decoy to get her into that booth. It was the Pietà that she was meant to find and own. In her mind there was no doubt about that at all.

Before she left the booth, she looked around at the rest of his inventory as if she might find some other reminder or reinforcement of her late husband. Unlike many of the more traditional country exhibitors, his mix was more sophisticated and eclectic.

Although he had a few exquisite pieces of American furniture, the bulk of his goods were European. There were other examples of statuary, both bronze as well as marble. He also had a delicate pair of French Provincial chairs that looked far too formal to be sitting in the middle of a field in Revolutionary New England.

Like many dealers do to encourage sales, his eyes followed her as she walked his booth. He spoke to her as she began to rub the palm of her free hand on the lime green, velvet seat of one of the chairs. "Those are period," he said, referring to the approximate year in which they were originally crafted. "Most of the ones you see around today are much later."

Feeling a sales pitch coming on, Zoe removed her hand and then physically stepped back from the chair to indicate that she was just browsing. "They're beautiful. In fact," she said, looking slowly around the booth and then at the bronze statue cradled in her arm, "everything you have is beautiful."

"Thank you," he replied with a gleaming smile.

"Where are you from?"

"Maine," he answered without a hint of Down East twang.

"Maine?" she said with surprise, looking around at the many antiques from across the Atlantic. "I never knew Maine to look like this."

"I get around," he laughed. "How about yourself?" he asked. "Where are you from?"

"Massachusetts. South of Boston."

"Nice city, Boston," he said. "I went to school there."

"Where?" she asked, expecting Boston University, Boston College or one of the other large campuses located there.

"St. John's Seminary," he smiled. "I was studying to become a priest."

As soon as he said the word "priest," she looked at his face closely. The word gave him a softer, more gentle look. "St. John's?" she said, almost in amazement. "How do you go from a seminary to Brimfield?" she asked.

"Good question. I think I initially enrolled out of guilt," he laughed. "A decade of Catholic schooling will do that to you, you know."

"I can understand that."

"But after a couple of years there, I realized that what attracted me to the Church even more than my guilt was the art in it. When I was a kid, my parents took me to Italy. The Vatican just blew me away. So I decided to become a priest," he said, grinning at his own twisted logic.

Zoe shook her head. "That makes sense," she teased.

"It took me awhile to figure out the error in my thinking," he laughed. "But I'm okay now."

For the first time since Zoe came into his booth, he looked at her as a woman and not just a customer., He looked right past her age and focused on her pleasing eyes and well formed lips. Then, being careful not to get caught, he stole the smallest of celibate seminarian glances of her firm mature body peeking out from behind the open yellow slicker. "I'm Christopher," he said, holding out his hand to shake hers, an excuse to touch the flesh he had just looked at.

"Nice to meet you. I'm Zoe," she said, putting the Pietà down carefully on an English sideboard so that she could return the gesture.

As the two shook hands a strange feeling came over Zoe, and she wanted to pull away but she couldn't. Her hand felt almost helpless in his grasp. Because of his mention of art in the Vatican, all she could think about was the Creation of Adam, Michelangelo's fresco on the ceiling picturing the outstretched hands of God and Adam. The fresco in which God, with the touch of a divine finger, was about to infuse the soul and all its desire into man for the very first time.

Without letting go of her hand, Christopher studied her

face carefully. "Zoe," he said approvingly, "that's a wonderful name. In Greek, zoe means life. Did you know that?"

"Yes," she answered, finally feeling her hand being released. "It's one of those love-hate names. You hate it when you're a kid because everyone makes fun of it, and then you get to be an adult and everyone thinks it's charming."

"Well, it's a beautiful name," he said with admiration.

Zoe blushed, not knowing how to respond. Then her own guilt kicked in, thinking she was somehow violating the spirit of her husband. Instead of saying anything, she picked up her bronze statue and tucked it under her arm. "I have to go," she said in a voice clipped of emotion.

Sensing the uneasiness of the moment, he immediately backed off. "Well it was nice meeting you, Zoe. Enjoy your Pietà."

"I will. Good luck with the rest of the show."

"You, too."

As she walked away with her icon, he watched her closely, and thought fondly, passionately of Italian art.

"You paid how much for it?" Melissa asked again in disbelief.

"He wanted three thousand...but I offered him two grand in cash and he took it."

"You're crazy, do you know that? Hey...since when do you have the kind of money to afford something so frivolous?" She laughed. "I didn't know you were such a rich widow."

Zoe hesitated. "I used our cash," she said apologetically. "But I'll pay it back."

Melissa tightened her lips in anger. "You used our money? The money we made this morning? The money you were supposed to use to buy more stock for the shop?"

"I'm sorry, okay? But he would never have accepted my offer if it weren't in cash. You understand, don't you?"

"What I understand is that my partner is spending money I need to live on to feed an obsession she has for Italy. And I don't think that's fair."

Zoe ran her fingers along the bronze as if she were stroking a pet. Even before she had gotten back to her booth, she knew Melissa would be upset at her disregard for their collective funds. "I'm sorry, Melissa. I know I shouldn't have done it," she said contritely.

"But you did it anyway, right? That hurts, Zoe," she said, zipping up her slicker. "Well, if you don't mind," she said caustically, "maybe you could watch the booth for awhile. I'm going for a walk."

"Take your time," Zoe said solicitously.

Melissa stepped out from under the tent and brusquely flipped her hood over her head to keep it dry from the vaporizer mist in the heavy air. Then she turned toward Zoe. "Get on with it, Zoe," she pleaded. "For everybody's sake."

Zoe stood there with the bronze cradled in her arms. "Melissa..."

Eye makeup running, Melissa turned away and walked off into the slosh of Brimfield, the low cloudy atmosphere pressing firmly on her head. As soon as she was out of sight, Zoe retreated to the passenger side of the van and removed the white wine from her backup bag. Before her partner returned an hour later, she drank the bottle—the first half in celebration of her Pietà—the back half to help forget her selfishness in its purchase.

The ride home was quiet except for the hum of the tires, and barely a word was spoken between the two women the entire way. Melissa closed her eyes and tried to sleep, but her anger, like too much caffeine, allowed her only a few minutes of surface dozing. Zoe, with both alcohol-impaired hands on the wheel, tried to stay in her appointed lane, and not drift carelessly as she had done when she used the shop's money for her own benefit. She was sorry that she hurt Melissa—that she violated the trust that is the rock of any partnership. On the other hand, she felt vindicated. In spite of Melissa's urgings to let go of Richard enough to allow someone else in her life, the bronze Pietà, Zoe believed, was concrete, cosmic evidence that she needed to do nothing of the kind.

3

Friday was Melissa's day to cover the shop and as usual, she showed up fifteen minutes before the normal eleven o'clock opening. When she arrived, Zoe was already inside waiting for her with her Nike baseball cap in hand. She was standing in the middle of the sparse shop like a customer who had no idea what she was looking for. She was a sight to be pitied.

"What are you doing here?" Melissa asked, slightly restrained.

"I came to apologize. Here," she said, handing her an envelope, "I went to the bank this morning and got the two grand. I figured you would want it in cash."

Melissa took the envelope and smiled at her partner. "You are something, you know that? I was so angry when I got home last night that I started pacing from room to room. Then I dusted everything in the house. Finally, I caught a glimpse of myself in the mirror whacking my collection of baby cups with the feather duster, and I realized how foolish I was acting. Then I started to cry," she laughed.

"I'm the one who acted foolishly," argued Zoe. "I shouldn't

have done what I did, and I'm really sorry, Melissa. Forgive me?"

Melissa played with her emotions just long enough to exact a spoonful of revenge. "I don't know," she said. "Maybe I ought to think about getting another partner...someone less flighty."

"Melissa! Don't even say that." She slapped Melissa's arm with the top of her hat. "I'm your partner, and I promise I'll be a better one from now on."

"Are you sure?" she teased.

"Yes." Zoe put her arms around Melissa's shoulders. "I wouldn't want to lose you as a partner...or as a friend."

Melissa smiled at her and they embraced.

"I got you coffee and a bagel," Zoe said, turning her face toward the desk.

"You are sorry, aren't you?"

"With extra cream cheese," she laughed.

While Melissa ate her bagel and looked over the mail, Zoe began to unload the van's remnants from Brimfield. Melissa offered to help, but Zoe refused. "It's the least you can let me do," she said.

After Zoe finished getting everything into a pile in the middle of the room, Melissa began to rearrange the shop with her intuitive decorator's eye. She was a master at making a statement with even the smallest, most mundane antique objects and collectables, mixing together glass, wood and metal to create photo-ready vignettes suitable for the pages of the most sophisticated decorator magazines. As Melissa reset the shop, she chatted about Brimfield with Zoe, who had begun to casually flip through the pages of *Antiques And The Arts Weekly.*

"So how does your bronze look at home? Are you happy with it?"

Zoe looked up from the trade paper. "I was so upset last night, I couldn't even take it out of the van. It's still out there," she said, pointing to the vehicle.

"Oh, can I see it?" Melissa asked genuinely. "I really didn't get an objective look at it yesterday, if you know what I mean."

Zoe was grateful for the kindness in her voice, and excited that she wanted to see it in the light of a new day. "Sure, let me get it."

She went out to the van and unwrapped it from the quilted moving blanket that she had put around it the night before, and brought it into the shop. She placed it gently on a wobbly, white wicker side table that had failed to find a new owner at Brimfield. As soon as she did, Melissa stopped what she was doing and came over to look at it.

"This is really great," she said. "I can see why you would want it. I've never seen the real statue myself, but this certainly captures the moment, doesn't it?"

"I had to have it, Melissa," she said, shaking her head. "I think I was meant to have it," she added with a shudder.

"Stranger things have happened," Melissa replied.

"And you should have seen the guy who sold it to me. Tall, handsome...an ex-seminarian to boot. I don't know," she said mysteriously, "there was something about him that made me feel funny."

"Funny? How?"

"Funny like boy meets girl. And I don't know for sure, but I think he had the same reaction."

"How old?"

"He couldn't have been more than thirty-five or six. Under forty, anyway," she qualified.

"And you think he was interested in you?" she teased.

"Actually, it kind of freaked me out...it was embarrassing."

"What do you mean?"

Zoe hesitated, then spoke slowly. "I felt like I was cheating on Richard."

Melissa thoughtfully pursed her lips, reviving her lipstick in the process. "Zoe...trust me. You weren't, okay?"

"I know, it's just that..."

Melissa interrupted her. "What's his name?"

"Christopher."

"Christopher what?"

"I don't know," Zoe shrugged. "I didn't get his last name."

"How could you not do that?" she scolded.

"Because it was a cash transaction, that's why," she said defending herself. "I gave him the money and took the bronze...end of story."

"Well, maybe you'll see him again when we go back to Brimfield for the July show."

Zoe smiled faintly. "I've already thought of that possibility."

By eleven-thirty, the shop was back in order with every piece meticulously in its place. However, it still looked empty enough to feel like it was going out of business.

Melissa perused the entire room carefully. "Not good," she said. "We need more stuff."

"I should have bought for the shop yesterday. I meant to. I'm sorry, Melissa."

"Stop apologizing and let's just move ahead, okay? We'll hit the yard sales heavy this weekend, and Monday we'll go to Mavilia's auction and see what we can pick up. I heard he's got some good furniture coming up."

"As long as you do the bidding. You're always complaining that I bid too high."

Melissa glanced at the Pietà. "You do," she laughed.

Even though it was her day off, Zoe hung around until noon. By then, the sun that had missed Brimfield had found its way back to Noble's Cove. Just as Zoe was about to leave, Elliot Baker pulled up in front of the shop and removed what appeared to be a dollhouse from the back of his van. As he got to the door of the shop, both women saw the round holes where the windows should have been and looked at each other. "Birdhouse," they said simultaneously.

Elliot lugged the painted Victorian home into the shop and rested it on the floor with a grunt. It still had straw and twigs sticking out of some of the holes. "Fresh from Brimfield," he smiled. "Any interest?"

The two women got on their knees and began to paw over the piece, looking for imperfections.

"It's all there," he said. "Except for the birds."

"It's got a great finish," Melissa said reverently, stroking the decades of dried and crackled green paint.

"Three-fifty," Elliot said efficiently.

"Elliot," smiled Zoe with a hint of manipulation, "that's your regular dealer's price. I know you can do better for us. Right?"

"Okay," he said, fully aware that he was being hustled. "Three and a quarter and it's yours."

"We'll take it," said Melissa without any hesitation.

While Melissa got up from the floor and went to the desk to get cash out of the envelope that Zoe had brought in, Elliot turned his attention to Zoe. She was still kneeling on the floor admiring the birdhouse. His eyes fixed on her rear, accentuated by the position she was in.

"I understand you had a good morning at Brimfield, Zoe," he said. "I came back to see you, but you were off picking the field. Did you find anything?"

Zoe turned and got up from the floor. "Yes," she said with excitement. "Wait till you see what I got."

She walked over to the wicker table and held the bronze proudly in front of her. "It's by a guy named Bellini, and it was done around eighteen-seventy."

Without saying anything, Elliot took the statue from her. He examined it slowly and carefully, turning it on all sides. Then he ran his fingers along the edges, feeling them with his years of experience.

Zoe grew impatient with his lack of response and thought his silence verged on rudeness. "Well, what do you think, Elliot? Isn't it great?"

Elliot looked up from the object with a serious expression on his face. "It may have been originally done by Bellini in the eighteen-seventies, but unfortunately, this was cast yesterday. It's a reproduction," he said with solemn authority. "Probably made within the last year."

Zoe turned pale. "A reproduction? Are you sure?"

Elliot nodded his head. "Absolutely sure. I hope you didn't pay a lot of money for it."

Zoe's mind raced back to Brimfield and to the handsome ex-seminarian who had sold it to her. How could she have been so wrong about his character, she thought. What bothered her most was how the forgery violated the spirit in which she bought it. It was a desecration of sorts, an assault on the memory of her husband.

"Well," asked Elliot, "how much did you pay for it?"

Before Zoe could mutter the number, Melissa spoke up. "She paid two thousand in cash for it."

Elliot frowned. "Welcome to Brimfield, Zoe. Remember what I told you before you went there? Huh? I told you that it's the ultimate one-night stand. I'm sorry," he said with compassion, "but you just had your first date."

Zoe looked like she was going to break into tears, but instead she composed herself and took the Pietà back from Elliot. "How much is it worth?" she asked softly.

"About three hundred dollars, I'd say. I mean it's decorative enough, but it's just not what it's supposed to be. You have to be very careful with bronze statues," he added. "They're very easy to reproduce, and my guess is that if there's one of these floating around, then there's more of them out there."

"What should I do? Try to get my money back?"

"Do you know who you bought it from?"

"All I know is that his name was Christopher, and he said he was from Maine."

"Did you get a receipt for it? Anything with a full name or address?" he asked.

Zoe's answer was barely audible. "No."

Elliot shook his head. "I'm sorry, Zoe, but I think you're out of luck. But don't be too hard on yourself," he continued. "All of us have made mistakes. All you can do is to chalk it up as a learning experience."

"I guess you're right," she said with resignation. "I don't know what else I can do."

Elliot's heart went out to the dejected woman standing in front of him. He also saw an opportunity to spend some time with her. "C'mon Zoe," he said, "come across the street with me, and I'll buy you a cup of coffee."

She was too beaten to argue. "Okay."

Zoe turned to Melissa. "Is that okay with you?"

"Zoe," she said, "it's your day off. Remember?"

"Oh yeah..."

"Elliot," Melissa said, realizing that she was still holding the money for the birdhouse in her hand, "don't forget this."

Elliot paused. "Just give me three hundred, instead of the three and a quarter."

"No," said Zoe. "We're not going to do that. The cup of coffee will be more than enough charity from you," she said adamantly.

"Okay. Whatever you say."

After the two of them left for the Wave Deli, a local ham and egger place just down the street from the shop, Melissa played with three or four locations for the birdhouse, until she found one that seemed right. She put it next to a chalkware figure of a cat which was sitting on top of an Irish scrubbed pine table. "Perfect," she said to herself. Then she sat down at the desk and waited for that elusive customer to come in.

As usual, she passed the time by reading. Her material of the day was the new issue of *Antiques And The Arts Weekly* which Zoe had casually thumbed through earlier. After a few minutes of reading, her eyes came to a screeching halt. She jumped up from the desk, set the "Be Back in Five Minutes" sign in the window, locked the door, and hurried down the street to the Wave Deli.

Melissa found Zoe and Elliot in a booth in the smoking section. Zoe was puffing away anxiously when Melissa got there.

"Move in," said Melissa. She pushed her small frame onto Zoe's side of the tattered and taped, red leatherette booth. She caught Elliot's look of disappointment for crashing his party.

Zoe could tell by the look on her face that something was wrong. "What's the matter, Melissa?"

"Look at this," she said, opening up the paper to the article that brought her to the deli. She pointed to a photograph of Zoe's Pietà. "It's your bronze, and it was stolen out of a summer home in Maine."

"Let me see," said Elliot. He leaned over the table, angling the paper slightly so he could read it. "It certainly looks like it."

The three of them poured over the article about a number of items, including a bronze Pietà by Bellini, stolen sometime over the winter from a summer home in Camden, Maine.

"So that's where it came from," said Zoe.

"Can't be yours," said Elliot.

"Why not?"

Elliot pointed to a paragraph midway through the article. "Because it says right here that the sculpture had been in the house for over forty years."

"Then where did mine come from?"

"It was probably cast from the one that was stolen. Yours was made from the original."

"Holy shit," Zoe said, taking a drag of her cigarette. "Well, at least mine's not stolen, right?"

"No, of course not. But if I were you, I'd put it away. If the police knew you had it, they would probably impound it as some kind of evidence after the fact, or some bullshit like that."

"I can't believe this," said Zoe.

"You got yourself into it this time, didn't you?" laughed Melissa.

"It's not funny, Melissa. How can you be so insensitive?" she asked, forgetting her own code violations the day before. "I'm out two thousand bucks, and somehow I'm connected to a burglary in Maine. That son of a bitch," she said, thinking of the smooth young dealer who took advantage of both her heart and her pocketbook. "I bet he stole it."

"Well," said Elliot, "just put it out of your mind. There's nothing you can do about it now."

"I don't know if I can do that," she said quietly, thinking of her last moments with her husband in front of the Pietà in St. Peter's Basilica in Rome. "It's a very personal issue with me."

By four-thirty, Melissa was ready to close the shop for the day. Brimfield had started to catch up to her, and she had dozed off more than once during the excruciatingly slow afternoon. All tolled, the shop had only grossed one hundred and twenty-two dollars for the day, not much to show for six hours of work, especially compared to the thousands they had done at Brimfield the day before.

Before leaving, she decided to go through the classified section of the local paper and make an itinerary of yard sales that she and Zoe could attack in the morning. As she circled an interesting ad with a red felt marker, the shop suddenly began to vibrate, forcing the marker to jiggle like the needle on a seismograph. Right away, she knew it was not an earthquake. It was the familiar rumble of her ex-husband's dump truck, hauling the flatbed trailer that carried his backhoe.

Because of the bent shape of the arm of the digger, Melissa always referred to his backhoe as his "praying mantis." Zoe, on the other hand, called it his "preying penis." Although Melissa sometimes objected to her raunchy humor, deep in her heart, she knew it was a more apt description.

Before he came into the shop, Melissa made a quick pass at the mahogany antique mirror next to the desk to make sure that she was presentable. Other than looking tired from her trip the day before, she thought she looked quite inviting. Certainly more inviting than that slut, Sheila Corcoran, she argued to herself.

Brad walked in with the same twinkle and swagger he had when she first started dating him as a teenager. It was a combination of alcohol and his "boys will be boys" personality, two facets of him that had caused them trouble for as long as she had known him. Right away, she knew he had been drinking.

"Hi honey," he said loudly.

Melissa smiled with tolerance at the tan, stocky man with the jowly moustache in front of her. "Hi Brad."

He looked around the shop, and although he admittedly had no use for antiques himself, he nodded with approval. "The shop looks good, 'Lis," he said. "Damn good."

"Thanks. Why did you come by?" she asked

He turned his attention to his ex-wife. "I just wanted to see how you did at Brimfield, that's all. So," he smiled, "did you make a killing?"

"I don't know if you would call it a killing, but it was

certainly worth the trip."

"That's great."

"How's your business going? Keeping busy?" she asked, knowing that he usually never worked past three in the afternoon.

"I'll tell you, 'Lis," he said, "with the new state law on septic systems, I've got orders for more holes than I can dig. Granted," he qualified, "they're not fancy house foundation holes like I used to dig. They're shit holes," he laughed. "But they're still holes, and the color of the money is just as good."

Melissa smiled at Brad's philosophical outlook on his lot in life. He had always been a man who did what he had to do—but only for as long as necessary. After his father died during his sophomore year in high school, Brad did his best for a couple of years to be a father to his younger sister. And when Melissa got pregnant the summer following their senior year in high school, it was he who insisted they get married. It was not that he wanted to. Marriage was the last thing on his mind, but he felt obligated to the forthcoming baby. Two months after they exchanged vows, Melissa miscarried. In a confused state of sorrow and anger, Brad blamed her for the loss.

In spite of a difficult start, the early years of their union were mostly happy ones. It was only after continuous failed attempts to conceive another child that the relationship began to fail. Brad took it as a personal affront that Melissa couldn't get pregnant, and his eyes as well as the rest of him, began to wander. While the medical community had no explanation, Melissa, no stranger to low self-esteem, believed she was at fault. As Brad began to stray, in desperation, she began to collect silver baby cups. It was not that she believed that they held any special powers. However, she felt that just being surrounded by the infant icons might in some way create an aura of fertility. Her rub-off theory failed to produce any results.

As the window of the childbearing years began to close, so did their relationship. To her credit, it was Melissa who demanded the divorce. It was not that she didn't love Brad or didn't want to be married to him. But she had come to the brutal realization that if she were ever going to be happy, then he would have to want to be married to her and accept the standards of fidelity intrinsic in a good marriage. Until that time they would be friends and occasionally, lovers—but not man and wife.

"How are things going with you and Sheila?" Melissa asked, turning her attention back to the her yard sale search.

Brad rocked back and forth in his mud-caked boots. "You know how it is. Women," he announced with the width of shotgun spray, "they all want the same goddam thing."

"And what might that be?" she asked unnecessarily.

"Vindication. You know, marriage." Brad put his hands deeply and defensively into the front pockets of his jeans and looked around the shop. "Well, I told her I'm not interested. I told her I already have a wife."

"Had a wife," she corrected him.

"As far as I'm concerned 'Lis, you're still my wife and a good one. I'm just not a husband, that's all. And that's not fair to you."

"I have never heard anyone speak out of more sides of a mouth, Brad. Do you know what you sound like?"

"I can't change," he said, shaking his head. "Doesn't mean I don't love you. It just means I can't change."

"Maybe if you tried harder..."

Brad shrugged and smiled. "What are you doing for dinner?"

"Nothing special. But I'm kind of tired from Brimfield."

"C'mon, he said. "Like I used to promise your dad, I won't keep you out late. Okay?"

Melissa remembered how sex had always made her late.

No matter how often she promised to be home on time, each heavy-petting night that she spent in the backseat of Brad's '57 Chevy always ended the same. Half dressed, she would jump up to check the time on the dimly lit, dashboard clock. To her horror it would always be after midnight—conveniently just a few minutes after Brad had gotten his—and unfortunately a few minutes before she would have gotten hers, when she got home to her angry waiting father. But coming home late paled in comparison to the consequences of her pregnancy. On the night she announced it, her father expressed his joy at the idea of becoming a grandfather by giving her the beating of her life.

Melissa softly stroked her cheek and thought of her father. "Okay Brad...we'll have dinner. But I want to be home by eleven."

"No problem," he said. "I promise."

Zoe and her daughter, Joanna, looked out of place at the table for two in the middle of the small, dining room. At Zoe's suggestion, they had met for dinner at Swider's Seafood Shanty, a fresh seafood restaurant in Noble's Cove. It was one of the oldest restaurants in town and looked it. Over the forty years that it had been in business, many renovations had taken place, all of them merely superficial. While other establishments in town gutted their interiors with each new gastronomical trend, Swider's only went as far as a new coat of paint or a fresh, food-free wall-to-wall carpet. But it didn't seem to matter to their patrons, most of them old as well and in need of renovations.

Swider's was a down-to-earth, close-to-death place that knew how to cook a piece of fish. It also knew how to price it. With little overhead, the restaurant could offer full course seafood dinners for around ten dollars. A similar menu at lunch could be enjoyed for around six dollars a person. So while other more beefy restaurants in town scrambled for the working lunchtime trade, the elderly, those with more free time than money, made their way to Swider's. They waited patiently in line, walkers and all, to partake of a Perfect Manhattan, straight up, and a perfectly broiled portion of fresh fish, complete with deliberately overcooked vegetables that were easy on the tooth.

The vesper hours between five and seven-thirty in the evening were always busy at Swider's. "Early Bird Specials for the tough, old birds," was how one rather youthful and insensitive waitress coined the time slot. The hours when those few hearty souls over seventy who were still capable of eating dinner after four in the afternoon without destroying their constitutions, would sit and sip their ancient cocktails from better days, then drive home—propelled by the lightheadedness of liquor and hampered by the dusk of failing eyes. That is what surrounded Zoe and her daughter on that Friday night—the tough, old birds of Swider's.

"Why do you love this place so much, Mom? The menu hasn't changed in years." Joanna looked at the three-fold embedded-in-plastic menu, which like the restaurant itself, was hermetically sealed to outside influences. "My God," she laughed, "if they added a new item, it might be too much for some of the old hearts in here to take."

Zoe smiled at the youthful glibness of her daughter. "I think you might be shocked at how much these old hearts have already taken." Zoe looked around the room, imagining herself and her late husband dining there in their old age. "Probably more heartbreak than you or I have seen."

"I suppose you're right," she said, taking a sip of her jug-quality Chablis. "And speaking of heartbreak," she said seriously, "let me tell you about Ramon."

Joanna proceeded to tell her mother about a conversation

that she had with Ramon the night before. After continually confronting him on his late nights at work, Ramon finally admitted that he was seeing another woman. He insisted that there was nothing to it, however, and it was merely a last fling before they got married.

Zoe listened intently as her daughter rubbed her hands nervously and then wiped her eyes as she began to cry. As she did, Zoe handed her the napkin from her lap.

"So what are you going to do, Jo?"

"I don't know. He told me he wouldn't see her anymore, but I'm not sure I believe him. Plus, I don't know how I feel about marrying a man who is already cheating on me. What do you think I should do?"

Zoe sat back in her chair and looked around at the elderly clientele in the room. "I wonder how many of these couples have been faithful to one another?"

"What's that got to do with anything?"

"I don't know," she said, "but my guess is that some of them cheated on their spouses and some of those that did, got caught. Instead of breaking up, they had the foresight to imagine themselves in old age, and decided then that they would rather not be alone at that point in their lives if they didn't have to be. Loneliness is a terrible thing at any age," she added with just a hint of sorrow in her voice, "and I'm sure it's particularly painful when you get old."

Joanna pushed back her blond hair as if to bolster her confidence. "I'm sure I could find another man," she remarked indignantly.

Zoe laughed. "That's not my point, Jo. How many flaws are you willing to accept in a partner? I know you love Ramon, and I would hate to see the two of you break up because of what's happened. On the other hand, I understand that you need to know whether he can really make the commitment. If he can't, then you want to know now."

"What would you do if you were in my position?"

"I don't know. Your father and I never had a problem like that. But I'll tell you what...if I could have him back right now, I wouldn't even care if he cheated on me."

"Dad would never cheat on you," she said defensively.

Zoe paused at the unconditional tone in Joanna's voice. "I don't know...but you know..." She smiled and shook her head. "I'm sure we had our moments."

"What do you mean? What moments?"

"I can't remember them right now." Zoe laughed. "So I guess they weren't that important."

The conversation was interrupted by their waitress, who plopped matching, rather mundane garden salads in front of them. "Your dinners will be out in a few minutes," she snapped. "Can I get you another drink?" she asked, staring at Zoe's empty martini glass.

"Yes, please."

The waitress then looked over at Joanna's half-full wine glass. "You're all set," she said, without even bothering to ask.

As the waitress flew off to another table, Joanna looked at her mother's glass, drained of everything except a small residual morsel of green olive, and spoke quietly across the table. "I didn't know you liked martinis that much."

"Like I said," Zoe smiled to take the edge off her words, "loneliness is a terrible thing."

"Well, don't get too chummy with those things," she warned. "They're not going to help."

"I beg to differ, Jo. If nothing else, they help me sleep. Otherwise, some nights I would be up all night. Would you rather have me on the pills again?"

Joanna was well aware of her mother's previous addiction. "Fine, but you know what I'm saying, right?"

"Don't worry. Anyway, I'm the mother here," she laughed. "It's my job to worry about you, not the other way around."

While they ate dinner, they talked more about Joanna's problem. In the spirit of shared woes, Zoe told her daughter about her trip to Brimfield and how she was burned by the Pietà. Joanna reprimanded her as only children can do, and told her she had no business spending that kind of money on something so sentimental.

"That's easy for you to say, but he was my husband. Anyway, I plan to get my money back."

"Just how are you going to do that?"

"I'm going to go to Maine next week and find him."

Joanna laughed at the absurdity of her mother's plan. "How are you going to find this guy in Maine? Do you have any idea how big that state is?"

"Of course I do. But I know the real Pietà was stolen in Camden, so I'm assuming he must be somewhere along the coast. You know, along Route One."

Joanna shook her head. "Mom, that's crazy, do you know that? Just forget about it."

"I can at least give it a try. There's no harm in that, is there?"

Joanna looked at her mother and could sense the unshakable loneliness inside of her, a loneliness she hoped she would never experience herself. "I suppose not," she answered. "Just be careful, that's all."

After dinner, Zoe invited her daughter to spend the night at their home in Noble's Cove, but Joanna insisted that she had to get back to the city. First of all, to make sure that Ramon came home. And second, because she had to work the next morning. As MIS manager of a small law firm, working on the weekends had become a common practice because she couldn't disrupt the systems during the week when the lawyers were busy with their clients.

After warm goodbyes, the two women went their separate ways. Joanna got back in her confident, red Saab convertible and drove off to Boston to check on her wayward man. Zoe went home and drank wine in the dark, staring at the silhouette of her fake bronze Pietà as she sipped.

4

Melissa and Zoe met for coffee at the Wave Deli at six-thirty Saturday morning. The weekend yard sales were calling, and they knew that if they expected to find anything good, they would have to get out early before the million other dealers with the same plan.

The place was crowded with the usual early Saturday morning types—local insomniacs, lawn service lackeys, lobstermen, and dressed down businessmen with newspapers, getting a jump start on their weekend. As always, Zoe and Melissa sat in the smoking section. Both of them were hung over from the night before. Zoe had sat up drinking wine with her bronze until three, carrying on conversations with herself as well as with Richard. Melissa, although home from dinner by eleven as her ex-husband promised, had invited him to stay for the night. Just like when she was a teenager, the sex made her stay up late, and the beer flowed freely between rounds.

While Melissa seemed serene from her night with Backhoe, Zoe was wired even before her second cup of coffee.

"What's wrong with you today?" asked Melissa.

"I have a lot on my mind. Joanna's having a problem with Ramon, and my fake bronze is like shit on my shoe. Even worse, I love it even though it's not real."

"Well then all is not lost, is it?"

"Listen," said Zoe, "can you work for me on Tuesday?"

"Sure. Why?"

"I'm going up to Maine on Monday to try to find the guy who screwed me on the statue. If I need to, I'll spend the night."

"How on earth are you going to find him?"

"That's what Jo said last night. But I've got to try."

"Get hold of yourself, will you? That's just not rational."

"Maybe not, but I'm going to do it anyway. If I can find him, I want him to give me most of my money back. I'm willing to pay what it's worth, but I don't like getting ripped off. So you'll cover for me on Tuesday?"

Melissa shook her head with disdain. "Of course."

As soon as Melissa agreed, Zoe dropped the subject and turned her attention to the yard sales that Melissa had circled in the newspaper the day before. Based on their locations and the times they opened, Zoe numbered them sequentially and figured they could hit the first one after a third cup of coffee.

By seven, they were walking out the door of the Wave Deli. Zoe stopped at the threshold, blocking the exit. "Why don't you go to the bathroom before we leave. Most yard sales don't have portable toilets," she laughed.

"Good thinking," Melissa said respectfully. "I'll be right out." Then she turned around and headed for the ladies room in the Wave Deli, a tiny closet with a dirty toilet, just one notch above those found outside in Brimfield.

Zoe barely slept on Sunday night. Even wine didn't seem to quell her anxiety about her trip to Maine. Finally she gave up trying to sleep, and got up at four. Within an hour and a half, she had already made it through the most congested part of her journey. Even at that time of the morning, getting through Boston could be a stop-and-go chore, but as she got onto the Mystic River Bridge, the traffic began to thin out nicely.

She and Melissa had enjoyed an excellent weekend of both yard sale purchases and shop sales, grossing almost eight hundred dollars on items that cost them less than two hundred. So she was in good spirits—so was her van. In preparation of her solo ride to Maine, Zoe had it tuned up on Saturday and it sounded up for the trip. As a widow, Zoe learned to depend more on herself, and the last thing she wanted was a breakdown somewhere in Maine. While many women can turn to their husbands, Zoe, out of necessity, learned to lean on AAA.

Camden was to be her first and farthest stop of the day. Because most antique shops don't open until late morning, she decided to go as far as Camden, about a five-hour ride from Boston, and then work her way back south. That way she wouldn't waste any time, and she would be that much closer to home when she finished. Her plan, although a long shot, was a simple one—stop at every shop along Route One until she found the man who sold her the bronze. Because she had looked at the items in his space at Brimfield so carefully, she felt confident that she would recognize them even if someone else were watching his shop at the time. Because it did not fit into her logic, she refused to consider that he, like Elliot Baker, might not even have a shop, which of course would make her entire plan flawed beyond repair. But Zoe would not even entertain that thought. She would have it her way, whether it made sense or not.

By eleven, Zoe hit her first shop of the day. Tattered Dreams was located right on Route One. The antique linens and lace, which hung like grandmother's laundry on a clothesline just outside the door, flittered in the light breeze of the

Maine morning. In spite of its workmanlike pose, there was something reverent about the clothesline, and the gentleness of the fabric that hung from it whispered something far more romantic than domestic.

Right away, Zoe surmised that this was not the shop she was looking for. Except for a few aberrations, most antique stores take on the personalities of the owners. Right down to the name of the shop itself, Tattered Dreams was too soft and too feminine to house a handsome young man named Christopher who had the gall to sell her fake merchandise.

As she suspected, the inside of the shop was a larger version of what hung on the outside. The pungent but well-intentioned odor of potpourri only added to the Victorian melancholy that already filled the air in the dainty tidy store. Sitting behind a white painted desk was a tiny, hollow-cheeked woman who acknowledged Zoe with the most gentle of smiles. Zoe returned an equally delicate smile and then slowly began to inspect her offerings.

"You have beautiful things," she said, holding up a throw pillow covered in vintage floral fabric that seemed out of place next to the tee shirt and worn jeans she herself was wearing.

"Thank you. Are you looking for anything in particular?"

Zoe thought about explaining the purpose of her trip, but she was too embarrassed to do so. "No. I'm just doing the shops along the coast today, that's all."

"You picked a fine day for it," the shop owner said sweetly. "Any luck yet?"

"You're my first stop. What other places in town should I go to?"

The woman told her of three other shops that she should visit in Camden, as well as a number of shops to the south that she shouldn't miss. In payment for that valuable information, Zoe spent more time than she had planned looking through her antique fabrics, although she had no intention of purchasing anything. After a long ten minutes, she said thank you and goodbye.

Within an hour, Zoe had finished with Camden and was on her way south to Rockport, the next town on her grand tour. After visiting four shops there to no avail, she continued onto Rockland, followed by Thomaston, Waldenboro and Damariscotta. By the time she reached Newcastle it was almost three o'clock, and she began to realize the frivolity of her thinking. However, her stubbiness kept her on track, and she took a left onto Route 27, the long asphalt finger with Boothbay Harbor at the tip.

Boothbay was at war with itself. It was trying to divvy up its precious and profitable waterfront between the fishermen who made a living from it, and the tourist businesses that, in good years, made a killing from it. By the number of restaurants and gift shops in the quaint seaside village, it looked like the tourist sector was winning.

The streets were busy with Dockers, Levis and Nikon cameras. Although the tourist season had not officially begun, many of the shops were already open to catch the late spring rush of those wise enough to visit Boothbay at a time when they could still find a parking space on the street and a seat with a view in a waterfront restaurant. Unlike the tourists, Zoe passed by all the gift shops and headed for the few antique stores in the area. The first one was what is called a "group shop," a multi-dealer shop that rents out space and requires no shop time of the dealers who exhibit there. As with most group shops, the quality of the merchandise was uneven, and the lack of presence by those who owned it added an impersonal touch to the experience.

In spite of the volume of stuff, none of it looked familiar to Zoe. She left and walked dejectedly toward the waterfront. Once there, she was confronted with a shop that looked like it was custom-made for the salty town of Boothbay. The sign above it was in the long thin shape of a ship's name board and read "Nautica Antiques," which was just what the front windows were full of. Even before she went inside, she realized that the shop was the complete antithesis of Tattered Dreams. Nautica Antiques was as masculine as Tattered Dreams had been for the ladies. She doubted that she would have any luck there.

It only took her a few minutes to confirm her original assessment. The shop shimmered with polished brass ships' binnacles, lanterns, and bells. The walls rocked with the waves of more than a dozen portraits of ships, bravely sailing the seas in search of nineteenth century worlds to conquer. Everywhere she looked there was another piece of nautical history, leaving little hope on the horizon of her own journey.

"If you need any help, let me know."

The pleasant voice behind her startled Zoe, and she turned in its direction. Leaning against a glass case containing scrimshawed whales' teeth and other sailor-made objects, was a large hull of a man who looked like a contemporary version of an antique sea captain. His cheeks were mapped with capillary vessels, rubicund estuaries formed by warm brandy and frigid gale force winds that flow from the spirit of every seafaring man. And his tightly woven beard, sans mustache, made him look like he would be at home in any Melvillian whaling port. He looked like a stowaway from another century.

Zoe smiled at him and imagined him dressed in uniform for some nautical reenactment. "Just browsing," she answered casually.

"Any questions, just ask."

"Actually...I do have a question," she said, picking up a large compass encased in a mahogany box.

"That's four-fifty," he offered, assuming the price was her question.

She put the compass back in place on a scarred, green sea chest. "I'm...looking for someone."

"Aren't we all."

"I know this is going to sound funny," she said with a blush of embarrassment, "but I'm looking for a dealer from Maine that I met at Brimfield. All I know is that his first name is Christopher."

"Maine's a big state," he said respectfully.

"I know," she sighed. "I just had the feeling that he was on the coast, so I've been hitting all the shops from Camden down to here, trying to find him."

"That's like trying to find someone lost at sea."

Zoe nodded glumly.

"Tough, but not impossible," he smiled. "What kind of merchandise does he deal in? I know quite a few dealers up here, and you'd be surprised at how many you can recognize by what they carry."

"That's what I thought. I'm Zoe Madden...from Boston," she said as she held out her hand.

"Blaine Flowers...from Maine."

After exchanging pleasantries, they sat at a highly varnished teak table made from the pilothouse door of an old tugboat. In place of the porthole was a fitted copper bowl with salt water taffy in it. Without hesitating, Zoe grabbed a lime flavored piece, unwrapped it, and popped it into her mouth. It was now almost four o'clock, and she hadn't eaten all day. Her stomach was physically whining for something to fill its emptiness.

"So tell me, Zoe, what kind of stuff does your friend Christopher sell? Americana? Marine? Art pottery?"

"Actually, his stuff was more European. In fact," she said, "I commented on it when he told me he was from Maine. I told him that I didn't know Maine had those kinds of antiques."

"Hmm."

"Oh," she continued, "and he really likes religious art."

"How old a guy?"

"Mid thirties, I guess. Handsome, too," she smiled demurely.

The nautical antiques dealer sat back in his chair and folded his arms. "There's a guy in Wiscasset...I don't know him at all, but I know his name is Christopher. Christopher..." He jogged his memory. "I think it's Doria. Yeah, like the ship."

"The ship?"

"The Andrea Doria. Went down in nineteen fifty-six. Forty-six souls lost," he added solemnly.

"I've heard of that."

"Yeah, that's why I remembered his name. It's a nautical thing," he joked. "Christopher Doria. That's it. And he's young, too. Not like most of us old geezers up here."

Zoe was exhilarated with the possibility that she had found her man and leaned forward in her chair, her breasts pressing against the edge of the teak table. "What's the name of his shop?"

"Relics."

"That figures," she said. "Where is it in Wiscasset?"

"As soon as you go over the Sheepscot River, it's up on your left about a hundred yards. You can't miss it."

Zoe looked at her watch. "Do you think I can make it before he closes?"

"Sure. Most of the shops there are open at least till five."

She stood up and took her canvas bag from the table. "Thank you so much, Blaine," she said. "You've really been a great help."

"No problem," he answered. "But," he cautioned her, "I can't promise that he's the guy that you want."

"It sure sounds like him," she said assuredly. "At least it's a lead."

"Good luck, Zoe."

"Thanks." She pointed at the bowl of salt water taffy. "May I? I haven't eaten all day."

"Take all you want," he offered. "There's plenty more where that came from."

Zoe grabbed a handful and threw them in her bag, and then took another from the bowl and unwrapped it. "I love the blueberry flavored ones," she said as she put it in her mouth.

"That's my favorite, too. Maine blueberry," he added with pride. He put his hand to his ruddy cheek. "Tough on my teeth, though."

"Do what I do. Suck on it until it melts," she recommended.

"I'll remember that," he smiled.

"Thanks again," she said abruptly as she shook his hand. "But I've got to get going."

"A hundred yards up on the left after the river," he said as Zoe walked briskly toward the door.

"I'll find it." She paused and turned toward him. "Have a great season, Blaine. You have beautiful things," she said with awe in her voice.

"Thanks." His capillaries filled like a high red tide.

By the time Zoe reached the bridge over the Sheepscot River, she had eaten a half dozen pieces of taffy. The inside of her mouth was arid from the sugar that coated it, as well as from the fearful realization that she might confront a man who would not take kindly to her accusations. Her strategy had been as ill planned as her trip, and she pulled over to a parking space on the right to finalize her approach.

She tossed her arguments back and forth between her rational and emotional sides like a Frisbee, and finally decided that she would take a "no questions asked" point of view. She would merely tell him that a very experienced and reputable dealer assessed that the bronze was not what it was purported to be, and was only worth a few hundred dollars. In light of that, she would ask him to give back seventeen hundred dollars. She would keep the statue, no questions asked. If he balked at that, then she would mention that the original bronze was stolen from a summer home in Camden, suggest that the two were connected, and that somehow, he was implicated. She hoped she wouldn't have to mention that, but she prepared herself for it just in case.

From her parking space, she could see the sign for Relics just up the hill on the left side of the street. It was located in what looked to be an antique home, and sat stoically about thirty feet away from the street. Like most of the buildings in Wiscasset, it was buffed and ready for the tourists for whom the town was either a destination or just an irresistible stop while heading north or south along Route One.

Instead of driving any further, she decided to leave her van and walk the rest of the way. She removed the bronze from the back of her van and wrapped it even tighter in the blanket that had protected it on the trip to Maine. It was not so much that she was afraid of damaging it on the short walk to Relics, but she didn't want to be seen in public with it, particularly in Wiscasset, a town strewn with antique shops and dealers who regularly read the trade publications. Uncovered, the statue could easily be mistaken as the one stolen in Camden.

As she approached the shop, she knew right away that it was the one she was looking for. Hanging in the left front window was the Italian gouache she had held in her hands at Brimfield. The sight of it brought her to a halt, and she took a step backwards in apprehension. Then she took a deep breath and walked through the front door, activating the metal bell that hung above it as she did. Under normal circumstances, the bell told the proprietor that a customer had entered the store. Zoe couldn't help thinking she was the cat with a bell around its neck, forewarning the rat inside of her presence.

The shop itself was in fact, a converted home, an oversized center chimney cape built in the early eighteen hundreds. The display area consisted of the twin front parlors, the common room behind them, and what was formerly a small kitchen in the rear of the building. Unlike the choking potpourri that filled the air of a few of the other shops she had visited that day, Relics was rich with the smooth arias of Pavarotti, emanating from compact white speakers in the corners of every room. It was an odd foreign sound for a town so steeped in Americana, yet it provided the perfect audio backdrop for the sophisticated antiques that were displayed there.

There were a few couples carefully exploring merchandise in the left parlor, so Zoe went to the one on the right. The room glittered with European elegance. Leaning against one wall was an imposing, French white marble fireplace mantle. Next to that stood an Italian marble statue depicting Cupid and Psyche that still had a slight green moss and pollen hue from the garden in which it must have sat. There were inlaid console tables from Italy and Germany, and on the walls, unsigned and flaking Old Master paintings of Christ and His saints in every variation. Everywhere she looked, there were vestiges of Western Civilization, including the early nineteenth century French chairs that she had also seen at his booth in Brimfield. Certain that she was in the right place, Zoe made her way to the back of the shop to find Christopher Doria.

The common room of the cape, most likely originally furnished with primitive American furniture made by novice New England carpenters, was full of more artifacts fashioned by the finest craftsmen from Europe. In a strange way, the purity, naivete and simplicity of the American structure provided a cultural counterpoint for the high art of its European ancestors.

As Zoe entered the room, she barely noticed the antiques

around her. Instead, she focused her attention on the man sitting at a seventeenth century, oak refectory table. Legs of mutton and slabs of beef and venison were long gone and replaced by a telephone, computer and fax machine.

Christopher Doria was staring intently at the computer screen and didn't notice Zoe until she was right on top of him. "Hello Christopher," she said coldly.

He looked up from the screen and recognized her immediately. Then he looked at the blanket under her arm and right away surmised what was inside of it. "It's Zoe, right?"

"Yes."

Christopher got up from the chair and walked around the table toward her. "I've been trying to find you," he said sincerely, "but I didn't know your last name and frankly, couldn't remember if you told me."

He looked around the room to see if anyone else was in it. One of the couples had made their way from the parlor into the common room and were much too close to allow a private conversation. "Come with me." He led her to the kitchen pantry, now a storage room for extra office supplies, and a small library for antique reference books. "Zoe…there's been a terrible mistake."

"I know."

"Yes," he nodded, "the Pietà I sold you was stolen. It's hot." He pointed to the blanket. "Is that it?"

"Yes but…"

"I'll be more than happy to refund your money. I'm really sorry," he said. "I'm so embarrassed this happened. I should have suspected something when I bought it. Let me take it," he said, reaching for it.

Zoe pulled back, and held the bronze tighter. "Wait a minute," she said, sounding confused. "You think you sold me the bronze stolen in Camden?"

"Of course," he answered. "I saw a picture of it in the paper when I got home. I assume that's how you found out, too."

Zoe was bewildered by the conversation and was taken totally by surprise at his seemingly proactive and sincere response. "You mean that you didn't know that the bronze you sold me is a fake?"

"What do you mean, a fake?"

Zoe began to unwrap it on the counter in the closet. "A dealer friend of mine looked at it, and he told me it was recently cast and probably made from the original that was stolen."

"Let me see," he said impatiently.

He picked up the Pietà and studied it. Then like Elliot Baker had done, he ran his fingers along the edges to feel their texture. "You're right," he said in disbelief, feeling the recent sharpness of the edges. "This is almost brand new."

"And you didn't know that when you bought it? How could you not?" she asked skeptically.

He shook his head. "I really didn't look at it that closely when I bought it. And the guy that I bought it from always brings me great stuff."

"Well, it's a repro," she announced.

Christopher looked at her intently. "Zoe, I hope you don't think I knowingly sold you something that wasn't right."

"To be honest with you, I did. And I was furious."

"That's not my style," he said in his own defense. He turned and took a locked metal box from the top shelf. "Now, let me give you your money back. In cash, of course."

"I want to keep it."

"Why? It's not right."

"I have my reasons," she said. "The dealer who looked at said it was only worth a few hundred dollars. So how about if you give me seventeen hundred and I keep the bronze?"

He hesitated. "Two problems," he said. "Without the statue,

it will be harder for me to get my money back from the person I bought it from. But," he added, "I can work around that. Secondly, if you keep it, keep it under wraps. If it's connected to the one that was stolen, it could be confiscated by the police."

"That's what my friend said."

"But you still want it, right?"

"Yes."

"Okay," he said reluctantly.

He unlocked the metal box, took three inches of bills out of it, and counted out the money. "Here's eighteen hundred," he said. "A hundred extra for your trouble."

Zoe smiled. "Thanks. And I'm sorry I blamed you."

He shrugged his broad shoulders. "Who else could you blame? I'm just sorry it happened."

After the transaction, Christopher showed Zoe around his shop. All the anger that she had brought with her to Maine had dissipated, and she fully enjoyed the guided tour of his merchandise. By six, he was ready to close up for the day and she was ready for the long drive back home. After locking the shop door, he walked her to her van.

"How about dinner before you go back?"

"What?"

"I'd love to buy you dinner. Sort of a peace offering, you know?"

Zoe blushed. "That's not necessary."

Christopher casually leaned against the van. "Actually, it's not a peace offering at all. I'd just like to have dinner with you."

Zoe didn't know how to respond and searched her mind for an excuse. "I'd get back too late," she said, unconvincingly.

"Then spend the night," he persisted. "You already told me that you planned too, if necessary."

"I have no place to stay," she argued.

He pointed to a bed and breakfast sign just up from the van on the right. "You can stay at the Parkhurst House. I'm sure they can accommodate you."

"I don't know..."

Christopher grabbed her by the hand and began to coax her in the direction of the Parkhurst House. "C'mon," he smiled. "Let's get you a room for the night. We'll have fun. I promise."

Zoe looked at the handsome young man in front of her and thought about how absurd the two must have looked to the few people around them. For the moment, she didn't care. "Okay."

Zoe arrived at Le Garage, a landmark Wiscasset restaurant overlooking the Sheepscot River. An hour earlier, she had checked into the Parkhurst House and showered in the shared bathroom adjacent to her second floor room. She made the best of her meager wardrobe—the oversized, just-in-case argyle sweater that she had brought with her covered most of the sins of her well-worn jeans.

In order to settle her stomach, growling from a lack of food and queasy from her lack of experience in matters of dating, she had arrived a few minutes early to acclimate herself to the unfamiliar surroundings. She found a vacant seat at the small but serviceable bar inside, ordered a martini straight up, and immediately put a quarter of it straight down. Although the gin burned, it also hosed down the butterflies. It made them flutter lackadaisically, giving them a false sense of security, a dangerous lack of regard for any entomologist of the heart who might wander by with a net.

Zoe wondered why she accepted such a blind offer. She'd never been a reckless person, particularly since the death of her husband. She had learned to live guardedly, holding on tightly to the hand of his memory for companionship whenever she went out, even if only to the mall or supermarket. Sitting at a bar in a Maine tourist town, waiting to dine with an attractive man more than a decade younger, was something out of the question. It was an off-the-deep-end madness, totally indefensible in her own eyes as well as those of a stern society that frowned on older women with younger men, just as it winked with titillation at the opposite combination. Those thoughts did their best to put Zoe under lock and key. Luckily with another sip of courage, she managed to escape their grasp.

"Hi."

Zoe looked up from her martini. "Hi, Christopher."

"You're early," he said, looking at her drink. "I wish I had known. I would have joined you. I've been ready for half an hour."

"Have a seat," she smiled.

Christopher sat down on the stool next to her and immediately swiveled it to his left so he could face her. As he did, his knees touched the outside lip of her stool and made the slightest innocent contact with the middle of her firm right thigh. Zoe's first reaction was to move her body to the left to give both of them, especially herself, more room. Then she remembered how she and Richard would sit in a similar perpendicular fashion. He would bury his knees into her thigh, moving them back and forth in a sensual manner, stroking her as gently with his knees as he had always done with his hands. Within seconds, Zoe slid back to the center of the seat, compassionately allowing herself to relax, to dip her toe in the unfamiliar waters of the company of another man.

Christopher ordered a twin to her drink, and the two sat there for awhile talking about the bronze statue until the topic was old news. Then he insisted on hearing about One Piece Antiques, wanting to know everything about her shop as well as her partner.

Zoe explained the origin of the name. How she had found an article in a decorator magazine that extolled the virtues of how one, wonderful antique can change the entire look of any room. She went on to say that, unfortunately, she and Melissa rarely found a piece that was visually strong enough to carry out such a weighty premise. "We could maybe make over a bathroom," she laughed, "but that's about it."

Zoe also gave him the surface details of the quirkiness of Melissa, being careful not to violate the friendship in any way. As always, she talked lovingly about her partner, and it was obvious to Christopher that the two were very close, both in and out of the business.

Once they were seated at a table overlooking the river, Christopher became more pointed in his questions about Zoe's personal life. Initially she was reluctant to talk about it, but after a bottle of wine she spoke more freely. At first, about her daughter, Joanna. And then about her life with her husband, and his sudden death in Italy.

"So that's why you wanted the statue," he said gently. "I knew there was something at work there. I just didn't know what."

"I had to have it."

"I understand, Zoe. I have a similar piece that means just as much to me. And just like yours, the value of it has nothing to do with how much it's worth."

Zoe seemed surprised as well as elated that he had a kindred symbolic object in his life. Sometimes in her loneliness she believed that she was the only person in the world incapable of letting go of grief, and while others finally pick up their wounded hearts and move on, she was frozen in place.

"What's your Pietà?" she asked.

He reached down into his neck behind his forest green, cable knit sweater and pulled out an oval, sterling silver medal and stretched it as far as he could toward her. "This," he announced.

Zoe leaned across the table to get a better look, but the restaurant was dark enough that it kept the face of the medal in the shadows of the room. "I can't really see it," she said.

"It's a medal of St. Christopher carrying Christ on his shoulders. I wear it for my brother."

"Is he..." She paused for a moment. "Has he passed away?"

Christopher hesitated and then deliberately looked away from her as he answered. "Yes...he died when I was thirteen."

"What happened?"

"A bike accident...he got hit by a car when he was seven and ended up paralyzed from the neck down. Even though he had a wheelchair, there was no such thing as a handicap-accessible house back then. So I used to carry him up and down the stairs to his room. I promised I'd carry him anywhere he wanted to go for the rest of his life if necessary. Unfortunately, he died a year after the accident. So now," he said solemnly, "I carry him around my neck."

"I'm sorry."

He put the medal back in its hiding place. "It's nice to meet someone who understands the significance."

"I do, Christopher," she smiled. "And I feel the same way. Melissa and my daughter are the only other people who know why I bought the Pietà."

"I feel honored, then."

Zoe smiled but said nothing. She studied the Mediterranean tone of his angular face and the unblinking gaze of his chestnut brown eyes, slightly recessed and vaguely watery from the wine and the secrets that slipped through them.

"What are you thinking?" he asked, knowing that he was being closely watched.

"About Richard, my husband," she said softly. "And about your brother."

"What about them?"

Zoe took a sip of her wine. "About how their unfortunate deaths have given us something in common. Isn't that weird?"

Christopher shrugged. "I think everyone who has lost someone feels that way to some degree," he said. "But not everyone keeps them so alive. Let me ask you something...do you talk to him?"

"Everyday."

"Me too," he laughed. "In a strange way, my brother's grown up with me and shared in every good and bad time I've ever had. I feel like I'm experiencing life for both of us."

Zoe sat up straight in her chair. "That's exactly how I feel," she said enthusiastically. "It's like he's part of everything I do and every decision I make."

"I hope he approves of our dinner," he joked.

She turned suddenly quiet, guilty that she was enjoying herself. Then she peered from side to side, as if she were looking for someone over her shoulder.

"What is it?" he asked.

"I can't feel him right now. This has never happened before," she said anxiously.

Christopher sensed the conflict that she was in—that even in death, she somehow felt disloyal. He put his hand on top of hers, and she instinctively pulled it away.

"No, Christopher."

"Zoe, it's obvious that you still love your husband deeply, but you have to understand that it's okay to go on. Take him with you if you want. But go on."

"I'm not sure I can," she said. "I'm not even sure I want to."

From there the dinner went downhill like half-eaten plates of food being scraped into the garbage. Neither finished the coffee or dessert that they had ordered. After waiting an eternity for the check, Christopher walked her to the Parkhurst House, and they clumsily said good night in the chilly Maine air.

"Will I see you in the morning?" he asked.

"No, I want to get an early start."

"Can I call you?" he asked politely.

"I don't think that would be a good idea."

Christopher could tell by the tone of her voice that it was not the moment to argue some form of inclusion in her life. That would have to wait for another time.

"Good night, Zoe," he said as he squeezed her hand. "Have a safe trip back...I guess I'll see you in Brimfield in July."

"Melissa and I will be there."

"I'll look you up."

"Okay," she said, forcing a smile.

5

June is a pivotal month for the antique trade, particularly in tourist traffic areas such as the coast of Maine. It is the beginning of an incoming tide of business that will peak in August and then ebb until the following spring, when the pull of new merchandise will bring them back again.

Unlike the gift stores that fight for the same tourist dollar, the antique shops cannot phone a toll-free number and order a dozen antique dressers or tables when their stocks run low. Every piece from the smallest to the most grandiose must be found by the dealer, either at auction, at other shops, or as was often the case with Christopher Doria, from dependable pickers like Benjamin Divers.

Benjamin Divers was an unlikable and nervous man who came from one of those unfortunate old New England families that was rich in lineage but financially no better off than your average gaggle of immigrants. If his family had in fact, come over on the Mayflower as he had claimed, then they traveled in steerage class, and even after three hundred-something years, had yet to improve their monetary lot. The conflict between his privilege and poverty rang with resentment, and he never passed up an opportunity to take advantage of the wealthy elderly who were kind enough to let him inside their well-furnished homes, and allow him to cull the best of their inherited finery.

He had spent the first two weeks of June picking on the road. His first stop, as always, was Relics, a couple of hours north of his unassuming home behind a discount outlet strip mall in Kittery, Maine, just over the New Hampshire border. At Christopher's insistence, Benjamin arrived at ten, an hour before the shop would open for the day. He backed his van up to the small storage barn behind the shop. Before he could get out of his van, Christopher was already next to his open window.

"How are you, Benjamin?"

"I could be better," he complained. "That goddam traffic. I'm telling you, it gets worse every year."

"Quit your grousing," Christopher smiled, "and let's see what you've got."

He walked past the rear of the van and slid open the twelve foot, green wooden door of the barn, which was already bursting at its post and beam seams with antiques.

Benjamin opened both doors to his van, equally sardined with merchandise, and then turned and looked into the over-flowing structure. "You're going to try to fit some more stuff in there? I don't think so."

"If you've got something worth buying, I'll find a place for it," he answered.

Benjamin shook his head. "Okay."

For the next half hour, Benjamin pulled item after item out of his van and handed each of them to Christopher. After quick inspection, Christopher made two piles. A large "no" heap, and a highly selective "yes" pile. Keepers included four pieces of Early American furniture and a number of ornate

European objects, including an elaborate pair of eighteenth century, carved and painted altar candlesticks.

"That's all you're going to take?" said a disgruntled Benjamin. "You're kidding me, right? I drive all over the place for you, and this is the thanks I get?" he said, pointing at the "yes" pile.

"You'll be well paid, as usual," Christopher assured him. "I'll give you eight thousand for the lot."

Benjamin groaned and started to pace back and forth like some distraught animal, something he did whenever he was trying to negotiate a price. "No way, Chris. No way."

"You know," Christopher argued like a true businessman, "I've got to make a profit, too."

"A profit, not a killing," he snapped. "No way, Chris. I need at least twelve."

Benjamin began to pace even faster, and his groaning got louder and more plaintive as he did. "Eleven then."

"I'll tell you what, Ben," knowing that he would go lower. "I'll give you ten grand under one condition."

He stopped marching in circles. "What condition?"

"You know the bronze Pietà you sold me?"

"What about it?"

Christopher sensed the apprehension in his voice. "Don't worry. It's already in a private collection."

"What then?"

"Some repros were made from it before I sold it."

Benjamin grunted. "I should have charged you more for the original."

Christopher ignored his remark. "The repros are too hot to be around here." He pointed at the "yes" pile. "I'll give you ten for that...if you deliver the new Pietàs to a friend of mine in New York City."

"Jesus, Chris," he whined. "I don't want to go to Manhattan."

Christopher smiled at the sour man. "It seems to me that it's also in your best interest that the fakes are as far away from Maine as possible. Don't you think so?"

"They're not mine," he argued.

"Do you think the police would care?"

Benjamin didn't have to wait to answer. "Okay, it's a deal. Where are they?"

Christopher pointed over his shoulder to the barn. "Way in the back," he laughed.

Before Relics opened to the general public, Benjamin Divers was back on the road with ten thousand dollars cash in his pocket, and five bronze reproductions of the Pietà stashed in his van behind all the merchandise that Christopher had passed on. He was not looking forward to being caught in the choking traffic of New York City. However, his consolation was knowing that the fakes associated with him would be hundreds of miles away from his home state of Maine.

While Christopher Doria was skimming the cream of the business, Zoe and Melissa were scraping the bottom. Like their higher end counterpart, they too were in search of merchandise, both in preparation for the summer trade and for inventory to bring to Brimfield in July. But unlike Christopher, who could sit back and wait for the goods to come to him, Zoe and Melissa, aside from an occasional piece brought in by Elliot Baker, had to go out and find whatever they could.

Following Zoe's return from Maine, the two women hunted frenetically for stuff. They hit all the usual local spots that, more often than not, turned up little worth buying. They stood for hours in the rear of insignificant cruddy auctions, waving their bid numbers high in the air until the price went beyond their reach. On weekends, in spite of knowing better, they gently pushed more timid and indecisive retail buyers aside at yard sales. And everyday they cruised the shelves and racks of the Salvation Army and other thrift stores in the area. Somehow, through their omnibus efforts, they were able to gather enough to keep the shop reasonably full, as well as to stockpile some inventory for the next Brimfield.

The two women had just returned to the shop with merchandise from a house call, that domestic virgin territory so lusted after by all dealers. However, as happens so many times, the homeowner had already invited an auction company in to take the best of the contents. Only a few musty cardboard boxes from the cellar remained for Zoe and Melissa to make an offer on. In their grab bag mentality, instead of looking through the boxes, they offered the woman fifty dollars. Rather than dig through the damp contents herself to see if she were giving anything away, she accepted.

After emptying the third box on the floor of the shop, they figured they were up about a hundred dollars and still had one box to go. Before they could get to the last, the phone rang. Melissa picked it up by the third ring. "One Piece Antiques," she said professionally.

"Is Zoe there, please?"

"May I tell her who's calling?"

"Christopher. Christopher Doria."

Although Melissa had never seen his face or heard his voice, she knew exactly who he was. She put her hand over the receiver and whispered to her partner. "It's the bronze guy in Maine...Christopher."

Zoe seemed almost as surprised as Melissa that he was calling. Although he had suggested that he would like to, she believed he was merely being polite. In addition, she had discouraged him from any follow-up contact after their dinner in Wiscasset. Then she thought it might have something to do with the stolen bronze. "I'll take it," she said.

Reluctantly, Melissa handed her the portable phone and hoped that Zoe was not in some kind of trouble because of her fake Pietà.

"Hello?"

"Zoe, it's Christopher," he said warmly. "How are you?"

"I'm fine," she answered "Are you calling about the bronze?" she asked apprehensively.

"No," he laughed. "I just bought a beautiful pair of eighteenth century Italian altar candlesticks, and they made me think of you. I know how much you like Italian art."

Zoe seemed relieved that it had nothing to do with her bronze, and assumed he was offering them for sale. "Eighteenth century Italian candlesticks? I'm sure they're great," she said, turning her head slightly toward Melissa, "but I'm not in the market for anything right now."

Melissa shook her head from side to side in a determined negative fashion, emphatically warning Zoe not to buy anything else from the dealer.

"I'm not trying to sell them to you, Zoe" he said. "It's just that they reminded me of you, so I thought I would give you a call to see how you've been."

"Oh..." Zoe thought back to the comment he had made at dinner about what Richard would have thought about her quasi-date.

"So...how have you been?" he asked in a tone somewhere between amicable and familiar.

"Busy. We've been trying to restock, which for us is never easy."

"Tell me about it," he replied.

The two talked shop for a couple of minutes, while Melissa squirmed and hung onto Zoe's every word, trying to decipher the gist of the conversation from her one-sided perspective. Although Zoe had declared him innocent of any wrong doing after her return from Maine, Melissa was still suspicious of the young dealer. Lack of trust is one of the guiding principles of the antique business, and every dealer, at one time or another, becomes a suspect in a less than righteous or less than fair deal.

While Melissa fidgeted and eavesdropped, Zoe became more comfortable on the telephone, even as the conversation turned less business-oriented. Perhaps it was the sheer physical distance from Christopher that put her at ease. Or maybe it was just the time that had passed since her night in Wiscasset, the clock allowing her to catch her emotional breath and feel her deceased husband's presence again. Whatever the reason, she seemed to be enjoying the male attention that she was receiving. As the conversation became more personal, she walked outside with the portable phone, leaving Melissa desperately trying to read her lips.

After a few more minutes of small talk, Christopher cut to the chase of his call. "Zoe, I know we said we'd catch up with each other at Brimfield, but I'm going to be down your way next week, and I thought that maybe we could get together for dinner...or if you're too busy, then just a drink."

"You're going to be in Noble's Cove?"

"Actually, Essex. I've got to pick up some pieces from a dealer there."

"Essex is not exactly down my way," she laughed. "It's over an hour from here."

"It is when you're coming from Wiscasset. What's another hour after that?"

"I suppose."

"What do you say? Next Thursday...can you make it?"

Zoe balked while she tried to find a reason to say no, but she couldn't find one, at least not in the moment she had to decide. Then as she often did, she let her heart speak silently to Richard, asking him for his counsel.

"What do you think, Richard?"

His answer was instantaneous. She could feel the warmth of his presence and almost see the smile on his face that spoke without words.

"All I want is for you to be happy, Zoe. That's all I ever wanted."

"Okay, Christopher. What time?"

"You can make it?" he said enthusiastically. "Great. I've got a two o'clock in Essex and that shouldn't take more than an hour. So I'll see you around four-thirty."

"Where?"

"At your shop, of course."

"Do you know how to get here? Noble's Cove is kind of out of the way," she said apologetically.

"Hey, you found me, didn't you?"

"Yes."

"Then I'm sure I can find you. See you Thursday."

Zoe said goodbye and stood in the parking lot with the phone down by her side. Within seconds, Melissa was by her side as well. "What did he want?"

Zoe turned to her and smiled. Her cheeks had the slightest flush. "He's taking me out to dinner next week."

Melissa was in shock. Zoe had never mentioned that she had dinner with him in Wiscasset, so the invitation took her totally by surprise. "He asked you to dinner? And you accepted?" she said incredulously.

"Yes. What's wrong with that?" Zoe asked defensively. "You're the one pushing me to start seeing men."

"Right," she agreed. "But this is different."

"Why?"

"First of all, he sold you a fake. Even worse, it was cast from something that was stolen."

"He didn't know it was a fake."

"How can you be sure?"

"I believe him, that's all."

By the tone of Zoe's voice, Melissa could tell that this argument was not one she could win. "Okay, so maybe he didn't know it. But you're still twice his age."

Zoe was insulted. "I am not. He's thirty-five. Do I look like I'm seventy?"

"Zoe, you know what I'm saying. He's too young for you."

"Wait a minute," she said. "When I first told you about him, you were licking your chops, too."

"I was just joking," she protested. "I never thought that you would ever see him again, and I was just teasing you."

"Well, I am going to see him again. Next Thursday. He's coming to the shop in the afternoon."

Melissa flipped through her mental calendar. "Thursday's my day off," she complained.

Zoe baited her. "Then I guess you won't meet him."

"What? Are you shitting me? I wouldn't miss that for the world. I'll be there."

Zoe laughed and put her arm around Melissa's shoulder. "You might even like him," she suggested.

Without thinking, Melissa began to fuss with her hair, adjusting it with the fingers of both hands. "I'll be the judge of that, thank you," she said sternly.

Zoe nudged her by the shoulder toward the shop door. "C'mon. Let's finish going through our house call."

Sometimes even the contents of a forgotten, water-stained cardboard box can reveal much about a family and the lives that formed it. The last box from the house call was one of those boxes—a corrugated diary of children, parents and grandparents, thrown together in good faith over the years, but ultimately unimportant enough to be relegated to any room except the cellar.

In between the afternoon's few browsers and buyers, Zoe and Melissa painstakingly excavated the layers of paper and paraphernalia inside the box. They laid the contents out on the floor, like so many fragments of some ancient, Etruscan urn that was once as whole as the family who used it. The largest fragments were the most recent—birth certificates from the late nineteen forties—three of them, two boys and a girl. There was also evidence of their childhoods in the form of Boy Scout and Girl Scout memorabilia, as well as one putrid report card received by one of the boys in the fifth grade that fully deserved the musty burial that it had been subjected to.

The fragments of the parents were fewer and smaller. A wedding picture dated nineteen forty-four of a young G.I. escorting his bride out of a church and into their uncertain future. On both sides of them were more uniformed men, crossing their unsheathed swords over the heads of the bride and groom like an armed canopy to protect the marriage from the ongoing war that would be their honeymoon. Thankfully, the honor guard's steadfastness worked. The same man, dressed in civilian clothes, was found in other photographs, bouncing post-war children on his knees. His wife, recognized by Melissa as the woman in the house call, stood or sat next to him in almost every picture.

The ages of the family grew as the two dug deeper into the photographs. Then the husband became conspicuous by his absence. After looking at a half dozen pictures without him, Melissa picked up a stack of greeting cards under the few remaining photos. They were tightly wrapped with faded black ribbon. She untied them and thumbed through them. Each was a sympathy card, extending the utmost of condolences on the death of "Frank." One of them was still in its envelope and was postmarked July twenty-seventh, nineteen sixty-three.

"God, Zoe," she said. "He was young when he died."

Zoe looked pensively at Melissa but didn't respond. Instead she began to dig deeper into the box. She pulled out a small, rusted metal container marked, "Papa" and opened it. On the very top was a crude but legible photograph of a man and a woman. The background looked like a New York ghetto around the turn of the century.

"They must be the grandparents," said Zoe respectfully.

While Zoe studied the picture, Melissa rummaged through the metal box until her hand hit something solid. "There's something here," she said with anticipation.

"What?"

From the bottom of the container, Melissa pulled out a pocket watch. "This has got to be his." She smiled. "Well, maybe this will make the house call worthwhile."

Neither of them knew much about watches, but the fact that it was gold told them that at least it was unusual.

"Let me see that," said Zoe.

Melissa handed it to her, and Zoe squinted to read the tiny name on the face of it. "Do you know who made this, Melissa?"

"I have no idea."

"It's a Patek Philippe."

"Who?"

"Patek Philippe. I know they're incredibly expensive watches." Zoe pointed to the reference books on the desk. "See if you can find it in Kovel's."

Melissa went to the desk where they kept their antique reference and price books. In the most recent *Kovel's*, the monetary bible of the business, she found what she was looking for. "Holy shit."

"What is it?"

"There are three listings here for Patek Philippe pocket watches." She paused. "Are you ready for this?" she said cautiously "From two thousand to six thousand."

Zoe grabbed the book from her. "Let me see." She ran her finger down the edge of the black and white type and read the listings for herself. "Wow," she said softly.

"Wow?" remarked Melissa. "It's more than that. This could be the biggest hit we ever had."

Zoe put the book down on the floor and studied the watch. Although it was beautiful to the eye, its thoroughbred value eluded her. She had not been in the business long enough to fully comprehend how any pocket watch could be worth thousands of dollars. However, she did understand its potential sentimental value. She picked up the photograph of the couple that they had identified as the grandparents and held it next to the watch. "You know, this is an important family heirloom."

"Not anymore," quipped Melissa. "It's inventory now."

"We can't keep this, Melissa."

"What are you talking about? We got it fair and square in a box lot."

"I know that, but I'm sure the woman we bought it from didn't know it was in there. We at least have to tell her about it."

"Are you crazy? Then she'll want it back."

For the first time since they had become partners, Zoe and Melissa approached the moral crossroads of the antiques business. That intersection of right and wrong that is inherent to the enterprise. Buy low and sell high are innocent enough principles, applicable to almost any business venture. Taking advantage of the ignorant is something else altogether, and many an elderly man or woman has been unknowingly robbed of the fair value of their earthly possessions by unscrupulous antique dealers.

Zoe turned to Melissa, who looked pale at the thought of giving the watch back. "You know as well as I do that it would be wrong for us not to let her know about it. "Anyway," she added, "how would you feel if someone did that to you?"

Melissa was cornered. "Of course I wouldn't like it, but this is different. We never get a chance like this."

"I'll tell you what, Melissa. Let's find out how much it's worth and then go back and tell her. If she wants to sell it, then we'll offer her a fair wholesale price, and we'll still make a decent profit. Plus," she smiled, "we'll still be able to sleep at night."

Melissa knew her partner's plan was right, but there was still a nagging part of her that wanted to treat it as found anonymous money, like a stack of bills on the sidewalk. What she couldn't get out of her head was the fact that she knew who had dropped it. "Okay," she said reluctantly. "We'll do it your way."

Zoe smiled. "Good."

"We'll never see a watch like that again, you know," she said regretfully.

"That's okay. Something else will come along with fewer strings attached."

Melissa shrugged. "I hope you're right."

During the week, Zoe anticipated her upcoming dinner date, while her daughter mulled over her lack of one. In the stress of an engagement closing in on marriage, Ramon and Joanna had, at least temporarily, gone their separate but unequal ways. To say that Ramon left her for another woman was not an accurate description. Even with Joanna's knowledge, he was unable to wean himself off the idea of variety. The other woman that he continued to see meant nothing more to him than the sexual freedom that, as a man, he felt was his inalienable right.

Joanna saw it differently. Having cold feet was something she could understand and accept. Being a coward to commitment was something she would not tolerate. Positioning herself firmly on that platform, she asked Ramon to leave the apartment leased in her name until such time that he was willing to give up his freedom for the greater and more succinct good of absolute fidelity. But in spite of her up-front resolve, the person behind the game face was frightened by the thought of living alone. Almost nightly, she leaned on her mother for support and advice.

"What am I going to do?" Joanna asked Zoe, in the crowded Early Bird evening at Swider's Seafood Shanty.

"Wait and see."

Joanna spoke louder in her frustration. "For what? For him to come crawling back? Because that's what he's going to have to do."

"God, you're a hard ass," she said. "Maybe you both have to crawl a little."

"I can't believe I'm hearing this from my own mother," she snapped. "I bet you wouldn't be so cavalier if you were in the same situation."

"Lucky for me, Joanna," Zoe said darkly, "I'm not. Nor do I plan to be in the future. I had my years in the wedding circle...fortunately, they were good ones."

Joanna stabbed at the last piece of swordfish on her plate. "So you're saying I should just ignore Ramon's screwing around?"

"Joanna," she said sincerely, "all I'm saying is that marriage is a crap shoot. I can't tell you if he's going to be faithful. Yeah," she added, "your father and I had a good marriage. But if I knew he was going to drop dead in the middle of our lives, would I still have married him?"

She looked at her mother and could see tears forming in her eyes. She knew it made no sense to press her for an answer. "I understand, Mom."

"Honey, the big difference between us is that those kinds of decisions are behind me now. I've good memories to hold onto...you still have yours to make. And there's no telling now whether they'll be good or bad."

"Okay, Mom, I'll wait and see what happens with Ramon."

Zoe took a long last sip of her martini. "Good. Now can we change the subject? How about another glass of wine? Or do you want to wait until we get back to the house?"

"Sure, I'll have another one."

"You are going to spend the night, right?"

"I might as well. It's no fun going home to an empty apartment."

"You too?" she laughed, just as the waitress approached. "Two more," Zoe said, gesturing with her fingers. "And make them big ones. We're almost within walking distance."

The waitress scribbled the request in her order pad. At the same time, she scrutinized the women just to make sure she wouldn't be overserving them. Each was on her third drink, at least one ahead of schedule for most early bird diners, and she knew that there was a lot of night left after seven-thirty. Just to be sure that they would leave relatively sober, she made a suggestion as she began to clear their empty plates. "Would you like the check now as well, or will you be wanting coffee and dessert?"

Zoe guessed her concern. "The check will be fine, thank you."

The waitress breathed the smallest sigh of relief. "I'll have your drinks and your check in a minute And I'll bring you some coffee on the house," she smiled.

"That's not necessary," said Zoe, "but thanks anyway."

"It will be my pleasure," she replied as she turned and walked away.

In the early years of mother and child, the two come together by way of their differences. One dreams, while the other faces reality. And each yearns for something of the other.

Youth desires the freedom of age. While age would trade almost anything to be among the young again.

Although the years never physically get any closer, the experiences of mother and daughter eventually cross paths as if they were born only minutes apart. In the case of Zoe and Joanna, both of them now felt the loss of the men in their lives. And neither of them looked forward to going home alone to a house furnished only with the shreds of memories. As one learns in swimming lessons for beginners, the "buddy system" can save you from drowning—in a lake, a pond or sometimes, even in your own deep reservoir of loneliness.

The thoughts and desires of Zoe and Joanna swam together after dinner that night in the shadow of the Italian gouaches on Zoe's living room wall. Quietly they sipped wine and shared moments of their separate lives that, up until that evening, were too personal to bring up. Joanna divulged her own infidelity during her relationship with Ramon. And Zoe carefully but casually announced her upcoming dinner with Christopher Doria, laughingly applying the same age differential that she had scorned Melissa for using.

To Zoe's surprise, Joanna seemed neither shocked nor angry that her mother was entertaining the advances of a younger man. As a child, Joanna learned about sex and procreation from her friends and peers. Like most children, she was abhorred by the thought of her parents "doing it." In the same way, at the time of her father's death, she selfishly could not conceive of her mother being with another man, let alone someone who was more age appropriate for her. But at that moment, mother and daughter and all the jealousies and expectations between them were mere figures on the shore. And the two grown women moved deliberately toward the deep end of friendship, until mother and daughter were completely out of sight.

6

The nineteen sixty-seven Austin Healy 3000 came to a graceful stop in front of Drake's Antiques. It was a perfect day for a vintage convertible—sunny, and about seventy-five degrees. It was also the perfect town for a vintage convertible. Essex is the quintessential New England seafaring town, having earned its reputation as a premier builder of ships during the very birth of America. Its heyday came in the late eighteen hundreds and early nineteen hundreds when it supplied some of the sleekest and fastest schooners that raced offshore to the Grand Banks, seeking their fortunes in American cod.

Using its maritime heritage as both anchor and compass, Essex successfully navigated into the late twentieth century and recycled itself into a home port for some of the finest antiques shops in the country. The main street looks like the template that a theme park designer would use to capture that elusive period in America's history. The nineteenth century buildings have been preserved, updated, and are now filled with antiques, some even nautical, instead of the sundries and supplies that they housed when it was a working fishing and boat building town. And like the craftsmen that preceded them, the dealers in Essex have a similar unequaled reputation for quality.

Christopher bent his body as far to the right as he could so his left leg would clear the low, open door of the Austin Healy. Although not the easiest car for a man his size to get in and out of, the joy of driving it eclipsed any ergonomic negatives. Like many dealers, he had an appreciation for almost anything old, including antique automobiles. He had taken it in trade for two oil paintings a year before, planning to keep it until he could make at least a twenty percent profit on it. In the meantime, he focused only on the pleasure of driving it.

Because he would meet Zoe later in the day, he was not dressed in his normal jeans and sweatshirt. He looked more like a sports car buff waiting for a rally to begin, rather than a working antique dealer. He was wearing a pleated pair of sand-colored, linen pants and a milk chocolate silk shirt, open at the neck. His Saint Christopher medal was fully exposed and glittered in the early afternoon sun.

Before he went inside Drake's, he studied the display in the window of the whitewashed brick building, and smiled to himself at the jumbled presentation of fine, nineteenth century objects. To say that they were thoughtfully arranged would be a gross overstatement. Arthur Drake, although one of the finer dealers in Americana, had no sense or care for merchandising whatsoever. As usual, his window offering reflected it. While many dealers spend hours creating perfect compositions to lure passersby into their shops, Arthur dumped his treasures in front of the glass, leaving it up to the window shopper to appreciate their historic or artistic potential. "They'll know it when they see it," was his argument. "Anyway, I'm a dealer, not a decorator."

His lack of retail sensibilities was one of the reasons that

Christopher enjoyed dealing with Arthur Drake. He was in the business because of his love for the objects, not how they looked in the window or on the selling floor. Christopher had a similar passion for what he bought and sold, although he couldn't be quite as cavalier when it came to displaying them in his own shop. Neatness, a virtue he had been taught as a young boy, was difficult to surrender.

Arthur was ceremoniously ignoring the few customers in his shop when Christopher walked in. He was dressed in madras plaid shorts and a blue shirt that was buckling at the buttons from his fast food belly. Adding to the stress was the coffee roll he was unraveling and holding over his mouth like a fish over a seal, before lowering it into the open cavity. At six foot five, he was as tall as an eighteenth century highboy, and his silky albino hair added an aura of eccentricity that made him the perfect sort for the business of secondhand artifacts.

"Hey," he said casually as Christopher approached him. "How are you, Guido?"

"Mr. Guido to you," laughed Christopher in his best Italian accent. "I'm good," he said, shaking his hand. "How about yourself?"

Arthur looked around the shop. "Aside from these pesky tire kickers," he said loudly enough that a couple of the customers heard him, "fine."

Almost on cue, the man and woman closest to him turned and walked toward the door.

"Have a nice day," Arthur said caustically.

Christopher shook his head. "Who are you, the manager of the sales prevention department?"

"They weren't going to buy anyway. They belong in a church bazaar," he added.

"You're tough, you know that?"

"Gotta be," he said. "I can't spend my day explaining why

a killer, grain-painted blanket chest costs four grand." He pointed to a copper weather vane in the form of a running horse. "Or why that weather vane is marked eight thousand dollars. If they don't know why, then they don't belong in here."

"I know what you're saying, Arthur, but you could try to be a little more discreet in your contempt."

"Nah," he said without giving it a second thought.

The two chatted until the shop was empty of customers, and then they got down to business. Arthur turned the swivel oak desk chair he was sitting in toward the file cabinet behind him. "I've got a couple of things you're really going to like," he said as he unlocked it. "They're not my cup of tea, but I think you'll be quite pleased."

He reached into the drawer and removed two clumps of tissue paper and put them on the desk. "They came out of a collection in Connecticut," he said as he unwrapped them. As he did, Christopher's eyes grew wide with anticipation. Arthur removed all the paper and laid the objects side by side. Then he pushed them across the desk toward Christopher. He picked up the copper figure, green with oxidation, and began to study it. It was a figure about six inches tall of what looked like a man with large ears and a pointed cap.

"Nice dunce cap on the guy," remarked Arthur.

"It's a headdress," Christopher corrected him. "And it's not a guy. It's probably a Phoenician god," he said respectfully. "Made around thirteen hundred B.C."

"That early?"

Christopher nodded. "It's great. And I've got just the collector for it. But first, I think I'll have a few new ones made from it. I'm sure we can make them look at least a couple of thousand years old," he laughed.

"Copper ages nicely, doesn't it?"

"The oxidation gets them every time."

Christopher turned his attention to the second piece on the desk. It was a five inch square, carved piece of ivory with finely incised figures on both sides of it. He gently rubbed his finger over the carved faces. "It's Byzantine...about nine hundred A.D., I'd say. It's a carving of Christ and, I would guess, some of his apostles. I'd like to keep this one myself...at least for awhile."

"I knew you would like them, Guido."

"How much for the two?"

Arthur shrugged his shoulders. "You're the expert on that kind of stuff. If they were Americana, I could give you a price, but you're going to have to tell me what you think would be fair."

"How hot are they?"

"Right now? Lukewarm. Believe it or not, they weren't even on display in the house. They were in storage, so my guess is that they won't be missed for awhile, maybe even years. The Revere silver, on the other hand, has already been reported stolen."

"An eclectic collection," remarked Christopher.

"Yeah, they had a little bit of everything, and it's all great. I got top dollar for the silver, and it's already safe and sound in another collection."

"I think thirteen grand would be a fair price, Arthur. I know I can get around nine for the Phoenician piece, and I'll take my chances on the repros of it. In any event, I'm going to have to sell them short. Now, on the other piece, my guess is that on the open market the Byzantine ivory would bring around twenty. However, since I don't have a ready buyer for it, I might have to firesale it at seven or eight grand."

"Like I said, you're the expert."

"I really appreciate your calling me on this."

"I knew they were you when I saw them, Guido. And it's always a pleasure doing business with you. By the way," he laughed, "I saw a mug shot of your bronze Pietà in the paper."

"Yeah, that didn't work out as well as I hoped. I had to move the repros to New York." He pointed to the copper god. "I hope the same doesn't happen to this."

"Well, I don't think you'll be seeing any pictures of this stuff in the paper real soon."

"Good. Because I hate the dicey part of the business."

"Comes with the territory, I'm afraid. We all have to pay our bills. And you certainly have your hands full," he added.

"Tell me about it," he replied. "I just can't stand looking over my shoulder all the time."

Arthur looked at him with affection. "Don't worry about it, Guido. You'll be fine."

"I hope so."

After paying Arthur thirteen thousand dollars in cash from the wad of money in the front pocket of his pants, the two of them walked outside. Christopher opened the tiny trunk of the Austin Healy and put his purchases in a small gym bag.

"It's a good thing you didn't buy anything big," joked Arthur.

"That's for sure," agreed Christopher as he carefully closed the trunk.

"Back to Maine?"

"No, I'm going to Noble's Cove. I've got a dinner date with a dealer there."

"Male or female?"

"Female," he smiled.

Arthur shook his finger at him. "Never date anyone in the business, my friend. It's a very dangerous concept."

"I'm being careful."

"Make sure you are. I'd hate to see you get in trouble. Even worse, I'd hate to see me get in trouble."

"I won't even mention you," he promised.

"You'd be surprised at what people tell each other when they're naked."

"It's just dinner, Arthur," he protested. "I'm not sleeping with her."

"No? Well give it time," he said. "Just don't bring my name up in your pillow talk."

"You're a piece of work, do you know that?"

"You too, Guido," he smiled.

By four o'clock, Melissa had planted herself in the front window of the shop and stared out at the vacant parking lot, impatiently waiting for Christopher to show up. Even though it was her day off, she had arrived around noon and kept herself busy by polishing every piece of silver plate that they owned. Zoe, much more at ease, spent her time polishing her nails a pale rose to coordinate with a new and somewhat sheer light green sundress that she had bought for the occasion.

"When do you think he'll get here?" Melissa asked impatiently.

"I told you before, Melissa...any time now. Jesus," she added, "you're so nervous you'd think that you were the one going to dinner with him."

"I'm nervous for you, that's all."

"He's not going to bite me," she laughed, as she went to the open front door and looked out into the parking lot.

As Zoe stood in the doorway, Melissa watched the facing sun illuminate the curve of Zoe's thighs and the straightness of her legs through the delicate dress. "Zoe," she said in shock, "do you realize you're not wearing a slip?"

Zoe turned to her. "I know I'm not."

"Well, you can see right through your dress!"

"How do I look?" she teased.

Melissa didn't know how to respond. "What?"

"How do I look?"

"You're crazy, do you know that? What kind of signal do you think that sends?"

"I'm not sending any signal," she laughed. "Anyway, do you want me to date or not? Let me know when you decide."

Before Melissa could respond, the British Racing Green Austin Healy purred into the parking lot of One Piece Antiques. The sports car definitely cut a masculine image and was an unusual sight in the lot, normally dressed in suburban vans and sport utility vehicles driven by forty-something, married women.

"Is that him?" asked Melissa.

Zoe watched Christopher extricate himself from the car. "That's him."

Melissa ran her fingers through her hair and took a peek at her face in the mahogany mirror next to the desk. Then she caught another glimpse of Zoe's lower torso shining like fire in the sun. "Get out of the doorway, Zoe. Don't be so eager to give it away."

"Melissa," she said with resolve, "I'm not going to give anything away." Then she left the doorway and went outside to greet him.

"Here goes nothing, Richard," she whispered to her husband, as she approached Christopher.

As soon as he saw her, he broke into a smile as wide as a high school prom. He held a gift wrapped package in his hand like a nosegay. "Hi Zoe."

"Christopher," she said as she reached him, "it's good to see you. Did you have a hard time finding us?"

"Not at all." He looked toward the shop. "It's a great location," he said approvingly.

"Thanks." She looked around at the empty parking lot. "It's a little slow today. It's usually a lot busier."

"We all have those days, Zoe. Here," he said as he handed her the package, "this is for you."

Zoe took it from him. "For me?"

"It's just a little something I had at home that I thought you might like. Open it."

While Melissa watched surreptitiously from inside the shop, Zoe ripped open the floral gift wrap. Inside was a beautifully lithographed book titled, *Napoli*. Embossed in the foreground on the cover were orange and lemon groves, and in the background was an erupting Mount Vesuvius.

"This is wonderful, Christopher."

"I'm glad you like it. It's a souvenir book from the thirties. See?" He opened it and pointed to the black and white photographs of tourist attractions found in Naples. "It's got all the hot spots in Naples," he laughed. "Including Vesuvius."

"Thank you so much," she said sincerely. "It will go great with my collection of gouaches."

"You're welcome, Zoe."

For a moment, they just looked at each other and smiled. Then Christopher took a step back and spoke. "You look great, Zoe," he said, quietly admiring the gauzy sensuality of her dress. "This is the first time I've seen you in a dress."

"Thanks." She blushed and stroked the front of her thighs with her hands. "I figured I would splurge for the occasion," she laughed nervously. "C'mon in the store," she said to get the attention off herself. "I want you to meet Melissa."

The two went into the store where Melissa was dutifully sitting at the desk. She was hunched over some papers and feigned attention to them. As soon as it was appropriate for the sound of their voices to interrupt her purported chain of thought, she looked up and smiled.

"Hello."

Christopher held out his hand. "Hi, Melissa. It's nice to

meet you."

Melissa looked at him closely. For a moment, his youth and his beauty left her breathless, and all the warnings she had bestowed on Zoe now seemed unnecessary and meaningless. "It's nice to meet you, too," she said, hoping he wouldn't hear her pounding heart. Then she looked at Zoe, and Zoe could tell right away that Melissa was quite taken with her friend.

"I've told Christopher a lot about you, Melissa."

"I hope only the good parts."

"All good," Christopher chimed in.

"Well," Melissa said uncomfortably, "would you like to see the shop? I mean...you're already in it, of course, but would you like me to show you around?"

"That would be great, Melissa."

Although not confident in her people skills, Melissa felt quite in control in and around antiques. Like a yard sale curator, she escorted Christopher through the shop, pointing out some of her favorite pieces and relaying any colorful information about them. When she got to the jewelry case, she singled out the Patek Philippe pocket watch. She told him the entire story about it, taking much more credit than she deserved for going back to the woman who unknowingly sold it to them and offering her two thousand dollars for it.

"It's a stunning timepiece," he said as he looked closely at it.

"It's a stunning price," remarked Melissa. "Thirty-five hundred is a lot for a watch, especially around here. So we figured we'd keep it for a month or so, and if no one buys it, then we'll put it in a good auction."

"I'll buy it," he said firmly.

Melissa thought he was just being gracious. "Don't be silly," she laughed. "We'll find a buyer."

"No, I'm serious. I know someone who collects these, and I can flip it in a minute and make a few bucks in the process."

"You're kidding, right?"

"No Melissa. I know a lot of high end collectors of almost everything, and watches like this one are hard to come by. Believe me, I'm not doing you any favors. In fact," he smiled, "you'll be doing me a favor by selling it to me."

By then, Zoe had joined in on the conversation and expressed a similar concern. "Are you sure, Christopher?"

"Zoe," he said, "you've been to my shop, so you know what kind of clientele I attract, right?"

Zoe looked around the store and laughed. "A different kind than we get. Okay, if you want it, it's yours."

"Thanks. Is cash okay?" he said as he took his roll out of his pocket.

"As long as it's in unmarked bills," she joked.

After the transaction, the three sat around the shop and chatted about the antique business, with Christopher doing most of the talking. The two neophytes were enthralled with the circles that he was part of and couldn't imagine traveling in them themselves.

"We're more country dealers," offered Melissa.

"Junk dealers is more like it," said Zoe.

"You have very nice things," said Christopher. "And I'm sure the people you deal with are a lot nicer than my customers. You wouldn't believe the egos that money creates."

"Oh, I don't think you have a monopoly on egos," argued Zoe. "We have a couple of women customers that treat us like personal shoppers. They take things home on twenty-four hour approval, and then we don't hear from them for a week. And that's only because we call them."

"You too?" he laughed.

"Yup," said Zoe. "They just don't spend as much with us, which makes it even more absurd. I mean how long does it take to decide whether or not you want to keep a forty dollar watercolor or a thirty dollar chair?"

"It's painful," added Melissa.

"I feel for you two," he smiled. "That would drive me crazy."

"It does," said Zoe, "and that's why we're going to close up right now, before anyone else comes in." She looked at her watch. "It's five of five," she said. "Let's get out of here and get a drink."

"Sounds good to me," said Christopher

Melissa brought in the flag, and Zoe put on a few lights in the shop so that after dark the merchandise in the windows could be seen from the street. Once locked up, the three went to the parking lot.

Melissa offered her hand to Christopher. "Nice to meet you Christopher. I hope the two of you have a good time tonight."

"Nice to meet you too, Melissa."

Zoe interrupted. "Melissa, why don't you join us for a drink?"

"Oh, no thanks."

"C'mon," she said. "There's no sense going home to an empty house."

"No, really..."

"Yeah," said Christopher. "Have a drink with us. It will be fun."

Melissa looked at Zoe. "Are you sure?"

Zoe hugged her with her eyes. "Absolutely."

"C'mon," said Christopher. "We'll go in my car."

"Great," said Zoe.

"I'll follow you in mine," said Melissa.

"No, we can all fit in the Healy," he said.

"The back will be perfect for you, Melissa," laughed Zoe. "You're tiny enough."

Melissa giggled. "I haven't ridden in the jump seat of a sports car since I was in high school."

"Well, then you're overdue." Christopher took her by the hand, walked her over to the Austin Healy, and opened the door for her.

"This is silly," she said.

"Quiet, Melissa," said Zoe as she got in the passenger side. "You need a little fun in your life."

"Okay. Whatever you say."

As soon as the women were settled, Christopher started up the vintage automobile and pulled out to the edge of the street. "Where to?"

"Left," said Zoe. "To the Jack Tar House."

"Just tell me how to get there." Christopher put the car in first gear and gunned it, leaving a length of rubber on the street behind. The quick movement jolted Melissa in the skimpy back seat, and she squealed with delight as he throttled down the street.

Drinking at the Jack Tar House offered patrons a choice between North and South Korea. The cocktail lounge and bar were separated by different ideologies about the consumption of liquor, as well as a physical line of demarcation—a narrow, chest-high pine partition with three bar stools on the bar side of it, that were usually filled with scowling alcoholic sentries staring at the less rude crowd on the lounge side of the room.

The threesome sat at a corner table in South Korea, as far away from the bar as possible. When they had pulled into the parking lot, Melissa spotted her ex-husband's heavy equipment, and tapped Zoe on the shoulder, pointing it out to her. She understood the problem immediately. When they entered the lounge, Zoe took it upon herself to find them as private a setting as possible, one where they would hopefully go unnoticed by Backhoe Lipton, a citizen in good, but sometimes unsteady standing, on the bar side of the Jack Tar House.

While Christopher and Zoe sipped their martinis, Melissa drank an uneasy glass of white wine. By the time she reached the cork residue in the bottom of the glass, Backhoe, with beer in hand, was standing in front of them. Since the two women sat on either side of Christopher, it was impossible to tell which woman was associated with him. In his liquored-up jealousy and sense of entitlement, Brad assumed the handsome young man was with his ex-wife, something he would not tolerate.

"Hi 'Lis," he hissed, as he stared at Christopher, who was baffled by his demeanor.

"Hi Brad...uh...I'd like you to meet Christopher. He's..."

"What's he doing with you, 'Lis?"

"He's Zoe's friend, Brad."

"I don't care whose friend he is. What's he doing with you?"

"Brad, you don't understand..."

He put his face right into Christopher's. "Hey buddy, why don't you chase someone your own age, huh?"

Before Christopher could say anything, Zoe got up from the table and grabbed Brad by the arm. "Brad, don't you get it? He's with me, not Melissa. We just invited her out for a drink, that's all."

"With you?" he said with disdain.

Zoe turned red. "What? Is there something wrong with that?"

"He's a little too young for you, don't you think?"

"Yeah," she snapped. "Like you're a little too drunk for Melissa."

Christopher jumped up from his seat and used all of his height to reach over the table. He grabbed Brad's dirty tee shirt right at the neck and twisted it until it was noose-tight. "Listen" he said calmly, "I don't know who you are..."

"He's my ex-husband."

Christopher loosened his grasp but still hung onto his shirt.

"Nice to meet you. Now, why don't you just leave?"

For a moment, Brad returned to his senses. "I thought you were with Melissa, that's all. You understand, right?"

"What I understand is that you're causing a scene. Now please, back off."

Christopher let go of his shirt, and Brad tried to press the wrinkles out of it with his hands.

"Melissa," Brad said softly, "can I talk to you for a minute?"

She raised her eyes from the table. They were damp with embarrassment. "Sure."

"In private," he said, pointing to the exit.

Melissa excused herself, and before they walked out together, Brad apologized to both Zoe and Christopher.

Neither of them responded.

"I'll take her home," he added.

Melissa tried to smile at Zoe and Christopher but was too upset. "I'll see you tomorrow," she said faintly, following her ex-husband out the door.

Dinner reservations were for seven o'clock at the Witch Haven Inn, a colonial road house that sat high on a bluff overlooking the harbor in Noble's Cove, and was supposedly the site of an eighteenth century coven of witches. The fare was steak and chops, and the quality and prices were more than a cut above those of the Jack Tar House. After their soiree with Backhoe Lipton, Zoe suggested that they pick up where they left off at the more civilized bar in the Witch Haven. After another round of martinis, they were seated at a table in the front window, which offered them an unencumbered view of the harbor, lit by the sinking sun.

To Zoe's relief, the meal was as good as expected, and Christopher complimented her on her fine choice of restaurants. She had initially made reservations at Swider's. But after considering the average age of the customers there, she felt that she would look younger in the Witch Haven Inn, a place pricey enough to attract a younger, more affluent crowd.

By eight-thirty, the sun was gone, and the candle that flickered in the middle of the table took on a new sense of importance. The conversation had finally moved off Melissa and her odd relationship with her ex, and focused more on the personal lives of the two diners. More stories of deceased loved ones were exchanged. Then they began to casually survey the likes and dislikes of each other, being cautious not to probe too deeply at such an early juncture in their relationship. Carefully, they removed layers of history from each other, until Christopher hit bedrock by asking if she thought she would ever marry again.

"What should I say, Richard? I would never deny you."

"Zoe, I know that. Live your life."

"I don't know how to answer that question, Christopher. I loved my husband very much, and even today I can't imagine being able to feel the same about another man." She shrugged her shoulders and smiled. "I don't know. And what about you?"

"What about me?"

"Marriage."

"I don't think it will ever happen."

"Why not?"

"Two reasons," he said. "First, I doubt I'll ever meet the right woman. Secondly, I'm already married to the business."

"The business is no excuse," she laughed. "And you've got plenty of years left to meet the right woman. And if you don't mind my saying so, I think you could have your pick. You're quite handsome, you know. You'd be quite a catch," she teased.

Christopher turned serious. "I don't know about that, Zoe," he said cryptically. "Like most people, I have my closet. And sometimes I feel it would be unfair to ask someone to share that side of me."

"What side?" she asked with concern.

"It's nothing worth talking about here," he said. "How about another brandy?"

Zoe knew by the tone of his voice that he wanted to change the subject. "Why don't we have one at my house?" she suggested without the least bit of a sexual overtone. "Anyway, I'd love to show you my Italian gouaches."

"And I'd love to see them," he smiled.

The two of them returned to the shop so Zoe could pick up her van, and then he followed her the short distance to her house on the water.

"It's not much," she said as they walked in the door, "but the view is great."

Christopher looked at the modest wall of glass facing the ocean. "It's wonderful. I could live here in a minute," he said enthusiastically.

"You freeze your butt off in the winter though. Somehow the northeast wind finds its way into the cracks. Anyway," she said, turning on the lights in the living room, "here's my favorite view."

"Nice collection." Christopher looked at the perfectly hung Italian gouaches. Below them on a table was the bronze that he had sold her. "The Pietà looks good here," he said, trying to hide the trouble in his voice.

"It does, doesn't it?"

He moved closer to inspect the paintings. "You've got some good pictures here, Zoe."

"Thanks. You look at them, and I'll make us a drink."

She went into the kitchen and removed two brandy snifters and a half full bottle of brandy from the cupboard. She poured an inch into both glasses, and held them up to the light to measure them.

"Richard, what am I doing?"

"It's okay, Zoe. Enjoy yourself."

She put the glasses back down on the counter and poured another half inch in both of them. Then she walked back to the living room. Christopher had removed one of the paintings and was looking at the back side of it.

"This Vesuvius is a really good one, Zoe."

"It is?" she said as she placed his drink on the table next to the Pietà.

"How much did you pay for it?"

"One-fifty, I think."

"It's worth about eight hundred. It's by Testoria."

Zoe moved closer to Christopher and the picture. "You're kidding me."

"No, I'll give you eight hundred for it right now."

Zoe thought of her late husband and the icons that her paintings had become for her. "It's not for sale, Christopher," she said without wavering.

He handed the picture to her. "Zoe, I'm only kidding. I know how much these mean to you. I'm sorry," he said, holding his hands in contrition. "I shouldn't have joked about it."

"Oh, I thought you were serious."

"I have a weird sense of humor sometimes." He took the picture back from her and hung it as straight and as carefully as she had done when she originally put it up. "There," he said. "Back where it belongs."

"Thanks," she said, sounding almost relieved.

For the next hour and a half, the two were deep in conversation and brandy, with the primary topic being Brimfield. The summer session was only three weeks away. While Zoe only planned to be there for a day, Christopher, as always, would spend the entire week there. He had long-standing reservations at the New England Motel, a small but convenient, single story motel located right on one of the selling fields. He rented two rooms, one for his stock and the other for himself.

"You're welcome to spend a night or two, Zoe," he said. "I can sleep with my inventory."

Instead of turning him down, the brandy inside of her said that she would think about his offer. That pleased him immensely.

By eleven, Christopher announced that it was time for him to leave. He had business the next day in Boston and had made reservations at a downtown hotel. Zoe walked him to the door and thanked him for a wonderful evening.

"Thank you," he said. "I really enjoyed myself, Zoe."

The two stood in the dark of the open doorway and looked longingly at one another. Zoe could feel the light summer breeze fanning through her delicate sundress.

"I guess I'll see you at Brimfield."

"I'll call you," he said quietly.

"Okay."

"Good night," he said, as he bent to kiss her on the cheek. As he did, her face moved in the direction of his and the two kissed.

"Richard, are you with me?"

"Yes, Zoe. I'm with you."

7

The instinctual physiology of sexual arousal escapes no one. Plumbers, prelates, housewives, and even chaste widows are powerless in the genital face of nature. For some, the urge is merely an innocent incident, like briefly waking from a fretful sleep only to fall back into the rapid eye movement of the night. For others, it is a true and troubling awakening—an unexpected crack in the wall of fidelity, large enough to gaze out at the desire reflecting like a mirror from the other side. To desire that desire, regardless of the consequences, is even worse.

Zoe was whetted by Christopher. Lubricated by their innocent evening together, she found that he had become part of her everyday life for the few weeks prior to Brimfield. Like a keepsake, she kept her thoughts of him hidden in a drawer of her heart. Only when no one was looking, would she open it and breathe in the intense emotions that she felt—emotions that she hadn't felt for a long time. Hiding from Richard was another matter. Even though she could feel his spirit of approval, her own guilt outweighed his loving indulgence and encouragement for her to go on with her life and embrace all that would nurture it.

Melissa could sense a change in Zoe. But even under the bare light bulb of her questioning, Zoe held her ground, admitting only that she was looking forward to seeing Christopher again at Brimfield. Because Melissa's own relationship problems had resurfaced the night that Brad confronted Christopher in the Jack Tar House, she ultimately let Zoe be with her own private thoughts, just as she had chosen to be with hers.

The night before Brimfield was wild with anticipation, particularly for Zoe. Christopher had called earlier in the evening to tell her how much he was looking forward to seeing her, and hoped that she would spend some extra time with him during his own extended stay. Although she had never agreed to his offer to spend a night or two at his motel room, she had packed extra clothing just in case. "We'll see," she said vaguely, never mentioning her backup wardrobe.

By nine o'clock she was in bed with a nightcap of white wine on the side table. As she was dozing off, the phone rang, startling her so much that she knocked over the glass of wine as she picked up the phone. "Hello?"

"What was that?" asked the voice on the other end.

"Oh, hi Jo. I just knocked over a glass of wine when I grabbed for the phone. Shit," she said as she looked down at the floor, "it's in a million pieces."

"Be careful that you don't step on them. You'll need both feet for Brimfield."

"Hang on for a minute, will you? I've got to throw something on so I can get this cleaned up."

"You're naked?"

"I'm in bed. I've got to get up early in the morning, remember?"

"Oh, I thought you were getting weird on me," she joked.

"I'll be right with you, hon."

Zoe put down the portable phone, threw off the sheet and stepped onto the floor, barely missing the broken glass. She walked quickly to her closet and opened it. As she did, she was confronted by the full length mirror on the inside of the door. "Jesus," she said out loud, "I'm losing it."

She crossed her arms and cupped her breasts trying to gauge the balance between their fullness and firmness. It had been a long time since that equation had been important to her. She could feel right away that although they were still as robust as they were in her youth, like the rest of her, they had softened with age. Then she ran her hands along the sides of her hips like a caliper. She knew they extended wider than the last time she had checked and lower as well. Finally, she turned her backside to the mirror and turned her head to view her ass. Once as taut as an unripened peach, it was just beginning to relax, subtly taking on the soft open shape of a cursive letter "W."

She began to feel foolish in her nakedness and wondered how she could have, even for a moment, believed that her own flesh could hold up pressed against the virility of Christopher's youthful body. How could he find her even remotely acceptable? She felt ashamed, as though age were something that we inflict on ourselves. Then she turned her head around and away from the mirror. Her reflection, like some side show oddity, was too much to bear. Without looking at herself further, she took out her robe and put it on, tying the cotton belt as tightly as she could.

"I'm back," she said softly as she picked up the phone.

"Did you clean it up already?"

Zoe sat on the edge of the queen-size bed and began poking the slivers of glass with her big toe. "No. I'll wait till we get off. So," she asked, "what's on your mind?"

Joanna noticed the change in her voice immediately. "Are

you all right, Mom?"

"Fine. Tired, that's all. So what's up?" she asked impatiently.

"I just wanted to wish you good luck in Brimfield."

"Thanks. I hope we do well."

"I don't mean with the antiques, Mom. I mean good luck with Christopher. You're going to see him, right?"

"Oh...I suppose so," she said ambivalently.

"What's wrong? I thought you were really looking forward to it?"

"I don't know, Jo." A fragment of glass caught the tip of her toe causing blood to trickle from it, but she was too numb to even feel it. "I think I'm being foolish. I'm fifty years old, and tonight I'm really feeling it."

"Don't be ridiculous," she scolded her. "You look great. Anyway," she laughed, "one of us has to have a man in her life, and right now that's not me."

Without even wincing, Zoe pulled the glass shard from her toe and applied pressure to it with her thumb and forefinger to make it bleed even more. "I'm just too old for this, Jo. And I don't want to embarrass myself."

"Why are you being so hard on yourself? You're always telling me to accept the flaws. Why can't you do the same for yourself?"

"I just don't think..."

Joanna interrupted her, and raised her voice to a maternal volume. "Listen, Ma, just go to Brimfield and give it a chance, okay? Because if you lose your self confidence now, you're going to feel like you're seventy, and you might as well book a table for one at Swider's for the rest of your life."

Zoe let go of her toe and reached for a tissue from the box on the night table and wrapped it around her toe to stop the bleeding. "Okay, Jo. I know what you're saying."

"Good. Then just go and see what happens."

"Okay."

"Now get some sleep."

"I will, hon."

"I love you, Momma."

"I love you, too."

"And Dad loves you, too. Don't ever forget that."

Zoe could feel tears forming in her eyes. "I won't," she quaked. "Good night."

It was a blue sky, coffee and donut morning at Brimfield, no tents necessary. By nine when May's opened, there were hints that the day would be a scorcher. It was already in the high seventies, and the dust kicked up with every aggressive stride of those who walked briskly or ran through the field as it opened for business.

With one Brimfield behind them, Melissa and Zoe were prepared for the onslaught. They had packed their van so that the most expensive and desirable pieces would come out first, a tactic that both sold goods quicker, and kept those who were waiting, hungry to see what would come out next.

In spite of their own personal demons, both women were in good spirits. Melissa seemed much less intimidated by the hysteria that is the nature of Brimfield. Wearing walking shorts and a plain white tee shirt, she looked very much the part of the triennial event.

Zoe was dressed for the incoming heat, as well as for Christopher, whom she planned to meet once the first wave of buying subsided. After the enlightened advice of her daughter, she decided to throw her fate and her fifty-year-old body to the wind. She realized that she could not spend the rest of her life apologizing for being less than perfect, or being subject to aging like the rest of the billions of people on the planet. With that in mind, she wore a pair of dark green shorts and a beige halter top with no bra. The ever so slight outline of her dark nipples was just enough to give her the sensual spin she was looking for, and her overall look did not go unnoticed, distracting neighboring exhibitors as well as the patrons eyeing the goods in her booth.

By late morning they were up three thousand dollars and down to the silt of their merchandise, the mundane pieces that they would most likely have to pack up later in the day and bring home. Fortunately, they had sold their heaviest pieces, passing the baton of lugging them around to a new group of dealers and collectors. What was left, if not good quality, was at least light in pounds, which would be more than a small consolation for having gone unsold.

The crowd was down to an occasional dealer or collector. Most of the buyers were now following the rotation of openings of the other fields of antiques, giving Melissa and Zoe a chance to catch their breath and take a portable bathroom break.

"You go first," suggested Zoe. "When you get back I'll go, and then I'm going to head over to Christopher's booth."

"It may take a while," said Melissa. "It looks like every other exhibitor on the field is there. The line's a mile long," she said, pointing to the row of outhouses a hundred feet away.

"I can wait."

"Good," replied Melissa. "Cause I can't."

While Melissa was off relieving herself, Elliot Baker came by the booth. Even more so than others, he took special notice of Zoe's wardrobe and had to work at it to keep from staring at her breasts. In his arousal, he began to imagine that she had dressed that way for him. Then his gaze became so obvious that Zoe firmly crossed her arms, covering his view. Her response brought him back to his senses, and he began to talk business.

The two of them compared notes on the early morning

rush, and Zoe was flabbergasted to hear that he had taken in over eight thousand dollars.

"I thought our three grand was good," she said.

"It's great," he replied. "Remember, I've been doing this a lot longer than you. Anyway, I'll have six of that eight spent before I leave here today. You know," he laughed, "buy more stuff, to sell more stuff, to buy more stuff. Hopefully, there's enough to live on somewhere in between."

"Thank God that Richard believed in life insurance. I don't know what I would do if I had to depend solely on this for a living," remarked Zoe.

"Just be thankful you don't." Elliot reached into the pocket of his jeans. "Here, I picked this up for you." He handed her a five inch high, greenish-colored plastic model of the Pietà.

"Thank you, Elliot," she beamed.

"At least it's not a fake," he said. "Genuine plastic."

"I'll put it with the other one," she said. "Maybe I can start a collection of them." As she felt the molded Mary and Jesus in her hand, her thoughts wandered back to Italy. Then she looked at Elliot, who at least in physical size and age reminded her of her late husband. "That was really sweet of you," she said, mentally forgiving him for his stares minutes before.

"It's nothing," he replied. "The guy wanted five bucks, but I knuckled him down to two."

Zoe laughed at the monetary context he had put it in. "Thank you, Elliot. I would have loved it even if you got it for a buck." Then she kissed him on the cheek.

Elliot was not expecting such an outpouring of physical gratitude. Many times he had dreamed of her lips on his face, and now he wondered how such a chintzy souvenir could perform such a miracle. "I tried to get it for a buck," he said sincerely.

"That's why you'll always make a living in the business," she laughed.

"Listen" he said, building on the peck on his cheek, "when Melissa gets back, would you like to have lunch with me? The dealer next to me offered to watch my booth for an hour."

"I can't, Elliot. I've got to meet someone."

"Who?" he asked with the privilege of one kissed.

"Christopher Doria. You know, the dealer who sold me the bronze."

"What are you meeting him for?"

Zoe could hear the disapproval in his voice. "Well," she hesitated, "we've become friends."

"Friends?"

Although Elliot was well aware that she had found Christopher in Maine, and had gotten most of her money back on the bronze, he knew nothing of their emerging social life. As best as she could, Zoe tried to keep her personal life separate from the gossipy auction halls of the antique business. Christopher, in a small way, had become important on that side of her life. She wanted to keep that as private as possible.

Yeah," she said, "friends."

"You should know better, Zoe. Don't think for a minute that he didn't know what he was doing when he sold you that bronze. If he's as experienced a dealer as you told me he is, then there's no way he didn't know your statue was fake."

Zoe's professional respect for Elliot wrestled with her own willingness to believe Christopher's oversight. "I honestly don't think he knew," she answered in Christopher's, as well as her own defense. "And he's a really nice man."

"Zoe," he said quietly, "remember what I told you about Brimfield?"

"How could I forget? You keep reminding me that it's Buyer Bewareland. And okay," she added as she threw up her hands, "I'll admit that I got screwed."

"Well," he continued, "objects aren't necessarily the only

fakes here."

"What do you mean?"

"Maybe your friend Christopher is not as nice as you think he is."

For a moment, Zoe felt like her private life was being impinged upon by someone who had no voting stock in her affairs. But instead of lashing out, she tightly squeezed the plastic Pietà in her hand. She knew Elliot well enough to know that he was sincere in his concern for her—magnified by his infatuation perhaps, but still genuine.

"Elliot, I appreciate what you're saying. I really do. But my gut tells me that he's a good person, and I hope you'll respect my judgment on that. After all, it's my life, you know."

Elliot shrugged and thought of how long it seemed since she had kissed him. He wondered if it would ever happen again. "I'm only thinking of you, Zoe. That's all."

"I know that. And I certainly respect your knowledge of the business. You know so much more than I do. However, I hope you respect my understanding of people...at least those in my own life. I think I'm a pretty good judge of character. Hey," she joked to brighten up the conversation, "I think a lot of you, right?"

Elliot smiled. "I get your point. Maybe we can have lunch together when we get back home."

"Absolutely."

"I'm going to hold you to that," he said as he turned and walked out of her rented field space. "In the meantime, I'll see if I can find you some more genuine plastic Pietàs."

"Any and all would be appreciated," she laughed.

"I'll see what I can come up with," he said, as he slowly walked off without a lunch date into the bright Brimfield day.

The food court at Brimfield is a U-shaped series of kitchen

trailers, as mobile as the bathrooms, that functions as the main commissary for the gastronomical needs of the thousands of people that trudge through the fields. In the international tone of the event itself, the menu offerings have something for every taste and palate, including Greek, Chinese, seafood and good old American barbecue. Although the food is not rated in any restaurant guide, anyone who has spent seven or eight hungry hours roaming the fields appreciates the satisfying grub that nourishes them sufficiently enough to continue on their journey.

The few picnic tables that occupied the inside of the outdoor cafeteria were full. Most of the diners were either standing, or as in the case of Zoe and Christopher, sitting in the dirt margin alongside the pavement of Route 20—eye level to the wheels of the cars that crawled along under the guidance of the experienced and patient Brimfield Police. Like everything else ancillary to the Brimfield experience, eating there is a compromise of sorts, a ritual reduced almost to pure function. To each person, what matters is the find, and shortcomings and defects in other normally important areas receive a dispensation for the day.

"I hope I'm not taking my life in my hands with this pork sandwich," Zoe said, licking the overflowing, sticky barbecue sauce from her fingers.

"I've been eating them for years, and I'm still here," laughed her companion. Christopher turned and took a long studied look at her. "Are you having a good time?"

Zoe's eyes moved deliberately from east to west as she gazed at the sea of people along Route 20. "I love this place. It's like nothing else I've ever experienced."

"It's amazing, isn't it? All these people in the middle of nowhere. In a few days, they'll all be gone. Like it never even happened."

"Maybe Brimfield is just a figment of imagination," she laughed. "Some sort of mass hysteria."

"No, it's real." Christopher put his hand on her forearm and rubbed it gently. "Not long enough, but very real."

In spite of the thousands of people around her, Zoe felt alone and intimate with Christopher. The unstated communion of Brimfield is that everybody there is looking for something. Regardless of the individual desire, the search for it is held in the utmost respect.

"I've got to get back soon and relieve Melissa."

"What about tonight? Can you stay?" He rubbed her arm even more gently, barely touching the hairs on it.

"I'll have no way to get home if I do. Melissa needs the van."

"I'll get you home, Zoe. Why don't you stay? Life is too short, you know? And Brimfield's even shorter."

"What should I do, Richard?"

"What you want to do, Zoe."

"I'd like to stay. As long as Melissa doesn't mind driving home alone."

"I'm sure she'll be fine." He leaned over and kissed her on the lips. "And we'll have a great time. I promise."

By five o'clock, the van was packed with the leftovers, and Melissa was ready for the solo trip home. Although Zoe had never previously mentioned her possible post-show intentions, Melissa was not the least bit surprised when she told her that she was staying over with Christopher. She understood first-hand how difficult it is to feel lonely, and cautiously encouraged her friend to enjoy herself. "Don't drink too much," she said. "And have a good time."

"I'll do my best."

The two women hugged, and Melissa got into the van. "I'll see you when you get back."

"Melissa..." She thought of herself naked in front of the mirror the night before.

"What is it?"

"Am I too old for this?"

"You're not dead yet, are you?"

"You know what I mean."

"You're a beautiful woman, Zoe," she said lovingly. "And not a bad person either."

"Thanks."

Melissa started up the van. "You're also one lucky old broad," she joked.

"See what I mean?" lamented Zoe.

"I'm kidding, Zoe. Have a great time, and I'll see you at home."

Zoe watched the van drive across the almost vacant field. Then she picked up her overnight bag and headed for Christopher's motel.

Brimfield is Vegas in the woods, a twenty-four-hour-a-day proposition. While there are no scheduled evening shows, the fields are darted with flashlights as the hunt and the deals continue in the dark. New vendors, planning to spend the night in their vans and trucks, arrive with fresh merchandise for fields opening the following day. Although no pre-show buying or selling is allowed, it is difficult to police, and some of the best stuff is gone before sunrise.

While the industrious worked by flashlight, Zoe and Christopher relaxed in the candlelight of the Yankee Tradesman restaurant—a ye olde Yorkshire pudding tourist eatery in Sturbridge, just six miles east of Brimfield, but in spirit very far away. While Christopher was making his final rounds for the day, Zoe had showered in one of his two simple rooms at the New England Motel and dressed in her casual clothes for her evening out—taupe cotton pants, a white silk blouse and blue linen blazer. It was a wardrobe that did not look out of place among the other diners, most of whom had spent the day at Old Sturbridge Village, a sort of Early American theme park.

Christopher had also dressed for the occasion, trading in his jeans for a more stylish pair of natural cotton pants, and his tee shirt for a long sleeve, green pullover. Together, they struck a pose more sophisticated than most in the restaurant, and of all, were the couple most worth watching.

The evening began with martinis for two and cigarettes for one. Luckily, they were able to get the last table in the smoking section. As an ex-smoker himself, Christopher didn't mind being surrounded by others who were still hooked, including Zoe, whose intentions were always on the losing side of her will power. Ultimately she justified her habit by claiming that smoking was a privilege of all widowed women.

In keeping with the culinary gist of the Yankee Tradesman, both of them ordered the "Gentleman's Cut" of prime rib served with all-you-can-eat popovers, the more comfortable and appetizing name for Yorkshire pudding. They were ravenous after their long day in the field and left nothing but bone. Brimfield stirs up many appetites, a taste for the carnivorous being just one.

They also drank two bottles of the best burgundy available, and finished the evening with the mellow, golden glow of brandy. With each sip throughout the course of the evening, they became more at ease, especially Zoe. Under the compassionate, loving eye of her husband's spirit, she gradually loosened her grasp on the foolishness of postmortem fidelity, and allowed herself the luxury to be a woman in the presence of a handsome man.

In spite of the amount of liquor they drank, the large portions of food they consumed kept them relatively sober, at least on the outside. Inside was a different story. Each felt tantalized by the other, and the liquor burned them with desire as it found its way into their bloodstreams. By ten, they were finished and ready to go back to the motel. Under the opportune pretense of stabilizing one another, they walked arm in arm to Christopher's Austin Healy, which he had transported in the back of the rented truck used to bring the rest of his valuables to Brimfield.

"I love this car," she said, stooping down to get inside.

"Do you want to drive back?"

Zoe was surprised and thrilled by his offer. "You'd let me?"

"Are you okay?"

"As okay as you," she laughed.

He walked to the passenger side and handed her the keys. "Here. Try to keep it under fifty, or you'll be spending the night in the Brimfield jail."

"I'll be good," she promised. Zoe jumped in the driver's seat like a kid and turned it over on the first try. The throaty sound of the dual exhaust pipes punctuated her excitement of the evening and the moment. "This is going to be great."

"Just be careful," warned Christopher as he nuzzled into the passenger seat.

"I will."

Both their necks snapped back as she popped the clutch in first gear and took off down Route 20 toward Brimfield.

"Take it easy, Zoe."

"You take it easy," she laughed. "Enjoy the ride."

Zoe was in the zone. With both hands on the wheel, she sat on the gas pedal and pushed the sports car through the soft country corners, hugging the inside as closely as she could. With the top down, her hair flew like a commercial in the crisp night air. For the first time in over two years, she felt good—drunk with the idea of just being alive. She looked over at Christopher, who was wearing the same face of fear that her husband had worn on a mad taxi ride that they had survived in Rome. "Enjoy the ride, Christopher," she roared over the noisy, vibrating racket of the antique two-seater.

Christopher was too frozen to respond.

After ten harrowing minutes, the Healy was safely back at the New England Motel.

"I can't remember when I had that much fun."

"I can't remember when I was that scared, Zoe." His voice carried the relief of someone just off a roller coaster. "Remind me never to let you drive again. Especially after you've been drinking."

"Don't be such an old fart," she chided in jest.

Christopher looked at her and smiled. "I'm glad you're having so much fun. You deserve it."

"I am, Christopher. I'm really glad I decided to stay."

"Then let's not stop now," he said. He reached over and took her cheek with his right hand and pulled her face toward him and kissed her. "C'mon," he said softly. "Let's go inside."

The room was what one might expect of a motel in the middle of nowhere. Country-simple and sparse, it was furnished with a suitable bed, dresser and night table, and was the most convenient accommodation in Brimfield. Located directly on a selling field, it offered luxuries that thousands of other exhibitors and buyers could only dream about. First and foremost was the most essential item of human decadence—a private, indoor bathroom. Second in importance was the hot water shower, the value of which could not be overestimated after a long dirty day in the fields. Finally, there was the room itself—plain drapes and white shades, but private enough to provide a sense of intimacy.

Zoe sat on the edge of the bed while Christopher went to the cooler in the bathroom to get them each a glass of wine. He had easily talked her into a nightcap before he himself would retire to the second room that he rented in the motel, where he would sleep, uneventfully, with his Brimfield inventory.

Within a minute, he returned with two plastic cups of white wine, fitting vessels for the casual environment. "I hope you don't mind plastic," he apologized.

"Are you kidding?" she laughed, looking around the room. "This is great. Compared to most of the other creature comforts at Brimfield, this is the Ritz."

Christopher sat down on the floor against the outside wall and stared up at her, taking a sip of his wine. "Zoe, can I ask you something?"

"Anything."

Christopher rested his cup on his left knee. "Do you believe in fate?"

She leaned forward on the bed. "What do you mean?"

"I mean you and me. If that bronze weren't a fake, then you wouldn't have come looking for me, and we probably would never have seen each other again."

"I've thought of that," she said softly.

"Do you think I'm too young for you?"

Zoe smiled. "Isn't that supposed to be the other way around?"

"No, I mean it. I don't know how you feel about it."

"Don't tell me you're feeling insecure about your age."

"Maybe a little." He blushed. "I hope you don't think this is some kind of infatuation."

"Well, join the crowd," she said. "I'm a middle-aged woman who spent most of her adult life with the same man, and the first one that I'm attracted to after he dies is someone fifteen years younger." Zoe laughed. "I don't think I have that much self confidence, Christopher. I don't know any woman who does."

He got up from the floor and stood in front of her. He bent down slightly and lifted her head towards him as he spoke. "Zoe, he said. "You're a beautiful woman that any man would want. Be confident in that."

"It's not that easy, Christopher. I'm new at this...and my age doesn't make it any easier."

He kissed her on the lips. At first, Zoe felt awkward, like she was cheating. Then she recognized her own desire in the moment, the same longing that had been present with Richard. It was not wrong, she told herself, just different—but equally as sincere.

Christopher slowly removed his lips from hers. "I think I should go to bed now."

"Okay."

He walked to the door. "I'll be with my stuff if you need me. Room twelve. There's a phone in it," he said, pointing to the one on the night table.

"I'll be fine," she reassured him.

"Good night, Zoe."

The echo of the kiss lingered on her lips, and she began to feel an overwhelming presence of her late husband, as if Richard's hands were caressing her face just as Christopher had done moments before. Her head felt like a bird in his gentle palms as he coaxed her.

"It's okay, Zoe. I will always be with you."

"Christopher..."

He turned just as he was going out the door. "Yes?"

"Stay."

"Are you sure?"

"It's okay."

"Yes," she answered unequivocally. "I'm sure."

8

The sexual awakening that Zoe experienced the night before was matched by the rude awakening she received from the boisterous Brimfield crowd doing business right outside the door at six in the morning.

"Jesus," she said, pulling the sheet over her breasts in modesty.

Christopher turned and kissed her. "That's our wake-up call."

"Is it always like this?" she asked, as if she believed the commotion outside were a counterstrike to her own sexual willfulness.

Christopher shrugged his bare shoulders. "It's Brimfield."

Zoe moved close to him and put her hands on his chest and played with his St. Christopher medal. "This is really weird. We're naked in the middle of a flea market. I feel like we're in a porno movie."

"They can't see us, Zoe," he laughed over the clamor outside the door.

"I know that...it's just not the way I expected it, that's all."

Christopher put his arm under her head and pulled it to his

chest to block the noise from her right ear. Then he cupped his
hand on her other ear and whispered in it. "Last night was
beautiful, Zoe."

She responded with approval by a long deep moan and a
full stretch of her body.

"In fact, it was the most beautiful night of my life."

"Do you mean that?" she asked insecurely.

Christopher tenderly pushed her away so that she was
lying on her back. He slid the sheet down to her waist and then
slowly stroked her nipples with his fingers until they became
erect. "Yes, I mean it, Zoe. It was like another world."

Zoe closed her eyes and fully accepted his attention, which
became more undivided with every stroke of his fingers. Soon
the noise was gone and all she could hear were the sounds of
intimacy, a man and a woman trying to crawl back into each
other, away from the hectic world outside.

By nine o'clock, the lovers had showered, dressed, and
were ready to roam the fields for the day. Since Christopher
had finished exhibiting for the week, he planned to concentrate
on buying from other dealers for the final three days. Zoe
hoped to buy for her shop as well, although she knew the quality
she would be able to purchase would not even come close to
what his keen eye would pick out.

At Zoe's request, before heading off, they went to room
twelve, the second room that Christopher maintained during
Brimfield week. When not on display, he kept the bulk of his
inventory in his rented truck. He used the additional motel
space to store his most expensive pieces of furniture as well as
valuable "smalls," an apt description for items small enough to
carry in one's hand. As with virtually all dealers at Brimfield,
Christopher brought more merchandise that he would sell, and
most of what was left in the room would return with him to

Maine.

"Be careful you don't trip on anything," he warned as he unlocked the door. "It's a mess in here."

The two entered, and Zoe immediately recognized a couple of pieces that she had seen at his shop, including the Italian gouache that first attracted her to his booth during the May session of Brimfield. "You still haven't sold that?"

"I almost did...twice."

"Does that include me?"

"No." He shook his head as he picked it up and inspected it. "It's getting to be one of those pieces...you know, like the guest that wouldn't leave?"

"I've got a number of those squatters in my shop, too," she replied.

Christopher inspected it even more closely. "It's a good picture," he said, "but I'm getting sick of looking at it. Here," he handed it to her, "take it home with you."

"I couldn't do that, Christopher."

"Think of it as a loan, then." He took her hand and placed it around the frame. "It will go nice with your collection," he smiled.

"Are you sure?"

He responded by kissing her. "Take it. Hopefully, whenever you look at it, you'll think of me."

"Thank you," said Zoe as she returned the kiss. Then she turned her attention to the picture and thought of their lovemaking the night before. She wondered how she could justify hanging his painting among the other gouaches in her home. "I don't know..."

"What's wrong?"

She turned and looked at him. "Nothing," she smiled faintly. "I'll take good care of it for you."

For the next few minutes he gave her an academic tour of

his goods. While he was pointing out the delicate inlay of a French satinwood table, her eye caught the rich green patina of three metal figures in a cardboard box underneath it. She bent down and picked one of them up. "What's this?" she asked. "It's really beautiful."

For a moment, Christopher was caught off guard. "Oh, it's a copper Phoenician god," he said casually.

As Zoe reached down to get the two other objects, she was startled to see that all three were the same. "Christopher...I don't understand." She turned and looked at him. "What's going on?"

"Nothing, Zoe. They're all repros."

"Reproductions? I thought you didn't..."

He interrupted her. "They're not mine."

"Then what are you doing with them?"

Christopher maintained his composure. "Zoe," he said emphatically, "I know what you're thinking." He shook his head. "Believe me...they have nothing to do with me. I'm just doing a favor for a dealer in Maine. I'm dropping them off for him to a dealer from Virginia who'll be up here tomorrow. That's all, okay?"

"Oh...okay. Well then," she continued, " is that dealer going to sell them as originals?"

"I have no idea what he's going to do with them, but I doubt it. Anyway," he said, as he put his hands on her shoulders, "it's none of our concern, is it?"

Zoe looked him straight in the eyes, searching for a hint of guilt. She found none. "I guess not," she answered. "I'm just glad they're not yours."

"I'd want the real thing," he laughed. "C'mon, let's hit the fields."

Zoe put the three figures back in the box where she found them and picked up the loaned Italian watercolor. "Can I leave this here until we get back? I'd rather not carry it around. It might get damaged."

He hastily took it from her. "Let's put it in the other room. Then we won't have to come back here."

Zoe looked down at the gods. "Good idea."

The Phoenician god was a pebble in Zoe's shoe throughout the day as the two walked hand in hand amidst the millions of objects for sale on the plains of Brimfield. It was only towards the end of the day that she began to feel comfortable and fully trusting of Christopher again. Perhaps it was all the fakes that he gladly, and without a hint of association, pointed out as they walked the fields. Although most booths were genuine in their presentations, there were some that were almost blatant in their misrepresentation.

As Zoe had already painfully learned, anything metal is the most dangerous. Christopher fingered dozens of reproductions in that medium, from iron door stops to painted tin advertising signs to bronze and brass figures. He also showed her country cupboards that had recently been nothing more than stacks of old barn board, now put together, painted and distressed to look like they had just come out of nineteenth century houses nestled in the hills of Vermont or upstate New York. In booth after booth, he found things that weren't what they seemed—signed pottery and paintings with counterfeit signatures, Currier and Ives hand colored prints that were nothing more than reprints of the originals, duck decoys and other wooden objects weathered and aged overnight in kitchen ovens, or in a matter of weeks by burial in the ground. Every category worth collecting was a candidate for merchandise designed to deceive those unsuspecting buyers whose love for the object made them blind to the truth. By the sheer number of pieces that he pointed out to Zoe, it seemed that there was an enormous, maybe even worldwide market of people who put passion before reason.

By four-thirty, their legs were giving out. Zoe, in particular, was starting to drag her feet, literally stubbing her toes in the ground. Deciding they'd had enough, the couple sought out one of the many lemonade stands along Route 20 to wash down the coating of dust that covered their throats.

Zoe watched with anticipation as the young woman behind the stand squeezed the fresh lemons into tall paper cups. "Well, at least there's nothing fake about the lemonade," she laughed.

"It's the best in the world," remarked Christopher.

Once served, they sat by the side of the road, sipped their lemonade, and watched the thousands of people lumbering by like porters in a cultural jungle—carrying architectural columns, paintings, floor lamps and furniture over their heads.

"This place is really unbelievable, you know that?"

"It's great," said Christopher.

"You can find almost anything here," she said, pointing to an elderly woman carrying a circa eighteen-fifty pine coffin, with an equally elderly man huffing on the other end of it.

"Actually," said Christopher, "I believe the objects find you."

"I don't get it."

"My theory is that every object on the field takes a lover. It picks someone out who will love and cherish it, in spite of its imperfections."

Zoe smiled. "That's an interesting way to look at it."

"Yeah...and while the retail customers promise death till us part to the object, the dealers, you and I, hope for a shorter relationship. A few hours...a few days...until we can pass along our brief encounter at a profit."

"You make dealers sound like pimps," she laughed.

"In a way we are. You buy it...you flip it."

"Not in my case," said Zoe. "My problem is that I buy

things that I love and then I don't want to sell them. Like my Italian watercolors. I'd rather spend money on them than buy stuff for the shop."

"You've got to learn to love 'em and leave 'em," he said pragmatically. "Otherwise, you'll never make any money in this business."

"But I love my paintings," she protested.

"I know you do, and that's fine. All I'm saying is that in general, you can't get attached to things."

"Don't you keep anything?" she challenged.

He shook his head. "Some things for awhile. But ultimately, when the right price comes around, the right opportunity, they go out the door, too."

Zoe was troubled by his hard-nosed approach. "And what about relationships with people?" she asked. "Are they disposable, too?"

"Zoe..."

"No, I want to know. I think I have a right to."

He turned to her and squeezed her hand. "We've only been together a short time, and I don't know where it's going, if that's what you mean. And I don't think you do either. However...I do know that I really enjoy being with you and want to keep seeing you. Can't that be enough for now?"

"I'm sorry, Christopher. It's just that...well...I haven't been with any other men like that, and I feel vulnerable, that's all."

He squeezed her hand tighter. "I understand. Just don't confuse my point of view on the business with my feelings for you, okay?"

"I won't."

"Now," he said, changing the subject, "we've got to get you home."

"Yeah," she frowned. "I've got to work tomorrow. I feel badly that you have to drive me. It's an awfully long round trip."

"I'm not going to drive you home."

Zoe went into a mini-panic. "You're not? Then how am I supposed to get home?"

He reached into his pocket and pulled out a set of keys. Dangling them in front of her, he smiled. "You can drive yourself."

"You'd let me drive your Austin Healy home?" Zoe was incredulous.

"I've got the truck, so I don't need it. And I've got my van at home. Anyway, that way, you'll be sure you'll see me again...and soon," he laughed.

"Are you sure?"

"You'll be the sportiest woman on the Mass Pike."

Zoe smiled. "When will I see you again?"

"I don't know. Maybe I'll try to get down late next week."

"I'll take good care of it."

"Just be careful driving, that's all," he cautioned. "There's no room for error in a car that small."

"I will."

He handed her the keys. "C'mon, let's get your stuff. If you leave now, you'll be home before dark."

Zoe breathed in the warm, late afternoon air and adjusted her baseball cap. "It's top down weather," she said.

Christopher leaned towards her and turned her hat backwards. Then he put his arms around her, and kissed her without reservation in front of the thousands walking along Route 20. "You're a top-down kind of woman, Zoe."

"I never thought of myself as that."

"What did you tell me last night on the way home from dinner? Enjoy the ride? That goes for you too." Then he kissed her again, long and hard, as the disinterested crowd passed by them, caressing their own objects of desire.

When Zoe pulled into the parking lot of her shop on Saturday morning, Melissa and Elliot Baker were bent over the open rear door of his van. The heavy breathing of the Healy's mufflers caught their attention immediately, causing them to look up from the carved Empire mirror that Elliot was trying to sell.

"Oh my God," Melissa said in awe, "she's got his car."

Elliot leaned forward to focus on the person driving the convertible. "Is that Zoe?"

"Yeah...in his car."

"Whose car?"

"Christopher Doria's. The bronze guy."

It didn't take Elliot a second to put one and one together. No man would casually turn over his automotive love on a whim. There would have to have been a major considera-tion—an exchange of something so valuable that the man was reduced to a deranged crew member on Ulysses' ship, pitifully jumping to his death while trying to reach the Siren on the island so far away.

"I wonder what she had to do to get that?" he asked rhetorically.

Melissa didn't respond, and briskly walked over to the car before Zoe had a chance to get out of it. As if the car weren't obvious enough, the sly smile on her face confirmed what Melissa suspected—that Zoe was a different woman from the one she rode to Brimfield with just days before. The chemicals in Zoe's body had changed, her hormone levels standing at attention from the masculine pampering that she had received. Zoe was flush with womanhood, something she had not experienced in a long time.

"Hi," said Melissa, loaded with innuendo.

"I know what you're thinking, Melissa," she laughed.

"What's the phrase? He drove me home?"

"I drove myself home, honey." Zoe stroked the pliant, worn brown leather on the passenger seat with her hand. "And I thought it was really nice of him to let me take his car."

"So...did you have a good time?"

"I had a wonderful time. Exquisite."

Melissa turned to Elliot who was watching them intently. "I want to hear all about it," she said. "Right after Elliot leaves."

"Okay." Zoe opened the door and awkwardly swiveled both legs out of the Healy, her short skirt hugging her thighs.

Melissa looked back at Elliot again. His gaze was fixed on Zoe. "Somehow, I don't think that's the right wardrobe for a car built so low to the ground," assessed Melissa. "You're going to get Elliot all worked up."

Zoe pulled her knees together as best she could and quickly stood up and adjusted her skirt. "I don't want to do that," she said sincerely. "He's hot enough for me already. And I know he doesn't like Christopher."

"Let's talk about it later," said Melissa. "C'mon...Elliot's got a great mirror for us."

As the two approached him, Elliot tried to brush off his jealousy. Like some fine piece of art that he had been eyeing for years, waiting for the moment that it would be offered for sale at auction, Zoe had been taken from him by Christopher Doria before Elliot even had a chance to make his bid. And the flash of her underwear that he caught when she got out of the car only served as a reminder of all that he would never know of Zoe.

"Hello, Elliot," she smiled. "I understand you've got a nice mirror for us."

"Hi, Zoe," he said almost coldly. "That's quite a car you're driving. Yours?" he asked, already knowing the answer.

Melissa glared at him.

Zoe picked up the mirror and tried to focus on the item for

sale. "This is really nice." She looked at Elliot. "The car? No. It belongs to my friend, Christopher."

"He must be a good friend now," he said with sarcasm.

"I got stuck in Brimfield. I stayed an extra day and I had no way to get home. So he let me take his car. That's all," she said firmly.

Elliot realized his interrogation was going nowhere and turned the conversation to the mirror. "I can let you have it for one-fifty. I think you can make a hundred on it."

"I really like it, Zoe. I think we should buy it."

"Sold. Why don't you bring it in and get Elliot his money." She looked at Elliot. "Cash, of course."

"That would be great."

While Melissa went to the shop, Elliot went to work on Zoe. "I haven't forgotten the lunch you promised. Do you want to do it today?"

"I can't, Elliot. It's my day to sit the shop. Melissa was just covering for me for the first hour."

"Oh. How about next week?"

"Sure," she said to appease him.

"What day is good for you?" he persisted.

"What day? Ah...how about next Friday?"

"Friday then. How's your plastic Pietà?"

"It's sitting next to the bronze one at home. Thanks again."

She was beginning to feel uncomfortable and was relieved to see Melissa walking toward them with his money. "Well," Zoe said, "I'm going to go in and get settled. Thanks for the mirror."

"You're welcome. By the way, Zoe," he pointed to the Healy, "how long are you going to keep that?"

"I don't know." She sounded perturbed. "Until he picks it up."

Before he could respond, Melissa handed him the money.

"I hope you don't mind ones, because I had to give you twenty of them."

"That's okay," he said as he began to count the bills.

Zoe took advantage of the diversion and turned to walk toward the store. "See you later, Elliot."

"Oh...bye, Zoe. Next Friday, right?"

"Yes," she answered curtly, and walked away.

"What's with you and Elliot?" Melissa asked when she returned to the store. "What's next Friday?"

Zoe shook her head. "He asked me to lunch when we were at Brimfield, and I told him we'd do it when we got back. It's the first thing he asked me this morning."

"He's on you now," she laughed.

"You know, I really like Elliot. I mean he's a good enough guy, but I have no interest in him. Doesn't he see that?"

"He only sees what he wants to see."

"Well, I don't want to wreck a friendship because he wants to take it beyond that."

"Don't encourage him, then."

"I'm not, for Christ's sake, Melissa," she said loudly, tugging on her skirt.

"Okay. Take it easy. We'll figure it out. Now," she smiled, "tell me about what happened with you and Christopher."

Zoe was glad to change the subject and told Melissa everything but the sexual details of their night together. She also told her that she was worried about where the relationship would go from there.

"Where do you want it to go?"

"I don't know. I don't know how to do these things, Melissa. I feel like I'm too old to date. It's so confusing. And his youth only adds to that."

"Do you think you're in love with him?"

"In love with him?"

"You slept with him," she argued.

"I don't know why I did that, but I'm glad I did. As far as love goes, all I can say is that I loved my husband. Outside of him, I don't even know how to define it."

"How does he feel about you?"

Zoe frowned. "I don't know. I know he wants to see me again, but he's already told me to take it day by day."

"That's probably good advice, Zoe."

Zoe nodded "It's just that I'm having these feelings that I haven't had for years, and as wonderful as they are, they're also confusing. I don't know what I'm supposed to do."

"Just relax, okay? See where it goes."

"Okay. I just don't want to get hurt, that's all. I'd rather not do anything than get hurt."

"I understand, Zoe," she said quietly. Then she put her tiny arms around her with great affection.

As if buoyed by the competition, Elliot Baker decided to find out more about Christopher Doria, to see if he could discredit him in front of Zoe. Although he had never met him, he was sure that he would know someone in the business who did. With Rolodex in hand, he spent Saturday evening on the phone to fellow pickers and dealers throughout New England. While some had heard of Christopher and had even been to his shop, most did not know him well, except for one picker who admitted doing business with him on a regular basis. That picker was Benjamin Divers.

Like all pickers, including Elliot Baker, Benjamin Divers was always on the road. Just as Elliot would drive north to Maine and New Hampshire to pick, Benjamin would drive south to Massachusetts and Rhode Island to do the same. Over the years, they had bumped into each other on numerous occasions, sometimes vying for the same items, with Benjamin Divers usually winning out because of his propensity for the devious. For that reason, Elliot did not hold him in high regard.

"Yeah," he growled into the phone, "I do a lot of business with Doria."

"What's he like?" asked Elliot.

Benjamin rarely had a kind word for anyone in the business, and Christopher Doria was no exception. "He's an uptown dealer, you know, mostly European stuff. And as far as I'm concerned, he's a cheap bastard."

"Why do you say that?"

"Because he never wants to pay my price. I drive all over the place for him, get him good stuff, then he kills me on price."

"Benjamin," he said, "you're not the only picker getting tanked on the price. Trust me."

The mention of trust burned Benjamin's ears. "Why do you want to know about him anyway?"

"I have my reasons. Let me ask you something."

"What?"

"Is he legit?"

Benjamin sneered. "What does that mean?"

"It's not a trick question."

Thinking about the reproduction Pietàs that he drove to Manhattan, Benjamin hesitated before he answered. "Listen, Baker," he said, "I don't know what you're getting at, but leave me out of it, okay? As far as I know Doria's no more guilty than anyone else in this business. And I know you can understand that because I know for a fact that you've moved questionable merchandise yourself."

"I can appreciate what you're saying Benjamin, but I'm not talking about a piece here or there. I'm talking about it in volume."

"Listen" he said emphatically, "as far as I know, he's straight, and I ought to know because he's a customer of mine. And if I were you," he warned, "I wouldn't be spreading rumors otherwise."

After that, the conversation went downhill quickly. Divers abruptly hung up, leaving Elliot with nothing to go on except his nagging suspicions and his desire to wrestle Zoe from Christopher Doria's grasp. He would have to find another way. He was just not sure how.

9

Friday was back-to-back men for Zoe. First, an indigestible lunch with Elliot, who decided he had hidden his feelings for her long enough. Right after the clam chowder course, he confessed that he had been taken with her since the first time they'd met at a local auction, shortly after she entered the business. Perhaps most telling of his affection for her was his admission that he often sold her goods for his cost, or just below.

"It was a way for me to treat you special," he said, "even if you didn't know it at the time."

With mournful eyes, he told her of his loneliness, and his desire to share his sunset years with someone of similar interests.

Zoe listened politely to the one-sided conversation, being careful not to encourage him in any way. It was not until coffee was served, when he asked her out for a dinner date, that she spoke her mind as gently as she could. "Elliot...I think you're a very nice man, and you've certainly been a big help to both me and Melissa. But you have to understand," she said, "I was married for a lot of years...and I loved my husband very much. You see," she stammered, "I really haven't had any interest in other men since he died. And as much as I like you...well...I think of us more as professional friends. Do you understand?"

"Maybe if you gave it a chance, that would change."

"Elliot, please."

"I'm not such a bad guy, you know."

"I know that. I just have no romantic interest, Elliot. I'm sorry."

Elliot's demeanor darkened. "What about Christopher Doria?"

"What about him?"

"Do you have a romantic interest in him?"

Zoe was angered by his forwardness. "Frankly," she said, "I don't think that's any of your business."

Her tone snapped him back into his good-guy mode. "I'm sorry. I shouldn't have asked that, Zoe. Well," he said, picking up the yellow credit card receipt, "I've got a couple of appointments to keep." He smiled genuinely. "I really had a nice lunch."

"Thanks for inviting me. I hope you understand how I feel, Elliot."

"I do, Zoe. But like everything else in the world, feelings can change too."

Zoe said nothing as he got up from the table. She began to feel uneasy about the man she thought was one of the good ones in the business.

"See you soon," he smiled.

As much as she hadn't been looking forward to lunch with Elliot, the reverse was true for her second masculine encounter of the day. Christopher had arranged a ride to Noble's Cove with Arthur Drake, who had been in Maine on business, and was heading to Provincetown on Cape Cod for the weekend, for a mix of business and pleasure. Christopher had been invited to spend the weekend at Zoe's, an invitation which he'd enthusiastically accepted.

They arrived at One Piece Antiques around four. Arthur commented right away about the Austin Healy parked in the lot. "Well, I see she's already got your license plate number," he joked. "It didn't take long for you to get wrapped around her finger, did it?"

"Cut the shit, will you Arthur? I told you, she had no other way to get home."

"Well, now you do," he laughed. "So why are you staying the weekend?"

"She's a nice person, Arthur. Which is more than I can say for you," he joked.

Arthur pulled into the spot next to Christopher's car, nearly catching its left, rear bumper as he did.

"Hey, take it easy, Arthur!"

"I wasn't even close. He threw the van in park. "Now, let's go meet this woman of yours."

"Don't be rude, okay?"

"When have I ever been rude?"

"Yeah, right."

Melissa was sitting at the desk when the two walked into the shop. She smiled as soon as she saw Christopher. "Hi, Christopher. It's good to see you again."

"Melissa...hi, I'd like you to meet Arthur Drake."

The albino-haired man put out his large hand. "Nice to meet you, Melissa. How have you been enjoying the Healy?"

"Oh, I haven't been driving it." She looked at Christopher for help.

"It's Zoe, Melissa's partner that took it home."

"Sorry Melissa," Arthur said. "I didn't mean to associate you with such a rogue."

"By the way," asked Christopher, "where is Zoe?"

"Out back," she answered, pointing to a door on the far wall. "Why don't you go get her?"

Christopher excused himself and went to the door leading to the shop's small storage room. As he opened it, he could see Zoe facing away from him, reaching for a bolt of vintage fabric on the top shelf. Her stretch lifted her white cotton blouse just above her midriff, and he quietly came up behind her and put his hands around her bare waist.

"Hey!" she screamed.

"It's me," he laughed, spinning her around toward him.

Zoe was momentarily out of breath. "Jesus, you scared me, Christopher."

"I'm sorry. I didn't know you were so hyper," he teased. He kissed her on the lips.

She settled in his arms and kissed him back. "Hyper? Wait till I find the right moment to do the same to you."

"I missed you, Zoe."

"I missed you, too...I'm glad you're spending the weekend."

"C'mon out," he said, pulling on her hand. "There's someone I want you to meet."

Once back in the shop, he introduced her to Arthur, who had busied himself by judging the quality of the merchandise on display. As soon as he saw Zoe, he understood why Christopher had loaned her his car.

"Nice to meet you, Zoe. I like your shop," he said. "It's a little too decorator for me, but it's nice."

"Oh..." Zoe wasn't sure what to say.

"Our customers love the way we lay it out," Melissa said defensively.

"I told you Arthur, don't be rude."

"I'm not being rude, Guido, just honest. I think they've done a wonderful job. It's just not my cup of tea, that's all."

"Guido?" laughed Zoe.

"It's just his twisted WASP sense of humor. Every Italian's a Guido to him."

"We're all entitled," insisted Arthur.

Arthur was one of those men that polarized those who met him. Melissa immediately disliked him, while Zoe enjoyed his full-speed-ahead honesty and point of view. They each reacted differently as he told them of his own disdain for most of the browsers that came into his shop.

"Have you ever thrown someone out of your shop?" he asked.

"Of course not," said Melissa.

"Try it sometime. It's a freeing experience."

On that note, he announced it was time for him to leave for Cape Cod. "I'll be picking and playing." He grinned broadly.

While Melissa deliberately stayed behind, Zoe and Christopher walked out with Arthur to his van. Christopher grabbed his overnight bag from the pile of movers' blankets in the back. "Thanks for the lift, Arthur."

"Any time, Guido." He looked at Zoe. "And have a good weekend. A real good weekend," he laughed.

Christopher put his arm around her. "I'm sorry, Zoe, the man can't be helped."

"We're all entitled." Arthur smiled and pushed his albino hair off his forehead. Then he got in his van and drove away. While they waved goodbye, Melissa, from inside the shop, wished him good riddance.

As Zoe and Christopher walked arm in arm back to the shop, Elliot Baker's van moved slowly up Church Street. He had picked up a couple of pieces in his afternoon appointments and wanted to offer them to Zoe, to demonstrate that he had no hard feelings about her tough stance on his romantic interest. He also wanted to keep the line of communication open with her. Continuing to offer her items would be the only way he would see her on a regular basis, as well as his best chance to get her to change her feelings.

Just as he put his blinker on to take a left into the shop

parking lot, Elliot spotted the Austin Healy, an indication that Zoe was there. Then he saw the affectionate couple walking toward the door. Right away he knew it was Zoe. Even from the back, he could recognize the wardrobe that he'd looked at so lustily during lunch. The pale peach skirt that he dreamed of lifting, and the white cotton blouse that he imagined unbuttoning.

Although he was too far away to see the features of the man, Elliot could tell from a distance that he was tall, and in much better shape than his own overweight body. He also had Zoe's arm tightly around him, leaving Elliot no doubt that it was Christopher Doria.

"That son of a bitch," he said, staring at the two.

The oncoming traffic had subsided and an impatient car behind Elliot prodded him with a beep. For a moment he did nothing. Then, as the couple disappeared behind the shop door, he sped away in anger, totally unsure of what his next move would be.

When a spouse dies, sometimes the desire to cook expires as well. There is little solace in endless nights of single servings, and more often than not, they're only bitter reminders of what was lost. In Zoe's case, cooking for her husband had been an act of love—as much a feeding of the heart as it was physical sustenance. It was not that she liked to cook, because in fact she didn't. She just enjoyed pleasing her husband, caring for him, whether at the kitchen table or by satisfying other appetites in the privacy of their bed.

It had been over two years since Zoe had cooked for another man, and she approached the dinner she would prepare for Christopher on Friday night with the same insecurities that marked their relationship in general. With that in mind, she planned to make it as fail-safe as possible—jumbo shrimp cocktail, boiled lobster, baked potato, and fresh steamed asparagus. The only risk would be to overcook the asparagus, so she dug out her egg timer from deep in the back of a kitchen drawer to make sure she would err on the side of crisp.

While Zoe ran cold water over the colander of shrimp, Christopher made two martinis. Once the shrimp was defrosted, the two of them made their way to the tiny porch with the splendid ocean view, that she had shared on so many other summer evenings with her late husband. In spite of a slight ocean breeze, the air blasted with mid-July heat, adding a meteorological tension that heightened the amorous feelings already swirling inside of them.

With the luxury of having no one to account to and nowhere to go, the two sat and drank for an hour and a half before having dinner. In spite of the unfamiliarity of an evening at home with a man she barely knew, Zoe became quite comfortable. She allowed herself to be in the purity of the moment, without looking behind or ahead, experiencing a peace she hadn't felt for a long time.

By the time they finished dinner, it was time to go to bed. While Christopher watched, Zoe poured two glasses of brandy to accompany them to the bedroom.

"Are you sure you want that?"

"Why? Don't you?"

"Have you heard the phrase, one and done?"

"Sure."

"Well, if I have one more, I'll be done," he laughed. "So I'll pass."

"I need it to sleep," she said, pouring half of his into her glass. She hesitated for a moment. "I used to do pills but I got in trouble with them."

"Don't let the same thing happen with that."

"I won't," she said defensively. "Anyway, you wouldn't want me up all night, would you?"

"That depends," he laughed.

"C'mon."

They walked the short distance to the bedroom. As soon as they were inside the threshold, Zoe froze. She knew that they were not in some neutral motel anymore. They were in the bedroom where she had shared every aspect of life and all its intimacies. While she felt uncomfortable about having a man other than her husband in the house, the idea of it took on surreal proportions in the bedroom. She felt as though she were allowing him to rip off the plywood from the windows of Richard's vacated life, encouraging Christopher to move in and pick up where her husband had so suddenly left off.

Christopher immediately picked up on her angst. "Are you all right, Zoe?"

She handed him the glass of brandy. "Hold this. I have to go to the bathroom."

Sometimes we see ourselves best when we're face down in our toilet bowl mirrors—coming to the realization that we are, after all, only human and limited to the amount of poison that we can hold down before it erupts out of necessity. As Zoe vomited, her entire being began to clear. She could feel the understanding hand of her late husband on her shoulder, steadying her in her grief and tumultuous guilt.

"Zoe, it's okay. It's your life now. It's no violation of us."

"Then why do I feel like it is?"

"I know things now that I didn't know before. You deserve to go on, and I want you to."

"Are you sure, Richard?" She could feel his grasp tighten with affection.

"Zoe...do you think you found that Pietà on your own?"

She got up from her knees and turned around, expecting to see Richard standing there. She felt almost miraculously relieved, as if she had regurgitated two years of gluttonous self

ﾋﾒﾒ

ﾒﾐﾒﾐﾒ

punishment.

"I will always love you, Richard." She walked to the door and opened it.

"And I will always love you."

Friday night was a turning point in Zoe's life. As fully as she could, she gave herself to Christopher. In turn, she allowed herself the pleasure of every inch of his body. Through Richard's intercession, she was able to temporarily let go of her ego, that nag inside of her spewing out illusions as if they were truths. She shed the vanity of believing that she would somehow wound her dead husband's spirit by being with another man in the bed that they once called their own. On that night, Zoe understood that nothing could take away what she and Richard shared, and that she was free, even entitled, to love again.

On Saturday morning, bacon and eggs were in order—that heady mix of cholesterol and fat, an appropriate dessert after a rich night of lovemaking. The culinary doubts that Zoe had the night before had evaporated, and no overcooked yoke or burnt piece of toast could cause even a ripple in her post coital confidence.

"I invited my daughter to dinner tonight," said Zoe between sips of her coffee. "She's dying to meet you."

"It's Joanna, right?"

Zoe nodded.

"What's the deal on her fiancee? Are they back together yet?"

"No. They're both unbelievably stubborn. So she'll be by herself tonight. Which is weird," she added, "because I'm usually the odd man out."

"Then I'll be sure to pay special attention to her."

"What does that mean?" asked Zoe in a temporary relapse of her new-found confidence.

"Zoe!" he laughed.

"It's the age thing," she said apologetically. "I mean, normally, you'd be with someone her age."

"It's only an age thing if you make it that." He leaned over the patio table and kissed her. "Anyway, I prefer someone with a little patina."

"Patina?" laughed Zoe. "That's exactly the word I used with Melissa to describe her wrinkles." She felt her own, early morning face. "Do I look all right, Christopher?"

"Fetching," he replied, as he put his own hand over hers. "So what are we going to do today?"

"Since Melissa offered to switch shop days with me, we can do anything we want."

Christopher looked out at the ocean. "Want to go to the beach? It looks like it's going to be a beautiful day."

"I was thinking something a little more private. Or at least a little more anonymous."

Zoe wasn't quite ready to go so public in Noble's Cove. Because of her years there as resident and shopkeeper, she knew the lion's share of people in town, most of whom liked nothing better than to chew mercilessly on the doings of other residents. And Christopher, because of his age, would be someone she would have to explain over and over. She knew that no matter what she said about him, the takeaway would always be the same—older woman with younger man.

"There's an antique show down in Plymouth. Why don't we go there?" she suggested.

"Wouldn't you rather have a day off from the business?"

"You know as well as I do that there's no such thing as a day off in this business."

"I'm already suffering from withdrawal," he joked.

"Then we'd better go," she teased. "Why don't you shower first, and I'll clean up this mess."

Christopher smiled. "I thought we'd shower together."

Zoe blushed and pushed her empty coffee cup away. "Okay."

Knowing Saturday was one of Zoe's days to tend shop, Elliot was in the parking lot waiting for her to arrive. In the back of the van were the pieces he had planned to show her the day before, his efforts having been thwarted by the presence of Christopher Doria. To his surprise, Melissa pulled in and parked next to him. Before she had a chance to get out, Elliot was at her open window.

"Isn't this Zoe's day to sit?"

"Good morning, Elliot," she said sarcastically "How are you today?"

"I'm sorry...good morning, Melissa. Isn't Zoe working today?"

"We switched. She's covering for me tomorrow."

"How come?"

Melissa thought for a minute about what she should tell him. She decided on the truth. "Because her friend, Christopher, is spending the weekend."

"What? You mean he didn't leave yesterday?"

"How did you know he got here yesterday? Did you meet him?"

"No, but I was driving by the shop and I saw Zoe out front with a guy. I figured it was him."

Melissa was well aware of the increased energy in his pursuit of her partner, as well as Zoe's total lack of interest in him. "Elliot," she said with compassion, "I know you're infatuated with Zoe, but I have to tell you...I think you'd better forget it. She thinks a lot of you, but not in the way you want her to. Plus," she said, "I think she's getting kind of serious with Christopher."

Elliot got visibly angry. "I'm telling you Melissa, just like I told Zoe. I think that guy pulled a fast one on her...and I think he's just as fake as that bronze he sold her."

"I can't answer that, Elliot. All I know is that she really likes him. He seems like a good guy," she argued.

"He's not." He pushed back his long black hair. "Melissa," he asked, almost begging, "could you put in a good word for me? Maybe if she heard it from you, she'd begin to feel differently about me."

Melissa shook her head and pleaded with him. "Don't ask me to do that, Elliot. I don't want to get in the middle of this. Anyway," she observed, "it's her life, and she's going to do whatever she wants."

Elliot was defeated for the day. "So she's in tomorrow?"

Melissa seemed concerned. "Yeah, but what do you expect to accomplish by badgering her?"

"I'm not going to badger her," he insisted. "I've got a couple of things in the van that I want to show her."

"Oh," she sounded relieved. "For the shop? I can look at them."

"That's okay." He started to walk to his van. "I'll show them to her tomorrow."

Melissa waved to him as he backed out of the parking lot, "Goodbye you antique asshole," she muttered as he drove away.

Zoe and Christopher got back to Noble's Cove late in the afternoon, following a productive day of picking at the antique show set up next to Plymouth Rock in historic Plymouth Harbor. They had lunched al fresco at a waterside Italian restaurant, and had easily covered the bill, and many more to come, by what they had bought at the show.

Just in case they got lucky, they had taken Zoe's van, leaving the Healy to sit for the day in her gravel driveway. Zoe bought four pieces of bulky country furniture that she could turn at a profit. Christopher, who would ultimately transport any purchases he made in the lilliputian trunk of his car, focused on smalls. He found a couple of pocket watches for short money, as well as a porcelain phrenology head for three hundred dollars that he figured he could flip to one of his physician collectors for around nine hundred.

Instead of going back to her house, at Zoe's wise suggestion, they stopped at the shop to unload her portion of the purchases. In carrying her end of anything heavy, Melissa always left a lot to be desired. It was a joy for Zoe to have a muscular young man on the other end for the first time since starting the business. She took full advantage of the opportunity.

"I love the cupboard," said Melissa as she watched them pull the massive pine kitchen piece from the back of the van.

"You wouldn't if you had to carry it," grunted Zoe.

"I don't think I could," Melissa said as she helped them guide it through the door of the shop. "Christopher, you're a godsend," she added.

He just huffed in response.

Once they rocked it into place, they unloaded the other more manageable pieces. Then Christopher offered to go pick up some soft drinks. Zoe pointed him in the direction of the Wave Deli.

Christopher looked at the three remaining pieces sitting on the ground behind the van. "Do you want me to help you with those first?"

Zoe waved him off. "Go. Melissa and I can get them."

Melissa flexed her potato stick arms. "I'll take care of it, Christopher."

He walked off to find the Wave, while the two of them moved the other pieces into the shop.

"Guess who was here this morning before I even got here."

"Who?"

"The other man in your life."

"Elliot?" Zoe moaned. "What did he want?"

"You. He knew it was your day to watch the shop."

"What did you tell him?"

"The truth."

"He knows Christopher's here?"

"He knew yesterday," she answered. "Apparently, he saw the two of you outside the shop."

"How's he taking it?"

"I'd say he's pissed."

"Great."

Melissa filled her in on the details of the brief conversation, and warned her to expect him on Sunday.

"I'll handle it," Zoe promised. "I'm really losing my patience with him."

"He is getting strange," Melissa remarked. "He used to be such a nice guy, too."

"Used to be," Zoe said regretfully.

As they began to rearrange the shop to accommodate the new additions, Christopher returned with three lemonades. "Not as good as Brimfield," he said as he handed one to each of them, "but they'll do."

"Thanks," said Melissa.

Zoe took a long sip of hers and thought of the time they had spent there. "No," she shook her head, "not as good as Brimfield."

A Saturday night table at the Witch Haven Inn was always a wait, especially during the summer months when the town filled up with tourists and seasonal residents, tanned and sandy-toed from a day at the shore. Zoe and Christopher were in the smoke-filled bar when Joanna arrived. As she walked toward them, Christopher surmised that the attractive young woman was Zoe's daughter.

Like Zoe, Joanna was above average in height. Her frame was the same as her mother's, only thinner by the years between them. Her long blonde hair had yet to turn with the foliage of age, and fluttered softly against her cheeks as she moved.

"That's got to be Joanna," he said. The youthful heart inside of him skipped an instinctual beat.

Zoe followed his gaze, spotting her daughter as she made her way through the chattering crowd. "How did you know?"

"It's you, twenty years ago."

The two decades difference made Zoe cringe. "Would you have liked me better then?"

"Not better, Zoe. Just as much as now." He patted her thigh. "Stop worrying about it, will you?"

Zoe sighed. "Okay. I just..."

Before she could continue, Joanna's arms were around her. "The Brimfield Babe," she laughed. "You look great."

Zoe exchanged affection and turned her attention to her guest. "Honey, I want you to meet my friend, Christopher."

Joanna, no stranger to meeting handsome, available as well as unavailable men in her law office, held out her hand with confidence. "Hi, Christopher. It's nice to meet you."

"The same," he smiled. "I've heard a lot about you."

"Oh, my perils?" she laughed.

"More than that, Jo," insisted Zoe.

Christopher stood up in the SRO bar and offered Joanna his seat.

"A gentleman as well," she said as she sat down. "Good going, Mom," she teased.

"What's with you tonight?" asked Zoe. "Did Ramon come crawling home?"

"Not exactly. But at least we're talking." She turned to her right and looked knowingly at Christopher who was standing between them. "So...how was Brimfield?"

Christopher passed the question to Zoe with his eyes.

"We had a great time," she said sincerely. "What would you like to drink?" she asked to change the subject. "White wine?"

"Sure. Chablis."

While Zoe flagged down the bartender, Christopher prudently decided it was time to go to the men's room, even though he knew he would do little more there than wash his hands. He excused himself and promised to check on their table before he got back.

As soon as he was out of ear shot, Joanna gave her assessment with a long nodding smile at her mother.

"What?" Zoe picked the olive out of her martini and bit off half of it.

Joanna reached over and took the remainder of the olive from her and popped it in her own mouth. "What?" she said incredulously. "He's wonderful."

Zoe blushed. "He is, isn't he?"

Without a hint of jealousy, Joanna took both her mother's hands in hers. "I'm glad you've met someone, Mom."

"And right now, someone is all it is. So don't get ahead of yourself, Jo. I don't know where it's going," she warned, "but so far, so good."

"He reminds me of Dad," she said.

"What do you mean?"

"Just the way he looks at you, that's all. I can tell he really cares about you."

"Jo," she argued, "you just met him, for God's sake."

"I've got an eye for love."

"Not lately," razzed her mother.

"Oh really?" she challenged, running her fingers through her hair in defiance. "Maybe I'm wrong about him. Maybe he'd like someone a little younger."

"Shit, Jo. Don't bring that up."

Joanna retreated to her compassionate self. "I'm just kidding and you know it. You make a nice couple."

"Yeah?" she asked, looking for reassurance.

Joanna picked up her glass of wine from the bar and gently tapped it against her mother's crystal stem. "Yeah."

The three sat in the sputtering candlelight of the living room, drinking wine and trading stories until two in the morning. Although Joanna had planned to go home after dinner at the Witch Haven, her mother convinced her that she was not sober enough to drive. Joanna agreed to spend the night on the pull-out living room couch. Once committed to the safety of the house, Joanna as well as her mother and Christopher, sipped with abandon. However Joanna, unlike the other two, was having trouble staying awake.

Even with all the liquor that she had consumed, Zoe's conscience was still lucid enough to make her feel uneasy as she tried to excuse herself and Christopher. As foolish as she knew it was, she struggled with the idea of going into her bedroom with a man other than her husband while her daughter was in the house. When Joanna began to nod off, Zoe took it upon herself to open the couch and get it ready for her. Then she gently nudged Joanna into place, clothes and all. She covered her with a sheet and waited until she was certain that she was asleep.

"I think it's safe to go to bed now," she whispered.

Christopher kissed her on the back of her neck. "Are you okay?"

"This is completely new territory for me. I'm sorry."

"I understand, Zoe."

Zoe turned and gazed at Joanna, who like all daughters could still be thought of as a child. She thought of the glorious day when she and Richard brought her home from the hospital. He had joked on the ride home that he would never give her away in marriage, that he loved her too much to ever let her go.

"She told me that she really likes you, Christopher," said Zoe, as if her endorsement would somehow justify their trip to the bedroom.

"I'm glad. I really like her, too. She seems like a really sweet woman."

"She is a sweet girl, isn't she?" Zoe took his hand and squeezed it. "Let's go to bed."

Although Joanna was more passed out than asleep, the two walked as quietly as they could to the bedroom, a mere ten feet from the living room couch. For a moment, Zoe thought of locking the door behind them, as if Joanna might wake like a five-year-old and enter her bedroom in the tears of a nightmare. She smiled to herself and closed the door tightly, knowing that no one would enter except her own ghosts of guilt, and no lock, however strong, would be able to keep them out.

The two undressed in the warm glow of the single table lamp. Unlike couples who have been together for many years, they were keenly aware of each other's body as they shed their clothes. Zoe got into bed and pulled the sheet up to her neck, while Christopher walked naked across the room to where his overnight bag sat on the floor. From it, he removed a plastic shopping bag.

"I have something for you, Zoe," he said, turning and walking toward the bed.

Zoe thought it was a strange time to be bestowing gifts. "What?" she asked apprehensively.

Christopher sat on the edge of the bed. "Here," he said, handing her the bag. "I found this at the antique show today. I bought it when you weren't looking."

Zoe sat up and reached into the bag. Her hand recognized the slipperiness of silk. "What is it?"

"Take it out," he encouraged her.

Slowly, she pulled the fabric object out of the bag until she could see what it was. With both hands, she held it up in front of her. It was a pale pink silk camisole with just a hint of white brocade on the edges. "It's beautiful, Christopher."

"Do you like it?"

"Yes," she smiled as she examined it.

"I found it at one of the vintage clothing dealers today. It's from the twenties. Feel it," he said. "You can almost sense the passion."

Zoe rubbed it with her fingers and thought of the woman who once wore it, and most likely made love in it. She thought of how special she must have felt—just as she would feel special wearing it herself. "I love it."

"Let me put it on you."

"Okay," she blushed.

She handed him the slight garment and then sat up on the edge of the bed next to him. Then, as if surrendering her will, she raised her arms and he slipped it over them, letting its slickness free fall to her waist.

"Stand up and let me see you."

Zoe got up from the bed and as she did, the camisole fell as far as it could, coming to rest just below her navel. "Do you like it on me?" she asked, looking for reassurance.

He put his arms around her and felt the softness of it on her back. Then he slid his hands down and embraced her bare buttocks, their silkiness eclipsing that of the camisole. "It's beautiful on you, Zoe." As he spoke, the grasp of his arms directed her to the bed, and her body willingly complied. Then he laid down beside her and touched her, bringing the camisole to life with pleasure. "I love you, Zoe."

Zoe moaned quietly and thought of Richard, still so close

to her heart. Then she thought of Joanna, her sleeping beauty just on the other side of the door. "I love you too, Christopher," she whispered, the words cutting the umbilical cord of her guilt, allowing her the freedom to be a woman again as well as the mother that she would always be. "I love you, too."

10

With Christopher's full frontal entry into Zoe's life, things changed forever, creating a new Zoe—a woman, like so many younger than herself, acute with sensuality, the touchstone of an amorous encounter. In the week that followed their two nights together, they talked on the phone daily, with Christopher promising to return on the weekend. However, on Saturday morning he called to cancel, saying only that "something had come up." Zoe offered to drive to Maine on Sunday, her day off, but he told her that he would be out of the area on both days, and would not be returning to Maine until late Sunday night.

"Where are you going?" she finally asked, almost possessively.

"New York City. I have to go look at some stuff."

"Oh," she said with relief, "it must be good stuff for you to go all the way there."

"It is. Hopefully, I can buy it right."

"Call me when you get back, okay?"

"I will."

"Christopher..."

"What?"

"I love you."

"I love you, too, Zoe. Talk to you Sunday night."

Christopher arrived at LaGuardia airport in New York on a flight from Portland around two Saturday afternoon. As he approached the main terminal, he found the cardboard sign with his name on it. The man holding it was dressed in a rumpled blue suit.

"I'm Mr. Doria," he announced as he reached the livery driver. "Is Mr. Drake here yet?"

"He's in the car, sir."

The driver took Christopher's single piece of luggage, and the two walked to the pick-up and drop-off section outside the terminal. More out of habit than respect, the driver opened the door for Christopher and he got in the Lincoln Town Car.

"Well good afternoon, Christopher," said Arthur. "I'm glad you made it here in one piece."

"I had a good flight. How about you?"

"Can't complain."

"I see you're dressed for the occasion," he laughed, pointing at Arthur's white short sleeve shirt and rust-colored shorts.

"You know me, Guido. I don't dress up for anyone."

"You look like a tourist."

"All the better then, isn't it?" He winked. "We need to be incognito in our line of work, don't we?"

Christopher frowned. "I guess."

On the trip into Manhattan, the two talked little about the business. Instead, Arthur probed Christopher's relationship with Zoe.

"So where's it going to end up, Guido?"

"I don't know Arthur. But it's getting serious."

Arthur shook his head. "She seems like a wonderful woman,

Christopher, but haven't you already got enough responsibility?"

"I suppose."

"Well," he said sincerely, "think about it, that's all."

"I will," he answered halfheartedly.

The off peak trip into the city took only about twenty minutes. By two-thirty they were at their destination, an antique store called Rinaldi's on Eighty Third Street and Lexington. To gain entrance to the store, they had to ring the buzzer. Within seconds, the door buzzed and they went inside.

The inventory of Rinaldi's was what you might expect in an Upper East Side antique store catering to the sophisticated surrounding brownstones. Gold leaf was everywhere in the store, as was bronze in the form of gods, nymphs, and other allegorical figures. Also in residence was a bronze Pietà, formerly from Maine.

Enzo Rinaldi, the proprietor, greeted them as they came through the door. He was a small man about forty, wearing a brightly colored silk shirt with exotic birds printed on it, and beige linen pants.

"Arthur," he said, kissing him on the cheek, "good to see you."

"You too, Ralph," responded Arthur.

Enzo put his hands on his hips and spoke effeminately. "Arthur, you know I don't go by Ralph anymore. That was my Bronx name. It doesn't fit the image."

"I'm just busting your balls, that's all."

"I wish you'd do more than that, Arthur," Enzo said suggestively.

Christopher interrupted the banter. "Hi Enzo." He held out his hand.

Enzo shook it gently. "Chris...good to see you. How are things in Maine?"

"A little slow, actually."

"I'm sure it's nothing compared to the city." Enzo did a three-sixty twirl around the store. "As you can see, all the antique collectors are out of town for the weekend."

"Just be grateful that none of us has to depend solely on the legitimate collectors to make a living," offered Arthur. "So," he said in a crisp business tone, "what are we looking at today?"

"Come with me," said Enzo. "I have something wonderful for both of you."

They followed Enzo to the back room of his store which was wall-to-wall objects, mostly flamboyant pieces perfect for the large egos who would ultimately purchase them. In the corner of the room was a metal flat file with extra wide drawers which could easily accommodate artwork up to two feet by three feet.

"Today is art class," joked Enzo as he opened the top drawer of the file. "Now Arthur," he continued, "I know you're the Americana purist, so this is for you." He removed a piece of fabric and slowly unrolled it on top of the file cabinet.

"A sampler?" asked Arthur.

"A great sampler," remarked Enzo. He finished unrolling it, and as he did, the colors exploded.

"Jesus," drooled Arthur, "it looks brand new." He then carefully studied the schoolgirl sampler. It was an elaborate, but naive scene of a house surrounded by livestock. In the background was what looked like Boston Harbor with a ship sailing majestically in it. The needlework sampler was signed "Anna Mary Bacon," and dated "Boston, 1813."

"I don't think it's ever seen the light of day," remarked Enzo. "That's why the colors are so bold."

"It's beautiful," said Christopher.

"You know," Enzo continued, "Sotheby's got over sixty grand for one last year, and I don't think it was nearly as good."

"I know the one you're talking about," said Arthur. "It couldn't touch this one."

"I knew you'd like it," smiled Enzo.

"How much?"

"For you, Arthur? Twenty grand."

"I can make money on that."

"Just don't display it in your shop," warned Enzo.

"No shit, Ralph. Anyway," he said, "that's what's great about this business. No matter what the category, there's always a greedy collector who's willing to look the other way to get the best. They don't care if it's stolen or not, as long as they get to look at it hanging on their own walls everyday until they croak. Then," he laughed, "they don't give a shit."

"Can you do cash?" Enzo asked.

"Absolutely."

Arthur unzipped his overnight bag and took out a bank money pouch. As he counted out twenty thousand in bills, Enzo reached into the file again and pulled out a flat piece of artwork, wrapped in plastic.

"Now for you, Chris...you like religious art, right?"

"What is it, Enzo?" he asked impatiently.

Enzo turned the piece over and showed it to Christopher. "You've heard of Durer, haven't you?"

"My old buddy, Albrecht Durer," Christopher said as he took the artwork from him. It was a dramatic, late fifteenth century woodcut, about eleven by fifteen inches, of an angel fighting a dragon. "St. Michael...it's from his Apocalypse series."

"You know your stuff, don't you?" Enzo said respectfully.

"Enough to get into trouble," he laughed.

"It's in good shape for something made five hundred years ago, isn't it?"

"Primo." Christopher studied it closely for a minute or so and then asked the price.

"Four thousand, Chris."

"That seems fair."

"Can you move it quickly?"

"I think so. I've got a collector who's into Old Master drawings and prints."

"Good. And the sooner I get it out of New York, the better."

"Oh?"

"It's like your Pietà out there, Chris," he said, pointing to the bronze statue in the showroom. "It just needs to be sold out of the area, that's all."

A cloud came over Christopher as he fanned out the four thousand dollars to cover the cost of the woodcut. As he picked it up and put it in his bag, he looked again at the angel thrust in the eternal fight with the dragon and thought of his own dragons, and how exhausted he felt from the fight that he was sure he would eventually lose. "I'm getting too old for this."

Arthur slapped him on the back. "Cheer up, Guido. You'll be fine."

Enzo seemed concerned. "Don't get chicken on me now, Chris."

He shook his head. "I won't."

After completing their business transactions, the two left Rinaldi's and hailed a cab to take them down to Eighteenth Street, where they had reservations at Trio's Hotel, an eighty-five dollar a night stopover for independent businessmen who traveled without the essential luxury of a company expense account.

"I would rather sleep in the Lincoln Town Car," joked Christopher as they walked into the lobby.

"Quit bitching," said Arthur. "It's clean...just a little rough around the edges."

Around six o'clock, they met in the lobby for dinner. Arthur dressed for the night out by changing into long pants, albeit wrinkled ones, but adequate to get him into places hungry for business on a summer Saturday night in New York City. They took a cab down to Little Italy, and found a small but affordable restaurant where they could dine on chicken and pasta for under fifteen dollars each.

After dinner, they decided to walk back to the hotel to work off the rum cake they'd both had for dessert. Their conversation centered around the difficulties of the business, and how both of them were momentarily disenchanted with it.

"Everyone thinks that just because you carry expensive stuff, that you're well off yourself," grumbled Arthur.

"It's a joke, isn't it? If people only knew how hand-to-mouth it is."

"It makes you do some nasty things," added Arthur. "Remember the dealer in Vermont who sold the same painting by Thomas Moran to three different chumps?"

"Billy Preston, right?"

"Yeah."

"Whatever happened to him?"

"He did the only honorable thing he could do," laughed Arthur. "He split with the money."

"Where is he now?"

Arthur shook his head. "I don't know, but my guess is he's doing the same thing under a new name."

"I wouldn't mind doing that myself," he mused. Christopher stopped in his tracks. "Arthur...have you ever thought of making one big score and getting out?"

"Many times."

"Then how come you haven't?"

"Afraid of getting caught, I guess."

"But you've already been pinched...just like I have."

"Not for anything really big, though."

"Sure, but you know as well as I do that we're active

enough now that, sooner or later, we're going to get nailed again."

"Chris...what are you getting at?"

"I'm just tired of the ugly part of the business, that's all. And now with Zoe..." He paused. "I guess I wouldn't mind making my day's work a little more honest."

Arthur put his arm around his shoulders. "Medical bills don't pay themselves, Christopher. Yeah, maybe you could earn enough to cover them legitimately, but it would be tough."

"I know..."

"So what do you want to do, Guido? Rob a museum?" he joked.

"No. Maybe just get out of the business altogether." He threw his arms up in the air. "It's making me crazy."

"Yeah, you could open a gift shop," Arthur cackled. "Then, you'd never have to hunt for stuff anymore. You could just call up and reorder some more scented candles."

"Please..." Christopher moaned.

"Or maybe some novelty coffee cups," he laughed. "Or New Age crystals. Hey, don't even bother with a store...sell it all on ebay."

Christopher smiled, "Okay Arthur, I get your point."

"We're stuck, Guido. Whether we make money at it or not, we're antique junkies. We wouldn't know how to do anything else."

"You're right."

"So buckle up my friend and buy what you can, when you can. You'll be okay."

"Thanks for the advice," Christopher said sincerely. "Are you up for tomorrow?"

"As long as there's money in it."

"At least the stuff isn't hot, Arthur."

"Theoretically."

"It's not," he argued.

Arthur shrugged. "Christopher, it doesn't matter to me either way, as long as there's money in it."

Christopher didn't respond.

The two men walked together in silence, separate in their own dark thoughts, the rest of the way back to the hotel.

"What time tomorrow?" asked Arthur as they entered the lobby.

"Our appointment's at noon, so meet me here about a half-hour before."

"I'll be there," Arthur said efficiently. "See you then."

St. Anselm's Catholic Church, a chiseled granite edifice on the Lower East Side, had once been the spiritual foundation for faithful immigrants who had made their way from Ellis Island.

Over the years, it had lost its sense of importance. Like so many other religious institutions, it paled in comparison to the temples of commercialism that had risen so quickly after Johnny came marching home from the war. No longer was it top on the list of financial considerations for its part-time parishioners. Instead, it took its place in a long line of out-stretched hands, most of which offered more alluring material pursuits.

Christopher and Arthur sat in the tiny waiting room of the rectory and waited for Father Ibsen to arrive. They were told by the octogenarian housekeeper that he had just finished the last Mass of the day and would be with them shortly. Arthur, not much for organized religion himself, felt uneasy in the surroundings, and fidgeted in the authoritarian, carved Gothic chair. He much preferred the simplicity of Shaker design—the Sect's own chair seats being just as hard on the backside, but somehow simpler in their faith, and without a hint of Gothic sanguineness.

Christopher was more at ease, although returning to the business side of the Church reminded him of his tumultuous days as a seminarian, and how he had vacillated back and forth, particularly in the area of heterosexual chastity. As a young man, his love of art and women was something he could not assuage. Eventually he had decided to follow a vocation outside the stringent rules of the Church's canvas.

"Good morning, Christopher."

Christopher looked up in the direction of the raspy smoky voice. "Father Ibsen." He got up from his chair and held out his hand. "Good to see you again. It's been a lot of years since Saint John's."

"It has, hasn't it?"

On seeing the man in the black cassock, Arthur stood up as if a judge had just entered the courtroom. His large frame and albino hair were hard to miss, and Father Ibsen immediately turned his attention to him.

"I'd like you to meet my associate, Arthur Drake."

"Your associate?" He seemed surprised.

"He's my financial partner in this deal, Father. It's not one I could underwrite alone."

"Oh...well I guess that's okay. Come with me, gentlemen. I've got three baptisms at two o'clock so I don't have much time."

The two dealers followed the prelate outside to a dungeon-strong metal door on the side of the church. Once opened, they followed him down the stone steps to the belly of the house of worship. Behind another locked metal door was what they had come for—approximately a hundred years worth of religious artifacts that sat like some Egyptian trove in the Catholic pyramid.

"This is it," said Father Ibsen. "As you can see, Christopher, there's a lot of quality here," he said, picking up a silver chalice from an entire box of them.

Christopher took it from him and studied the ornate, nineteenth century embossing. "This is wonderful." He handed it to Arthur.

"There must be thirty ounces of silver here," Arthur said, ignoring the aesthetics of it, and focusing on its metallurgical value.

"There's probably a dozen more chalices," chimed Father Ibsen. He began to walk around the dusty storeroom, pointing out other valuable silver and gold religious objects. Then he flipped through the paintings stacked against each other on the left wall—some nineteenth century reproductions of earlier religious scenes, as well as paintings from the sixteenth, seventeenth and eighteenth centuries.

"If you don't mind my asking," said Arthur, "why are you getting rid of this stuff?"

"I didn't get into details about your reasons, Father," volunteered Christopher.

"Years ago Arthur, the value of all these pieces was strictly ritual. They were part of everyday life in the Church. But times have changed. Rituals went the way of the Latin language in the Church's effort to be more accessible. User-friendly I think they call it today," he laughed. "In any event, devotion isn't what it used to be, particularly financial devotion. Frankly, this parish, like most, needs money just to stay open."

"I get it," said Arthur.

"Now," added Father Ibsen, "the Church brass in all their wisdom look at this collection as a line item on the asset side of St. Anselm's. That's all well and good, but doesn't do much when the winter heating bill is due. And they want to keep it as a line item because it makes the parish seem more valuable and in the black. But," he said solemnly, "it's not anywhere near black. And that's why I'm selling."

"Do they know it?" asked Arthur.

"Not exactly," said the priest, "but...the line of fiscal

responsibility for the parish is hazy enough that I can get away with it and deal with them later. I just have to get a valid price for all of it, which is why I called Christopher."

Arthur looked toward Christopher. "It's a hundred grand for the lot, right?"

Christopher nodded.

"A fair price, I think," said Father Ibsen. "Christie's took a look at it and estimated its auction value around two hundred. But of course," he added, "I can't be that public about it, so I'm willing to take less by selling it privately."

"And he'll take a check too," laughed Christopher.

"Cash or check" the priest added wryly.

"What do you think, Arthur?" asked Christopher. "Perfect Brimfield stuff."

"I'm in," he answered without hesitation, and reached for his checkbook.

One Piece Antiques was unusually crowded for a Sunday afternoon. Between browsers, Melissa barely had time to go to the bathroom, a bodily function that seemed to press her harder every day. Fortunately, Zoe stopped by around three and took over for Melissa, allowing her to relieve herself.

"I don't know what's wrong with me," she whispered to Zoe when she came out. "I'm peeing my brains out."

"Pregnant?" joked Zoe.

"Really," she answered with disdain. "Sheila Corcoran might be," referring to her ex-husband's girlfriend, "but I'm not."

"I thought Brad was getting tired of her?"

"He can have her for all I care," she said angrily. "I told him that as long as he's seeing her and as long as he's still drinking, then I didn't want to see him at all anymore."

"What did he say?"

"It's not worth repeating."

"When are you going to find someone else?" Zoe asked.

"Oh, the tables have turned, haven't they?"

"What do you mean by that?"

"Now that you have Christopher, you get to lecture me on men."

"I'm sorry, Melissa. I don't mean to be preachy."

"Then don't be," she said firmly. "And I'm sorry too. I'm just pissed at him. "Now," she said in a more civil tone, "it's your day off...why don't you take advantage of it. Anyway," she added, "if Elliot sees your van here, you know he'll stop by."

"Please," Zoe said, "I had him in here yesterday He's really getting relentless."

"You'd better figure out how to shake him."

"I don't know how much more direct I can be. He just doesn't listen."

"Keep trying," she encouraged her. "What's going on with Christopher?"

"He'll be back from New York tonight. I hope to see him this week."

"What was he buying there, anyway?"

"He didn't tell me. Just that it was good stuff."

Melissa looked around the shop. "We could use some good stuff ourselves. Especially for the next Brimfield. It's only about a month away."

"Well, we've got the house call tomorrow."

"Let's hope it hasn't already been picked over by some auction company, like the last one."

Zoe smiled as she picked up her car keys from the desk. "I've got a good feeling about this one. See you here in the morning."

"I'll bring the coffee."

"Large," insisted Zoe, as she walked out the door.

Benjamin Divers showed up unannounced at Relics on Monday morning with a vanload of goods. He was as giddy as a man whose ship had come in. He had an Alzheimer's house call over the weekend, and he took full advantage of the forgetful elderly man and his somewhat more coherent wife, paying them only cents on the dollar for what their antiques were really worth. However, he still had to lay out over ten thousand dollars of his own money, and like all hard pressed pickers, he immediately became anxious to get his money back out of it. Because the antiques were more Continental than American, he felt he would have a ready buyer in Christopher Doria. In his greed, he did not think past him.

"Wait till you see what I got," he cheerfully announced as he walked in the door of the shop.

Christopher looked up from the oil painting he was painstakingly cleaning with a Q-Tip. "This is an unpleasant surprise," he laughed. "What's up?"

"I've got a load, and it's all fresh." He pointed outside toward his van.

Christopher put down the Q-Tip. "I'm tapped today, Ben."

Benjamin was stunned. "What do you mean? I just drove all the way up here from Kittery. And it's mostly European stuff. Just what you like."

"I'm sorry, but I just spent a ton of money in New York, and I can't do anything until after Brimfield."

Benjamin started to pace and became more agitated as he thought about how much money he had tied up in the goods in his van. Then he lost it. "After Brimfield? Listen Chris," he said, pointing his finger at him, "I've been giving you first refusal on my stuff for years, and I've always accepted your shitty prices, too. And now you're going to fuck me?"

"I'm not trying to fuck you, Ben. I just don't have the money."

"I can't believe this," he yelled. "Now I've got to schlep all over New England, which is not exactly a locale in love with European antiques. I'll tell you what, Doria. This is the last time you're going to screw me, understand? From now on, you can find yourself a new picker."

Christopher got up from his chair and moved toward him. "Take it easy, Ben. You're getting yourself all worked up."

"I am fucking worked up," he screamed. "We had an understanding, didn't we? I pick it. You buy it."

"Benjamin," he said calmly, "I can't buy everything. You know that."

"All I know is that I've got to move what's in my van." He pointed disparagingly around the shop. "I can't sit on it like you can. I don't have a shop, remember?"

"Look, I'm sorry. But I can't do anything until after Brimfield."

"You'll pay for this, Doria," he threatened. Then he turned and stomped out the door.

As soon as Zoe and Melissa pulled up in front of their house call, all the anticipation they brought with them exited through the open windows of the van. Even in their limited experience, they had come to the realization that more often than not, the outside of a house was a good indication of the contents inside.

The one they were staring at held very little promise. It was a Jetsonesque, single-story ranch house built in the fifties. It was covered in dull yellowed aluminum siding probably sold by some overly aggressive salesman in the sixties, with the promise that the owners would never have to paint the house again. In the picture window on the left side of the front, they could see a collection of elongated red glass cats and ceramic clowns, objects true to the age and value of the house.

"It's not exactly one of Noble's Cove's historic homes, is it?" remarked Melissa.

"Maybe we'll be surprised," said Zoe.

They got out of the van and walked up to the front door. Next to it was a concrete birdbath. Although not particularly old, it had weathered nicely over the years, giving it a hint of character.

"We could sell that," said Zoe as she pointed to the bird jacuzzi. "It's got a good look."

"Let's hope there's more than that inside," said Melissa as she knocked on the door.

After three knocks, the door opened slowly, revealing a frail wrinkled woman in a perfectly ironed, floral house dress and a dark blue sweater, a somewhat out of place article of clothing for the eighty degree day.

"Mrs. Corbeil?" asked Zoe.

"You must be Zoe," she answered warmly.

Zoe nodded. "And this is my partner, Melissa."

"Nice to meet you, Mrs. Corbeil."

"Come in," she said enthusiastically. "I've been waiting for you."

As they entered the living room, their suspicions were confirmed. The room was furnished in garish pieces from the days when cars had fins and television came in only two colors. Although there was a small but sophisticated urban market for "Fifties Funk," it was not something that they would ever dream of putting in their own shop. In their own minds, they had more integrity than that. Or at least egos large enough to dismiss any decorative value for the used furniture in the room.

"Have a seat," said the elderly woman as she pointed to the once-bright, vinyl orange couch.

"I remember a couch like this as a kid," said Zoe as she sat down.

"We bought it the year we moved in," smiled the old woman. "That was nineteen fifty-seven." She pointed to the coffee and muffins on the coffee table in front of the couch. "Help yourself."

Normally, house calls were all business for the two women. On occasion they would encounter a woman like Mrs. Corbeil, a lonely soul more interested in companionship than the sale of the no longer valuable objects of her life. Out of respect, Zoe poured coffee for herself and Melissa. "Would you like some, Mrs. Corbeil?"

"No thank you. I just had some tea."

The coffee break lasted over twenty minutes as the widow filled them in on her last twenty years without a husband. She also provided vital information on him, as if to prove that he once existed in the first place. By day, he had been a sheet metal worker at the Fore River Shipyard, proudly making his contribution to the American Naval inventory during the Cold War. At night, he had been a drummer in a five-piece band that played the forties with a passion that only men of his generation could attest to. While Zoe listened intently, Melissa's eyes roamed around the room trying to find something worth buying. Unfortunately, most of what she saw was nothing more than yard sale stuff for the indiscriminate.

"Let me show you the house," offered Mrs. Corbeil.

"Great," said Zoe, getting up from the couch. "I really appreciate that you called us in."

"I'm too old to keep up the house anymore, dear," she said without regret or guilt. "Much to my son's dissatisfaction, I'm moving in with him and his family, and he's already told me that he barely has room for me, let alone my furnishings."

Zoe wanted to hug the woman. "I'm sorry to hear that."

The old woman smiled. "It's okay, Zoe. It happens to all of us someday."

The two dealers followed her from room to room. Everything she was interested in selling was displayed in an orderly fashion, and she had obviously spent a good deal of time getting ready for their visit. While they passed on most of the goods, they selectively picked items that they knew they could sell in their shop—old books, china and some faded and worn oriental scatter rugs.

As they rummaged through Mrs. Corbeil's life, Zoe felt a sadness come over her. Then an anger that even she sometimes valued old things over old people.

"Mrs. Corbeil," she said, "I hope you understand that we can't use everything. But," she continued, "we know another dealer that we can recommend who will buy whatever we don't."

"That's very thoughtful of you," she said, taking Zoe's hand. "I thought I might have to pay someone to clean it out,"

"Don't worry about it. He'll take whatever we don't."

"Good," she answered, sounding relieved.

Once they finished touring the first floor, they followed the woman to the basement. It was unevenly split into two sections. On one side, was what you would expect in a cellar. It was packed with boxes of junk from the workaday aspect of owning and maintaining a house. The other side was a more colorful and poignant story. It was an adult playroom with a speckled linoleum covered floor and a ten foot long, red vinyl bar, complete with eight chrome and red vinyl bar stools.

"We used to have parties down here every Friday and Saturday night." She smiled like a much younger woman. "We had some fun."

Zoe picked up an oversized glass tumbler packed with hundreds of plastic drink stirrers from different restaurants. She could almost feel the laughter of the liquor. "It must have been great," she said with respect.

"It was." She took a framed, black and white photograph from the wall. "Here's me," she laughed, pointing to a woman in the shot of six adults. Then she pointed to a man in the picture proudly holding a chrome cocktail shaker in his hands. "That's Charlie, my husband."

Melissa and Zoe studied the robust young man with the shaker. "He was a handsome guy," said Melissa.

"He was," she said fondly.

Zoe didn't say anything. Her mind went through her own photo albums of similar pictures of Richard. She thought of how full of life he had been and how they, too, had their glorious nights of shaken, not stirred.

"Here's one of Charlie at his drums," she said, pointing to another picture on the wall.

They turned their attention to the man in the white tuxedo jacket and bow tie in a Gene Krupa pose behind the set of drums. Printed on the bass drum were the initials, "C.C."

"Charlie Corbeil," surmised Melissa.

"All the women loved him. I had all I could do to keep him," she laughed. She pointed to a set of drums in the opposite corner of the playroom. "I thought those were going to end our marriage."

"Is that the same set that's in the picture?" asked Zoe.

"Yes, although I'm not sure they're in very good shape anymore. They've been down here a long time."

Zoe walked over and gently ran her fingers over the tightly stretched gut of the bass drum. Then she took one of the sticks and tapped on one of the cymbals.

"It's been a long time since I heard that sound," Mrs. Corbeil said sadly.

"Are they for sale?" asked Zoe.

"I have no need for them now. Maybe you can find some young musician."

"We'll take them," she said without checking with her partner or asking a price.

Zoe went back to the bar, mesmerized by its time-capsule

quality. At some point the fun, as well as a husband, had abruptly ceased to exist. She stepped behind it and looked at the dusty glassware on the shelves underneath it. Then she turned and looked at the mirror behind her, the shelves on both sides of it lined with dozens of varieties of hard liquor, all in nip-size, miniature bottles. She also caught a glimpse of her aging face. It was then that she realized the full meaning of the deserted bar. She picked up a nip of Four Roses whiskey and noticed that even though it had never been opened, through the corruption of time, half of the liquid inside had evaporated, as if Father Time himself had greedily imbibed. She picked up others and found the same to be true. They were also sadly unused, but still relentlessly stolen by time.

"Life does not stop, Zoe. Neither can you."

She picked up a nip of gin that had no more than a spoonful left in it, although the cap was as tight as the dry gut of the drum that she had felt only minutes before. She cracked it open, and the brittle metal cap creaked with over twenty years of loneliness.

"Now I understand, Richard." She thought of a new life with Christopher. *"And I know you do, too."*

11

The more Elliot thought about Zoe with Christopher Doria, the more obsessed he became. He was determined to find a way to reveal him as the thief Elliot thought he was. In every antique shop that he stopped in during his normal course of picking, Elliot looked for other reproductions of the bronze Pietà. Even after visiting hundreds of shops throughout New England, he had not found one.

On Wednesday, Elliot's first stop of the day was the York Antiques Gallery in York, Maine. It was a group shop with a reputation for carrying high quality merchandise. Although he had no luck in picking there before, the cardinal rule of the business was to never give up. Sooner or later, a piece would slip through the cracks, and he wanted to be there when it did.

After a depressing hour of browsing and turning over price tags, he had found nothing that he could easily resell at a profit, and decided to move on to other shops in southern Maine. As he left the building to head up Route One, a van screamed into the parking lot and almost hit him as he walked to his own.

"Hey, watch where you're going!" Elliot shouted.

The driver of the van shook his fist at Elliot as if his own flagrant driving were his fault. "Screw you," he yelled out the window.

Elliot, angry and empty-handed, was not in the mood to put up with someone's road rage and quickly confronted the driver. "Who do you think you are?" he yelled. As soon as he got close enough to the van, he recognized the hostile man behind the wheel. "Hey...Divers...how the hell are you?"

In his anger, it took Benjamin a few seconds to recognize his fellow picker. "Baker?"

"You're as rude on the road as you are on the phone," Elliot joked.

"It's my prerogative," snapped Benjamin. "Maine's my home state."

Elliot could see that the van was loaded, and his dealer curiosity canceled out any ill feelings. "Anything good?" he asked as he peered through the driver's window.

"It's all good. Fresh from a house in Maine."

Never one to pass up an opportunity to sell, and especially eager to move the remainder of the merchandise he had originally offered to Christopher, he got out of the van and walked toward the back. "Let me show you what I've got." He opened the rear doors of the van, giving Elliot a clear view of the contents.

"Hmm. I can't do much with Continental stuff. Got anything American in there?"

Benjamin scowled and muttered loud enough that Elliot could hear him. "That fucking Doria."

"Christopher Doria?"

"Yeah."

"What about him?" asked Elliot.

"I bought this lot of European stuff because I know that's what he likes. And when I offered it to him, he turned me down. Now I'm working my ass off trying to get rid of it piece by piece"

Elliot seized the opportunity. "Yeah? Well let's see what you've got."

For the next few minutes, Elliot sifted through the van and found three pieces that he thought he could sell. As he committed to each one, he quizzed Divers about Christopher Doria, knowing that the money that would change hands would help in his cause.

"I've got a friend who bought a fake bronze from Doria at Brimfield. A woman friend, do you understand?"

Benjamin grinned lecherously, and made an obscene gesture with his fingers. "I think so."

"Anyway, she's kind of hot on him, and I'm trying to convince her that he's a crook. If I can, then…you know…I think I can get him out of the picture."

"And you think I might know something, right?"

"I would never say where the information came from, Ben," he promised.

In spite of the possibility of implicating himself, Divers couldn't pass up the chance to hurt Christopher. As it had in the past, his anger clouded his thinking. And since he knew that the stolen original had passed through the hands of at least three other dealers before he got hold of it, he thought his own risk was minimal. Anyway, he reasoned, he didn't make the fakes. Doria did. He just drove them to New York.

"There was a bronze Pietà stolen from a house in Camden," Divers confided.

"That's the one it was cast from," said Elliot. "I saw a picture of it in the trade press."

"Exactly."

"I figured there's more around, and I thought if I could find one, then I might find Doria behind it."

"You might," he agreed. "But I don't think you'll find any

in New England."

"No?"

Divers shook his head. "But...you might try Manhattan."

"That's a lot of area to cover, Ben"

"Try Rinaldi's on Eighty Third Street."

"You think so?" asked Elliot.

Benjamin shrugged. "Maybe." His demeanor changed and his face turned red. "Just keep me out of it, that's all," he requested and threatened at the same time.

"Absolutely," smiled Elliot.

Elliot pulled into the small garage on Eighty Second Street late Thursday morning and immediately got into an argument with the attendant. Like most out-of-towners, he was not used to the usury disguised as parking fees, and he could not imagine why he would have to spend sixteen dollars to park when he would only be about an hour. Like everyone else before him, he lost the battle, and then grumbled all the way around the corner until he got to Rinaldi's.

Enzo buzzed him in and looked him over, but Elliot was dressed for the ruse. He did not want to look like either a dealer or a knowledgeable collector because either one would potentially question the authenticity of the bronze. He wore a palm tree covered Hawaiian shirt, a pair of tan shorts, and dress sandals. He also wore some of his professional inventory of men's gold jewelry, which included two thick gold chains around his neck. Also on his neck hung a thirty-five millimeter camera.

"If I can help you with anything, just let me know," offered Enzo as he shut the door behind him.

"Actually, you can," Elliot said. "I don't know much about antiques myself, but my wife loves them. It's her birthday, you know..."

"I see."

"Yeah," he said proudly, "I snuck out of the hotel on her this morning to get something. I want it to be a surprise."

"Good for you," Enzo said, stroking him. "What's her taste?"

"Gee, I don't really know. But I know she likes sculpture."

"Marble or bronze?"

"You ask some tough questions, don't you?"

"I'm sorry. Anyway, as they say, it's the thought that counts."

"Right," laughed Elliot. "As long as it's backed up by money."

Enzo took him by the arm and began to lead him toward the bronze Pietà. "I think I have something that she will just love," he gushed.

Elliot smiled to himself as they reached the statue. "That's quite impressive," he said. "What's it a statue of?"

Enzo had to resist rolling his eyes. "It's a copy of Michelangelo's Pietà."

"It's a Michelangelo?" he asked in awe.

"No, it's a Bellini," he said, pointing to the signature on the base. "It's a nineteenth century copy of Michelangelo's work. And a very good one, too, I must say."

"I think she'd love it. How much?"

Enzo looked at the price tag. "The retail on it is three thousand, but I could let you have it for twenty-five hundred."

The dealer in Elliot couldn't resist the haggle. He shook his head. "I really can't spend more than a couple of grand. I mean, I'm not saying that she's not worth it. It's just that she spends her share of my money on her un-birthdays. Do you know what I mean?"

Enzo laughed. "I certainly do, sir." He paused for a moment. "I guess I could go two."

"Then I'll take it."

While Elliot wrote out two thousand dollars in traveler's checks, he asked that Enzo write up a detailed receipt. "I'll never remember who did it or how old it is," he said apologetically, "so I would really appreciate it if you could put it in writing for me."

Enzo hesitated, but concluded that the tourist in front of him presented very little risk. "No problem," he said.

Once the transaction was completed, Enzo walked him to the door. "I'm sure she'll love it."

Elliot looked down at the brightly colored gift-wrapped package under his arm. "I know she will," he smiled. "Thanks. You've been a real lifesaver."

"I'm glad I could help."

"You did," he laughed and thought of Zoe. "More than you know."

Waiting for Sunday seemed like an eternity to Zoe. It was her day off and Christopher was coming down from Maine to spend it with her. Ever since her moment at the vinyl bar during her house call earlier in the week, she could not wait to see him. She had come to realize that she could no longer let life pass her by. That she had every right to pick up the pieces and move on. Any ambivalence she had about the future was now gone, and more than anything, she knew that she wanted to spend the rest of her life with Christopher.

He arrived as scheduled, and as soon as he was at the door, she threw her arms around him with an aggressiveness that took him by surprise. "I missed you so much," she said as she kissed him.

"I guess you did," he laughed. "What got into you this morning?"

Without letting go of him, she spoke. "Something happened at a house call I had this week that helped me understand what I'm supposed to be doing with my life."

"What happened?"

She shook her head. "It doesn't matter. What matters is that now I know that I'm supposed to get on with my life. No more guilt...no more hand-wringing."

"You deserve it, Zoe," he said gently. "More than anyone I know."

Zoe stepped back from him. "I love you, Christopher. I never, ever thought I could say that to anyone with as much conviction as I said it to Richard. But now I can."

"I love you too, Zoe."

She put her arms around his neck. "I need you to love me, Christopher."

"Let's go in the house," he said softly. Then with her arms still around his neck, the two walked into the house and went directly into her bedroom. Not once did she think of anyone but Christopher as she passed through the threshold.

Zoe and Christopher spent a quiet, intimate day together and at her coaxing, he decided to spend Sunday night with her and not leave for Maine until Monday morning. Thrilled about their extra time together, and enthusiastic to share her new-found happiness, Zoe decided to invite Melissa over for a cook-out after she finished work. To Zoe's great surprise, Melissa asked if she could bring Brad. Rather than ask her the gory details of how he had weaseled his way back into her life again, Zoe simply told her to bring him along.

The estranged pair arrived around five-thirty, with Brad holding the mandatory bottle of wine. Both women had warned their men to be on their best behavior, and not to bring up any reference to their tiff at the Jack Tar House. Brad was especially well-scrubbed and tanned, looking more like a sailor than the ditch digger that he was. He was wearing a white polo shirt with plaid shorts and leather boat shoes. His bushy mustache was well-curled. Melissa, on the other hand, looked pale and thinner than normal. The pink sundress she had on hung from her shoulders as if it were on a hanger rather than a human body.

Once they were settled on the porch, Zoe brought out a tray of simple appetizers and Christopher took orders for drinks. As usual, Melissa asked for white wine. Brad asked for a soft drink.

"I've been drinking too much," he openly confessed to the group. "For a long time," he added.

Melissa reached over and took his burly hand. "It's been four days now," she said proudly. "He's doing great."

"That's wonderful, Brad," said Zoe, who was already on her second martini. "It's an easy habit to get lost in," she added, thinking of her own drunken nights since the death of her husband.

"I'm trying." He looked lovingly at his ex-wife. "Melissa's been a big help already."

Zoe had been so caught up in her own life that she had failed to notice the change in Melissa's. On the other hand, the "cry wolf" relationship of Melissa and Backhoe was such that no one could tell if they were ever serious about getting back together. But even Zoe knew that his swearing off the bottle was a first, and indicated that he was at least sincere about turning things around.

"Your ultimatum worked?" Zoe said, once she got Melissa aside. "Why didn't you tell me that he was on the wagon?"

"I was afraid if I did, he would fall off it. Anyway," she said hopefully, "it's a start."

"What about Sheila Corcoran?"

"He's abstaining from her too. We'll see."

Zoe hugged her. "I'm happy for you, Melissa." As she squeezed her with her arms, she could feel Melissa's skeleton. It was too close to her skin. "Are you losing weight?" she asked with concern.

"Just a little."

"Are you feeling all right?"

"You know how I've been urinating all the time?"

"Yeah?"

"Well I went to the doctor, and he told me I probably had a bladder infection. So I've been taking antibiotics."

"And?"

Melissa shrugged her tiny shoulders. "It hasn't seemed to help."

"Go back and see him then. This week."

"I will, Zoe."

Throughout the dinner, Zoe audited her partner to make sure she was eating enough. She could tell by her earlier conversation that Melissa was concerned about her urination problem. Like most women, Melissa knew her body best.

The one consolation of the evening was Brad. Not only was he more than civil toward Christopher, he was almost doting in his attention to Melissa. Minus the normal multiple ounces of liquor, he was quite a gentleman, and obviously still very much in love with his ex-wife.

The quiet evening came to an end when the company excused themselves at nine-thirty. After Zoe and Christopher cleaned up the minimal mess that the grilled chicken and corn on the cob had created, they decided to call it a night themselves. By ten, they were in bed. Zoe held Christopher tightly, troubled by thoughts of Melissa, until she eventually gave way to sleep.

Elliot showered and shaved and applied some Old Spice to his full cheeks with two slaps of his palms. Rather than his normal pair of picking jeans, he put on a pair of clean khaki walking shorts and topped them off with a short-sleeve white shirt. While dressing, he took long glances at the gift-wrapped box containing his Pietà. He smiled to himself at his own ingenuity. Although two thousand dollars was a ridiculous amount of money to pay for a fake bronze, he felt in the long run it would be well worth it. And since he ultimately planned to go to the police with his information, he was reasonably sure he would get his money back from Rinaldi's in New York.

At exactly nine, he called Zoe and told her that he had information for her that was of vital importance, and convinced her to allow him to come by her house to tell her in person. Once she agreed, he wasted no time. He took one last look in the mirror, loaded the package into his van, and headed for Zoe's.

As he got out of his van, Zoe could see him from her front window. She thought is was odd that he had a gift-wrapped package with him. She shuddered, thinking it was some kind of gift to get in her good graces.

"Good morning, Elliot," she said as she opened the door. Right away, she could smell Old Spice in the air.

"Hi, Zoe. Thanks for seeing me. It's really quite important."

"Come in," she said curtly.

She walked quickly toward the living room, continuing to speak as she did. "So what's so important, Elliot?"

He followed her in his normal slow pace, and she was already sitting down on the couch by the time he entered the room. He took a seat across from her and put the package down on the floor. He began his preamble. "Zoe, I've already made it clear how I feel about you, and I've always tried to help you in the business. I never wanted to see you get burned. That's why I was so upset when you bought that," he said, pointing to her Pietà. "I also told you I was convinced that your friend Christopher knew what he was doing when he sold it to you."

"Get to your point, Elliot."

He pushed the package across the floor towards her. "Open it."

"Is that a present for me?" she asked caustically.

"Not exactly. You'll understand once you open it."

"Okay," she snipped. She picked it up from the floor, and the weight of it surprised her. It belied the dainty floral paper that covered it. "It's heavy enough," she said. Then she ripped the paper off and removed the masking tape from the top flaps. With some trepidation, she opened the flaps and looked inside. "What is this?" She put both hands in the box and felt the metal and its familiar shape.

"Take it out."

Without hesitating, she pulled the bronze out of the box and held it in shock in front of her. "What the…?" She shot a glance at her own. "It's the same thing."

"Exactly," smiled Elliot. "I told you there'd be more than one."

"Where did you get it?"

"New York City."

"Is it the real one, or a reproduction?"

"It's fake," he announced.

Zoe looked at it closely and then looked at hers again. "Well, Elliot," she said, "I guess I should congratulate you on your fine detective work." She paused. "Elliot," she asked in confusion, "what's your point? You've always thought that there was more than one repro of it."

"My point is Christopher Doria."

"Wait a minute," she laughed at his logic. "Just because you found another Pietà doesn't mean he had anything to do with it."

"That's where you're wrong, Zoe. The only reason I found it is because I was told by a picker who does a lot of business with Doria, where to look. He told me exactly which shop in

Manhattan to go to."

Zoe's mind flashed to the three, identical copper reproductions of the Phoenician god that Christopher had in his motel room at Brimfield. "What are you saying, Elliot?" she pleaded.

"What I told you all along. That he's a crook. That he's behind it. And now I know that for a fact."

Zoe was speechless. She felt totally betrayed. She walked over to inspect her own Pietà just to be sure. There was no doubt in her mind. They were exactly the same. "Elliot, are you sure he's involved?" she asked, sinking into the couch.

"Unless my source is lying, yes. And I have no reason to believe that he is. Like I said, he does a lot of business with Doria."

Tears began to form on the lower lids of Zoe's eyes as she thought about how she had misjudged Christopher. Elliot had been right. Christopher Doria was no more authentic than all the fakes that he had pointed out to her at the previous Brimfield. He too, was just another Brimfield forgery.

Zoe's emotional vulnerability triggered something in Elliot. All of the months that he longed for her converged in that moment, arousing his feelings and clouding his judgment at the same time. As her tears became more visible, he got up from his chair and sat down next to her on the couch. "I'm sorry, Zoe," he said, "and I'm not trying to say I told you so, but I was right about him all along. He's just a piece of shit who took advantage of you. Something that should never have happened."

"I can't believe it," she said softly.

"Put him behind you, Zoe. You can do a lot better than Doria." As he spoke, he put his large arms around her and pulled her toward him.

The sudden embrace startled her. "Elliot, what are you doing?"

He moved his head toward hers and tried to make contact with her lips.

"Elliot!" She struggled to turn her head away from his. First to the left, then right.

"You know how I feel about you, Zoe," he said, ignoring her resistance.

On the swing back from right to left, his lips finally caught hers. The pressure of them on her mouth made her feel like she was being smothered. All she could smell was the overpowering wave of Old Spice. Zoe used all her power to try to free herself from him, but he would not relinquish his grasp. Finally, in her struggle, her left elbow caught him right under the chin, throwing his head back, allowing her to jump up from the couch.

"What the fuck are you doing?" she screamed.

"Zoe." His eyes were bulging maniacally in their sockets as he got up. "I could take such good care of you. We could be in the business together."

"You're fucking crazy, Elliot! Now get out of here!"

He moved toward her with his arms outstretched. "But I saved you from Christopher Doria."

"Just get out, Elliot!" she screamed, backing up to the wall.

He kept coming, and she frantically reached behind her until she could feel the torso of her metal Mary on the table behind her. She grabbed the bronze as tightly as she could and swung it around until it hit him squarely on his shoulder. The force of it knocked him to the right, and at least temporarily, knocked some sense into him, causing him to back off.

"I'm sorry, Zoe," he said, massaging his shoulder. "I just thought..."

Still holding the torso of the Pietà, she interrupted him. "You just thought if you could bury him, then you could have me, right? Wrong, Elliot," she screamed. "Now get out of here before I call the police." She turned to the table behind her and with her free hand, picked up the plastic Pietà he had given her. "And take this piece of crap with you," she yelled, aiming for his face and catching him on the left ear.

Slowly, Elliot picked up the plastic statue from the floor. "You don't want this then?" he asked sarcastically.

"Just get out," she said quietly, her eyes filling with tears.

He put his bronze Pietà back in the box and put it under his arm. "Okay." Then he looked at the plastic icon in his hand and turned his attention to Zoe again. "This is the thanks I get, huh?"

Zoe didn't respond.

He shook his head back and forth in mock disgust, and then turned and walked to the front door. As she heard it close behind him, Zoe fell onto the couch and wept.

Melissa was rearranging the shop when Zoe came in. Right away she noticed something was wrong. The glow on Zoe's face from the night before was gone and her eyes were rimmed in red. Melissa put down the painting she was about to hang on the wall. "Zoe, what is it?"

"Christopher," she said softly.

Melissa immediately thought he might have been in a car accident in his British death-mobile. "What happened to him? Is he all right?"

"He's fine."

"Then what's wrong, Zoe?"

"My Pietà," she said. "He knew it was a fake when he sold it to me. He's been lying to me all along."

"What?" Her voice rose in disbelief.

Zoe sat down and told Melissa about her visit from Elliot Baker that morning, and how another picker told him that Christopher was definitely involved in the bronze forgeries.

Then she told her about Elliot's attack on her.

"That bastard," said Melissa in anger.

"Which one?" Zoe joked darkly. Then she began to cry.

Melissa walked over to the front door and closed it. She put up the "closed" sign, walked over to Zoe, and put her arms around her. "I'm so sorry, Zoe. Are you sure Elliot was telling you the truth...or was it just another way to get at you?"

Zoe shook her head. "You know him as well as I do. If nothing else, he's thorough. I'm sure he's right. I just can't believe Christopher's been lying to me all this time."

"What are you going to do?"

"I guess the same thing I did when I first bought the bronze...confront him."

"Why bother? He'll probably just try to talk his way out of it. Just forget about him."

"How am I going to do that, Melissa? I'm in love with him. Or at least I was last night."

"Zoe," she said softly, "how can you love a man who's been deceiving you like that? Huh? There's no future in a man like him."

Zoe looked at Melissa and did her best to smile. "Isn't it strange how things just happen? How they turn around? There I was...ready to spend the rest of my life with Christopher, and now I find out he's not the person I thought he was. And here's you and Brad," she continued, "looking like you're going to get back together again." Zoe sighed. "It's amazing, isn't it?"

"Zoe...I wish I had an answer for you...I don't."

"How are you feeling today?" Zoe asked, changing the subject.

"About the same. I called my doctor this morning, and he set up a Cat Scan for me on Thursday."

"What for?"

Melissa shrugged. "He didn't say, but you know how vague

doctors can be."

For the moment Zoe put her own troubles aside and thought only of Melissa. "Is there anything I can do?"

"Just keep your fingers crossed," she said, trying her best to smile.

12

Zoe cried on and off, all the way to Wiscasset. Against Melissa's advice to just forget about Christopher entirely, she decided to meet him face to face. She left early Tuesday morning without letting him know that she was coming. In the back of the van was a cardboard box with all the reminders of him. There was her bronze Pietà which she no longer wanted to lay eyes on again. In addition, there was the tourist photo book from Napoli, the Italian gouache he had given her on loan, and finally, the antique camisole that she had worn so intimately during their lovemaking. What she would give back, she thought, couldn't even come close to what he had taken away.

By the time she arrived his flag was blowing fiercely in the southwest breeze, indicating that he was already open for business. She pulled up in front of his shop, took her box from the van and went in. The bell above her head at the doorway tolled as she did.

Christopher was sitting at his elaborate oak refectory table when she approached him. Although there were a few people in the shop, she did not seem to notice or if she did, she did not seem to care if they witnessed the conversation that was about to take place. As she moved toward him, he looked up.

"Zoe," he smiled. "What are you doing here?"

She plopped the cardboard box on the table. "How could you, Christopher?" She spoke loudly enough that the few customers in the immediate area moved off into other parts of the shop.

"What are you talking about?" He looked in the box and recognized all the items. "And what's this?"

"You lied to me, Christopher."

"What?"

"About the Pietà."

As soon as he heard the reference to the bronze, he got up from his chair and walked around to where she was standing. "Come outside," he demanded.

Before she could answer, he whisked her out the front door. "What are you talking about, Zoe?"

"You knew it was a fake when you sold it to me, didn't you?"

He didn't answer.

"And you sold others, too," she accused. "I know that for a fact."

At first, Christopher stood there in shock. Then he turned away from her, as if to gather his thoughts. "I'm sorry, Zoe." His words were barely audible.

She grabbed him by the shoulder and spun him around toward her. "Sorry? Is that all you can say? I loved you, Christopher. I trusted you." She began to cry.

"Zoe, I never would have sold it to you if I knew we were going to get together. And when we did, I didn't know how to tell you."

"Well, now I know. Where's the real one?"

He hesitated.

"Where is it?" she yelled.

"In a private collection."

"Yours?" she asked with disdain.

"No."

"And what about the Phoenician gods? Your fakes, too?"

"Yes, but I can explain."

Zoe seemed deflated. "Christopher, there's nothing to explain. I never want to see you again."

"Zoe..."

She turned away from him and stared at the front of his shop. "Never."

"How did you find out?" he asked.

She turned around. "What? Afraid of getting caught?"

"That's not why I asked."

"A dealer I know was told by one of your pickers where to find one just like mine. He got his in New York City. Sound familiar?"

Christopher knew right away that Benjamin Divers was the connection. "Yes," he said. "Zoe," he pleaded as he moved toward her, "can I just explain?"

She backed off.

"I love you, Zoe, and I don't want to lose you because of this. I told you a long time ago that there was another side of me. I'm just as screwed up as everyone else."

Zoe was too hurt to be compassionate and stood there like stone.

"Please, Zoe."

She turned and walked quickly toward her van, refusing to acknowledge him. Without further ceremony, she drove away.

Christopher drove like an outlaw down Route 95, the mournful bronze bouncing in the back of his van with every bump that he hit. Although he had no definitive strategy on what to do next, he knew that he could trust Arthur Drake to help him with his problems.

By the time he arrived at Arthur's shop in Essex, he was an emotional mess. Christopher was convinced that he would be caught, which would mean an end to his freedom and his income. And he believed he had lost Zoe, something he regretted even more. He came as close to tears as he had in decades.

As soon as he came into the shop with the bronze, Arthur took it from him and put it in his back room.

"At least it's out of your place," said Arthur as he came back to the selling floor. "I'll get rid of it permanently as soon as I can."

The thought of how much it meant to Zoe blurred Christopher's reason. "Don't get rid of it yet, Arthur."

"Aren't you in enough trouble, Guido? Forget about her and do what you can to cover your ass."

"But I'm in love with her."

"Since when is love a good excuse?"

"If it weren't for that asshole, Divers, I wouldn't be in this position," he lamented.

"It not all his fault."

"Are you defending him?"

"Of course not. But if you had just sold her the piece and had not gotten involved with her, then you wouldn't be in the soup you're in now."

"That's easy for you to say." He began to pace nervously. "Can I use your phone?"

"Go ahead, my friend. Make it even harder on yourself."

Christopher dialed Zoe's number. After three rings he heard her recorded voice. Even one magnetic tape tone rekindled him. "Zoe," he said, "I've already left three messages. Please call me back. I'm at Arthur's in Essex. Or call me on my cell phone. I can explain everything, if you just give me a chance."

As he hung up, Arthur looked at him with pity. "So you're going to tell her, huh?"

"I have to, Arthur."

"I'm surprised. I know how personal it is to you."

Christopher looked him directly in the eyes and spoke with conviction. "So is she, Arthur."

Zoe was disheveled with love and liquor, and as sorrowful as she had been since the death of her husband. As soon as she arrived home from Maine, she started drinking, right into the evening. The more she did, the more despondent she became. She called Joanna for moral support, but what she received was far from it. Joanna scolded her for not heeding her own advice.

"You were the one who told me not to expect perfection in a partner, Mom," she said. "Why can't you do the same?"

"He lied to me," she muttered through the smoke of her cigarette.

"So he's a liar, so what? My God, Ma, you're the one who's always telling me how beautiful old furniture looks with nicks and scratches. Why can't you cut the same slack with people?"

"It's different, that's all."

"Bullshit. You told me that if you could have Dad back, that you wouldn't even care if he cheated on you. Remember?"

"No..." The sound of ice cubes rang in the receiver as she took a sip of her drink.

"Trust me...you said it. Anyway," she said sternly, "you're not so perfect yourself. If you don't stop drinking, you're going to turn into a major alcoholic. How perfect will that be?"

Zoe responded by hanging up, leaving her with one less shoulder to cry on. She made herself a fresh drink, and sat in the dark with her wall of Italian gouaches. She began to cry.

"Zoe, it doesn't have to be like this."

"I'm so hurt, Richard."

"It's only your ego that's bruised."

"What am I supposed to do?"

"Accept him. Just like you accepted me and my many faults. Just as I accepted you and yours."

Zoe staggered to the wall and removed one of the pictures of an erupting Mount Vesuvius. It reminded her of the many eruptions in her relationship with Richard—the petty and not so petty arguments, the jealousies and indictments, the wrong-side-of-the-bed days, the unspoken malaise so prevalent in long-term relationships—even the unthinkable, unsubstantiated whiff of infidelity. And yet all of those negative memories had been the first to go with his death. What she held closely was their love for each other—some days better than others, but there everyday, just the same. It was then that she realized that the only facet of their relationship that had been perfect was the ability of their love to turn the other cheek and move on. To rejoice in the nicks and scratches. Forgiveness, she thought—the difficult but perfect response.

In her drunkenness, Zoe struggled to rehang the picture, and it took her four tries before the wire caught the hanger. Once it did, her total lack of dexterity made it impossible for her to get it straight on the wall, as it, and all the other pictures had always hung so rigorously. Finally, she conceded that it didn't matter if the picture was crooked. The false god of symmetry no longer held her in its grasp.

Elliot's phone rang just as he was about to leave for the day. He was shocked to hear Zoe's voice, the last person he expected to dial his number. "Zoe, I was going to call you."

"About what?"

"About my inappropriate behavior. I'm really sorry...I don't know what got into me."

Zoe was surprised by his demeanor and wondered if he was afraid that she might bring charges against him. "Can we meet for coffee, Elliot?"

"Sure. When?"

"At the Wave in fifteen minutes."

"I'll be there."

Zoe looked in the mirror before she left and decided that she needed a little makeup to cover her indulgence of the night before. Not for Elliot's benefit, but for her own self-esteem. She knew that Joanna was right about her drinking, and mixed in with her morning's remorse was at least the desire to do something about it. Anyway, she thought, if Brad Lipton could abstain, then anyone could.

When she arrived at the Wave, Elliot was already sitting in her favorite booth in the smoking section. Just seeing him made her angry and she had to remind herself of her reflections on forgiveness the night before. When she reached the booth, Elliot stood up like a gentleman to greet her.

"Hi Zoe," he said timidly. "I ordered you coffee already."

"Thanks." Zoe sat down, took a sip from the cup, and then lit a cigarette.

"Listen," he said, stirring his coffee, "I was wrong the other day. I had no right to force myself on you. It's just that I'm really fond of you." He paused. "And very lonely."

"I understand very lonely, Elliot. I've been that for two years. And that's what I want to talk to you about."

"Okay."

"I know you don't like Christopher, but you know what? I'm in love with him. For the first time since my husband's death, I feel like a person again. And I don't want to lose him."

"But he's a thief, Zoe," he protested.

"And you, Elliot," she said with planned consideration, "are an attempted rapist."

Elliot squirmed in his seat.

"I've already told you my feelings for you and none of them include us as a couple. I've made that quite clear. All I'm asking is that, from this point on, you accept that. I can't fill your void... but I can be your friend."

"Okay, Zoe."

"Now, the big question..." She took a long drag on her cigarette. "Have you gone to the police about Christopher?" Zoe held in the smoke, waiting for the answer.

"Not yet."

She exhaled. "Thank God. You know Elliot," she continued, "you keep calling Christopher a crook, but aren't we all?"

"Of course not."

"Sure we are. When you buy something that you know is worth a lot of money from some unsuspecting party, you're stealing, too. It's just a different way of doing it, that's all."

"Well I don't see it like that," he argued. "I've spent over twenty years gathering the knowledge that I have now, and I don't see any problem with using it to my advantage."

"Elliot," she said with authority, "I understand that. But you know as well as I do that the antique business walks a fine line between honesty and dishonesty everyday. And every dealer, myself included, has violated it at one time or another. Look...I'm not saying what Christopher did was right. It wasn't. All I'm saying is that sometimes we're just as guilty."

"It's just the way the business is, that's all," he said in his own defense.

"I'm not here to argue about the ethics of the business, Elliot. I'm here to ask you not to go to the police with what you know about Christopher," she said sincerely. "I want to be with him and you can help me do that. Or," she added bluntly, "you can ruin my life."

Elliot mixed his fondness for Zoe with her words, *attempted rapist.* "Okay, Zoe. I'll keep it to myself. But I'm warning you... he'll probably keep working the underside of the business, and sooner or later he's going to get caught. I'd hate to see you in the middle of that."

"Let me worry about that, okay?"

He shrugged. "Have it your way."

She reached her hand over the table. "Deal?" She smiled at him almost seductively.

He put his hand in hers, and realizing that it was probably for the last time, squeezed it tightly. "Deal."

Within an hour Zoe was headed for Maine. The long drive gave her time to consider what she would say to Christopher about his criminal activities. Although she certainly couldn't endorse them, and would use his close call with Elliot and the Pietà as leverage to encourage Christopher to conduct business more honestly, she ultimately decided that, if necessary, she could live with his lifestyle. "Turn the other cheek," she kept telling herself, until she arrived in front of Relics.

Christopher beamed at the sight of her, and kissed her with an intensity usually only seen at airport arrival gates. "I thought I'd never see you again, Zoe...I'm so sorry I hurt you."

"We have to talk, Christopher."

He looked like a man waiting to hear his sentence. "I know."

Since it was almost noontime, the two decided to discuss it over lunch. They walked down the street toward the Sheepscot River to the Country Tureen, a homemade soup and bread stop. In the August heat, they both opted for cold cucumber soup with peasant bread. The simple offering seemed to ground them in the basics of rebuilding a relationship. In that context, while Christopher ordered a glass of house white wine, Zoe prudently asked for a Diet Coke.

She took Christopher through her entire range of feelings—

from the immediate attraction she had felt for him when they first met at Brimfield, to her strong desire to spend the rest of her life with him. Finally she spoke of the sense of betrayal she felt when she discovered that he had knowingly sold her the fake, and how disappointed she was that he never had the courage to tell her.

"And how do you feel now?" he asked tentatively.

Zoe explained her catharsis of the night before, and how, since her husband's death, she had repressed the fact that their relationship had its bumps as well. "Death has a very selective memory," she said. "Richard reminded me of that last night."

"You talked with him last night?"

"At great length."

"And?"

"He said to accept you." She took a sip of her Diet Coke. "Just like he accepted me."

Christopher was relieved. "I'm so sorry I hurt you," he said again. "After lunch, I want you to come down to Bath with me. Although there's no excuse for what I did, I do have my reasons. I think it's time you knew about them."

Zoe was confused. "What's in Bath?"

"Just wait till we get there, okay?"

Zoe agreed, but continued to express her concerns to Christopher. She told him that she didn't condone his illegal actions, and hoped that he would find it in him to put an end to them. Christopher promised her that he had been trying to do just that for a long time, and perhaps the most recent incident was the impetus he needed. Finally, Zoe told him about Elliot Baker, and how his infatuation with her lead him to reveal Christopher as a thief. "He thought if you were out of the way, then he could have me," she said.

"He's my problem now, isn't he?" he observed with concern, knowing that a second arrest would lead to more than the probation he was given on his first offense.

"Not anymore."

Zoe told him about their discussion earlier in the day and how, out of respect for her wishes, Elliot promised that he would not go to the police with his information about Christopher. She never mentioned the other reason behind his cooperation.

Christopher felt like he had been given a reprieve, a true second chance from Zoe as well as from the illegal activities that had chased him for so long. "I feel so fortunate, Zoe," he said, taking her by the hand.

Zoe thought of the crooked Vesuvius painting on her living room wall and the freedom it represented. "So do I."

The city of Bath is about sixteen miles south of Wiscasset, and is as industrial as Maine gets. Located on the Kennebec River and home of the Bath Iron Works, it is a center that has always made its living with ships and their repair, going all the way back to the early seventeenth century. Even today, it is easy to get a sense of America at work as you cross the thin and high Carlton Bridge on the way into the blue-collar borough.

Since Zoe planned to go back to Noble's Cove that afternoon, she followed Christopher in her van so she could continue south after going to Bath. Although she lost him a couple of times at traffic lights, the Austin Healy was easy to find again. Once over the bridge she followed him past signs for the Bath Maritime Museum, and Zoe began to suspect that the antiques that the museum housed had something to do with their visit there.

As she past the museum, she realized that she was wrong. Soon the landscape thinned out and looked more like Maine again. After a few more miles, Christopher put his right directional light on. As she took the turn herself, a red brick, institutional-looking building loomed in front of her. She followed the long circular driveway, and then veered off to the right into the lot where Christopher had just parked. As she did, she could read the chiseled name, Mayer Rehabilitation Center, over the double front doors.

"Christopher, why are we here?"

"Come with me," he said, taking her by the arm.

They walked through the front doors and entered the cavernous front hall. To the right was a reception desk where an elderly woman sat. As soon as she saw Christopher, she smiled and spoke. "Good afternoon, Mr. Doria."

He walked over with Zoe still on his arm. "How are you Lucy? Everything under control?" he joked.

"As always," she laughed, and then turned her attention to Zoe. "I see you've brought a friend today."

Christopher introduced them. Then, as if he had been there many times before, he excused himself and began to walk Zoe down the wide corridor on the left side of the building.

"Why are we here?" she asked again.

"You'll see."

After they passed a dozen doors in the quiet corridor, he stopped in front of number sixteen. In a sliding chrome bracket next to it was the name, "P. Doria."

"Who's P. Doria?" she asked.

Christopher took hold of Zoe by her forearms. "My brother."

"You have another brother? You never told me that."

"Zoe," he said as he tightened his grip on her arms, "it's my brother Peter."

Zoe closed her eyes as she felt the lie coming on. "What?"

"Let me explain..."

Zoe pulled away from him.

"The bike accident he was in, Zoe. It was my fault."

"What do you mean?"

"I dared him to ride on the handlebars of my bike...he was

screaming at me to stop, so I did. That's when he went flying in front of the car, Zoe." Christopher focused his eyes on the floor.

"Christopher..."

"Peter was a tremendous amount of work for my parents. As much as they wanted him home, it ultimately became too much for them. They had to institutionalize him."

"But why did you tell me he was dead?"

"Zoe," he said, "I was only thirteen at the time, and I was devastated by their decision. It was all my fault...the accident... and then his leaving home for good." His eyes began to fill with tears. "I couldn't manage the guilt, Zoe. And the only way I could rationalize it at the time was to pretend that he was dead. The more I suppressed it, the more real his death became." He wiped his eyes with the back of his hand. "I'm sorry. I didn't mean to lie about him, but that's how it's been since I was thirteen."

"My God, Christopher," she said, reaching up and putting her arms around him, "why didn't you tell me before?"

"I keep it to myself. Very few people know about it. Arthur is the only person in the business who knows about Peter."

Zoe looked down the wide, freshly-painted white corridor. "It must be expensive to keep him here."

"On an antique dealer's salary it is. Like I told you, Zoe, there's no excuse for my actions, but at least now you know my reason."

"I understand perfectly, Christopher," she said compassionately. "Can I meet him now?"

"Sure. Just don't expect much. He's degenerated a lot over the years and he's also had a couple of strokes. Right now he can't move much or speak more than a mumble."

Zoe's heart went out to him. "Okay."

They entered the small private room and Zoe immediately

recognized Christopher's influence on his brother's surroundings. The walls were covered in antique oil paintings, a mix of canvases to feed mind, body and soul. There were soothing luminous landscapes for the mind to romp through, as well as beach-scapes to skip stones along the pigment of their calm waters. There were pictures of suffering saints to draw daily strength from, and paintings of heavenly ascensions full of hope for the future. Finally, there was a small collection of naked Victorian nymphs, from comely to voluptuous, nineteenth century pin-ups pleasing to all young men for all time.

Zoe's eyes quickly found the bed in the room and the specter that was Christopher's brother. She had to hold her breath to keep from letting out a gasp as she looked at the form in the bed, curled up like the letter "S." Although she knew him to be a young man, the entropic years since childhood had brought on an almost extraterrestrial visage to him, both frightening and beatific at the same time. Directly over his bed hung a large oil painting of St. Christopher carrying Christ on his shoulders, the same composition as the medal that Christopher had worn around his neck for so many years.

Without hesitation, Christopher walked over to the bed and kissed his brother on the cheek.

Zoe was frozen in place.

"How are you, Peter?" he asked cheerfully.

His brother didn't move, but a moan of acknowledgement emanated from his mouth.

"I want you to meet someone, buddy." He turned to Zoe. "Zoe," he said, "it's okay." He gestured for her to come over to the bed. She walked over to Christopher's side and gazed at Peter's face. He had Christopher's eyes she thought, only they bulged with the animation of someone whose pupils had to also be their arms, legs and speech. They spoke clearly and calmly to her.

"This is Zoe, Peter. I'm in love with her," he said, putting his hand over his heart.

"Hello, Peter. It's nice to meet you."

A small noise came from his mouth and his eyes blinked.

Zoe bent down and kissed him on the forehead. "I've heard a lot about you from your brother. He loves you very much," she said. She turned and looked at Christopher. "And I love him very much."

Peter sounded another groan. Zoe hoped it was one of approval.

Christopher pulled up two chairs and they sat for an hour at Peter's side. While Zoe didn't say much, Christopher carried on a conversation as if his brother were participating in it telepathically. It made her think of her own conversations with Richard—how in spite of even the most daunting obstacles, love somehow finds a way to express itself. As she listened without shame to Christopher's chatter about how beautiful she was naked and what an extraordinary lover that she was, she thought back to the night when he told her that in a way, he was experiencing life for both of them. She felt honored to be part of such an imaginary ménage à trois.

Zoe watched Christopher's arms and face move with an enthusiasm that his brother could only dream about, and she prayed that Christopher could let go of the guilt that drove him to his denial. She then glanced up at the painting of Christ and St. Christopher over the bed, and thought about the brotherly love that had kept Peter alive inside of his failed body for so many years—a love she was grateful to share.

13

Life is essentially a barter system that never seems to give anything without taking something away. It constantly exchanges good for evil, right for wrong, and pain for pleasure. In Melissa's case, the trial reconciliation with Brad was to be traded for the gruesome discovery of a potentially life-threatening tumor attached to her uterus. As her situation so dramatically demonstrated, bartering is not always a one-to-one proposition.

Zoe was in the best mood of her life when Melissa walked into the shop on Thursday afternoon. With Elliot off both hers, as well as Christopher's back, Zoe was able to enjoy the nuances of being in love. Everything she did now had meaning, with even the most mundane thoughts and actions taking on a special nature. It was as if the world were now covered in a thin film of gold dust—a sort of pollen from the trees of passion that made everything and everyone, including the most sour-looking customers, beautiful to her sight. Zoe's optimism even extended to Melissa's Cat Scan, and she bet her lunch at the Wave that it would turn up nothing. The look on Melissa's face when she arrived told Zoe otherwise.

"What is it, Melissa?" Zoe got up from the desk and walked over to her.

Melissa removed a large cardboard box from under her skinny arm, and plopped it onto a salmon-colored, painted commode next to the front door. The contents of it clanged as the box hit the wooden surface. "At least now I know why I've been going to the bathroom so much."

"Why?"

"Because of the tumor on my uterus. It's pressing against my bladder."

Zoe was stunned. "A tumor?" She put her strong arms around her friend as Melissa began to sob.

"I can't believe this, Zoe. I'm not back with Brad for five minutes and this has to happen."

"What are they going to do?"

"They want to remove it right way. Next week."

"Okay," Zoe said with a hopeful voice. "I know it will be benign."

"Benign? How many tumors are ever benign, Zoe?" Melissa shook her head. "Remember Gretchen Canon? Cindy Krintzman? Joan Hall? They were all malignant, Zoe."

Zoe looked at her sternly. "You can't think like that, Melissa. You've got to be positive about it."

Melissa picked up the box she'd brought with her. "Yeah right, Zoe." She turned it upside down, sending the contents bouncing off the table and onto the floor. "Just like these helped when I was trying to get pregnant again," she said scornfully.

Zoe recognized the shower of objects. It was Melissa's collection of silver baby cups that she had amassed in connection with her tumultuous marriage to Brad. "Melissa," she said in horror, "what are you doing?"

Melissa shook the box until the last cup fell to the floor. "I'm getting rid of them, Zoe."

Zoe hastily bent over to pick up the cups. "Why? You've always loved them."

"I was so foolish, Zoe," she yelled. "After my miscarriage, I thought that Brad would come back if I could get pregnant again." She kicked one of the cups across the floor, just barely missing Zoe. "So I started collecting these stupid things, thinking they would help. They helped all right," she added. "Now I've got a tumor growing there instead of a fetus. Perfect," she laughed, "isn't it?" She began to cry again.

Quietly, Zoe gathered the eighteen cups together, carefully putting them back in the box. "Please Melissa, try to be positive, okay?"

Melissa shuddered and sniffled. "I'll try. But it's hard not to expect the worst."

"I know it is, but as long as they get it all, you'll be fine. Right?"

"I guess so," she said unconvincingly.

"Does Brad know?"

"Are you kidding? This really screws things up now."

"What do you mean?"

"Once he finds out about this, he'll never leave."

Zoe was confused. "What's the problem with that?"

"The problem is that now I'll never know if he really wants to come back. He'll stay with me out of sympathy...or at least that's what I'll think."

"Jesus, Melissa. Stop thinking like that, will you? You're going to destroy yourself."

"I can't help it, Zoe. I'm just so mad that this had to happen now. Well," she said darkly, "at least I get a free lunch out of it."

As if tumors and anger were contagious, Zoe's mood dropped to the depths of Melissa's for the rest of the day. After

Melissa left the shop, Zoe spent the rest of the afternoon polishing all of her partner's baby cups, and then, according to Melissa's instructions, priced them well below market value. As Zoe cleaned them, she rubbed each piece aggressively until all the tarnish disappeared. She prayed as she rubbed, hoping that the growth on Melissa's uterus would disappear as well.

With all hope of capturing Zoe's favor gone, Elliot turned his attention to getting back the two thousand dollars he had paid for the Pietà. Rather than squandering time and money to travel to New York, he decided he could accomplish the task over the phone. Sitting alone and holding the detailed receipt in his hand, he called Enzo Rinaldi.

"Rinaldi's," answered the lean voice on the other end of the line.

"Enzo, please."

"Speaking."

"Enzo, this is Elliot Baker. I bought a bronze Pietà from you."

"Of course," he said. "How did your wife like it?"

"She didn't," he answered, thinking of Zoe's reaction.

There was silence on the other end.

"Enzo."

"Yes?"

"We have a problem."

Elliot revealed himself as an established person in the business, and went on to tell Enzo that he knew everything about the fake bronze, as well as its origin. Without getting into the details, Elliot told him the reason he bought it was because of a personal problem with Christopher Doria, and now he wanted his money back. At first Enzo balked, but at Elliot's suggestion, he looked at his copy of the receipt and realized that his own false statements about the age and maker would be all the evidence necessary to potentially put him behind bars.

After assuring Enzo that once he received his money, the issue would go no further, Enzo agreed.

"I'll have a check out to you overnight," he promised.

"Good," said Elliot. "And I'll send back the bronze as soon as it clears."

Enzo never wanted to see the fake again, but he certainly didn't want it circulating beyond his control. "Okay," he agreed.

"Nice doing business with you, Enzo," he said glibly.

"Fuck you, Baker," he sassed. "You'll have your check in the morning."

As soon as he hung up with Elliot, Enzo called Christopher. Although Christopher had planned to call Enzo to tell him what had happened, Elliot, anxious to get his money back, had beat him to it. Enzo was both angry and nervous on the phone.

"Listen Chris," he said, "those bronzes aren't worth the risk. I don't want to be in the middle of some personal vendetta that some dealer has with you."

"I understand, Enzo," he said calmly.

"Those Pietàs are bad news. With the one coming back, that leaves me with three...and I don't want them anymore. That guy Baker really freaked me out. They're not worth shit, anyway."

Christopher remained calm, and suggested that Enzo destroy the rest of them. Since it didn't cost much to reproduce them in the first place, Christopher would be more than happy to give Enzo his money back.

"I know someone who can get rid of them for me," said Enzo. "Hopefully, we'll never see them again."

"I hear you, Enzo."

After Christopher, Enzo made one more phone call. It was to Carmen Huerto, a nine-dollar-an-hour employee of an in-home carpet cleaning service in Manhattan. Carmen freelanced by cleaning out some of the valuable art and antiques in the townhouses where he scrubbed the social wine stains of the wealthy. Some of the residences were so full of valuables that he reasoned that a piece here or there wouldn't be missed.

More often than not, Carmen sold the items for next to nothing on the street. Which was exactly how he had met Enzo. Although Carmen knew nothing about antiques, he was wise enough to work the streets where there were antique shops and galleries. The first time Carmen approached Enzo, he bought an English sterling silver kettle for a hundred dollars that he sold within hours for three thousand. From that day on, Enzo was hooked, and became a regular customer of Carmen Huerto. In addition, Enzo occasionally hired him as a runner, making both legitimate and illegitimate deliveries for him around Manhattan.

After three rings, Enzo got Carmen's recorded voice and left a message for Carmen to call him at home when he returned from work.

Early in the evening, Carmen returned the call. Enzo explained what he had, and what he wanted Carmen to do with them. "I want them dumped into the East River," he said with finality.

"Dónde?" he asked in disbelief.

"The East River, Carmen."

It was a strange request, Carmen thought. He worked hard and dangerously to find things for Enzo. Never had he been asked to get rid of anything of value for him. His voice shrugged, "Okay."

While Melissa was unsure that she would be able to make the trip following her surgery, the September Brimfield was just a few weeks away. Over the weekend, she and Zoe hit every yard sale they could, amassing a pile of odds and ends that, along with the inventory in the shop, they hoped to sell at Brimfield. Both women were preoccupied with Melissa's upcoming operation, and the running around helped take their minds off the unthinkable negative possibilities of it.

As expected, the news of her condition became an even stronger glue for Brad to stay with his ex-wife. Although Melissa would have preferred a reason based solely on love and devotion, she was frightened enough to welcome his support under any circumstances.

While Zoe and Melissa were picking front yards, Christopher was picking through the lot of religious antiques that had arrived by truck from St. Anselm's in New York. In spite of the fact that he and Arthur were financial partners in the deal, Arthur knew nothing of religious art, nor did he have a ready market for it. It was up to Christopher to move it. Although he planned to sell most of it at Brimfield, within a day of its arrival, he sold over fifteen thousand dollars worth of silver articles to one collector alone. He was sure that after making a few key phone calls to other collectors and dealers, telling them what to expect at his booth in Brimfield, that he would unload most of it during his few days there.

While he was going through the merchandise, he was suddenly taken by a small oil painting that he hadn't noticed when he was in New York. It was a nineteenth century copy of an earlier Renaissance work titled, *Flight Into Egypt*. The narrative it presented was of Mary, Joseph and the just-born Jesus fleeing to Egypt by donkey, after being told that King Herod was going to kill the newborn.

As Christopher looked at it, he had a strange premonition about Brimfield, as if something would go wrong there. He thought about the religious lot that he would bring there and its questionable ownership, but dismissed any problem with it based on his assurances from Father Ibsen. After studying the painting for a few minutes, he could come up with nothing, and ultimately attributed his apprehension to his recent run-in with Elliot Baker and the fake Pietà. He put the picture of the three fugitives back with the rest of the paintings, and continued his survey. But no matter how hard he tried to put it out of his mind, the foreboding about Brimfield stayed with him.

Thursday couldn't come fast enough or slow enough for Melissa. On the one hand she was anxious to have the tumor removed, but on the other, she was worried about what else they might find, as well as their prognosis for her future. She had known so many women who had gone under the knife full of hope from less than forthright physicians and once opened, found that the cancer had spread to other, sometimes inoperable parts of their bodies. She shuddered at the thought of becoming another contributor to that statistic.

Zoe sat in the back seat of Brad's Jeep on the dawn ride into Brigham and Women's Hospital in Boston. Traffic and conversation were light. Hearts were heavy. Brad was especially quiet. His ineptness at understanding the inner workings of women, both physical and emotional, made it difficult to relate to Melissa's condition. He could understand lung or liver cancer, as well as a beef-and-french-fry-induced heart attack. But the word uterus was foreign to him, as distant and mysterious as Mars or Venus. Uterus was also in some far off galaxy, one he would never comprehend. Rather than try to, he simply held Melissa's hand all the way to the hospital.

Since the surgery would not take place until later in the day, once they delivered Melissa to the medical authorities, Brad and Zoe said their goodbyes, and reluctantly left and drove back to Noble's Cove. Brad, seemingly in the need of companionship, invited Zoe for coffee at the Wave. She accepted. He passed on his normal breakfast of three eggs over easy, and held the thick white mug of coffee with both hands, making it more of a hand warmer than a beverage.

"Zoe," he asked, his eyes pleading, "do you think she's going to be all right?"

"Let's hope so."

"But what do you think?" he persisted.

Zoe sighed. "It doesn't matter what I think, Brad. You know as well as I do how unpredictable tumors are."

"What should I do?"

Zoe thought of the many years that Christopher had taken care of his brother, Peter. "Just be there for her. Like you have been recently," she smiled.

"I feel like such a shit," he said. "I hope it's not too late."

Zoe put her hands around his. They were warm from the coffee cup. "It's only too late if you don't do something about it. And you've already taken the first step. Just keep doing what you've been doing."

"I will," he promised.

"One other thing, Brad." Zoe hesitated.

"What?"

"Melissa's baby cups..."

"Her baby cups?" He was dumbfounded. "What about them?"

Knowing Brad as well as she did, Zoe was sure he had no idea of the significance of Melissa's collection. She explained the meaning behind them, and suggested that Brad was germane to her need to collect them in the first place.

"I never meant to blame her for the miscarriage or the fact that she couldn't get pregnant again, Zoe...really. I just say the wrong things sometimes."

"We all say things we don't mean," she said compassionately. "I just thought you should know so you can be more sensitive in the future...especially now."

Brad removed his hands from his coffee cup and Zoe's grasp, and put them on top them of hers. His calloused surfaces felt strangely gentle, almost vulnerable. "I love her, Zoe."

"Then keep showing her you do."

Carmen Huerto arrived at Rinaldi's at eight o'clock in the morning to pick up the bronzes. Enzo, in his nervousness to get Elliot's Pietà back so he could get rid of it with the rest of them, had sent him a bank check, guaranteeing a swift return of the fake. Once he had it back with the remaining two, he had called Carmen immediately so that he could get them out of his store, and onto the bottom of the East River.

"They're in here," Enzo said, pointing to his back room.

The thin, young carpet cleaner followed him to a table on which the three identical pieces sat. "Santa Madre," he said as he blessed himself.

"They're fakes," said Enzo, making a sour face, "so there's nothing holy about them. They won't work," he added with sarcasm.

"Oh..." Carmen seemed relieved, as if authenticity had something to do with their ability to accept or act on devotion. "It don't look fake to me," he said as he picked one up. "Throw away, eh?"

"They're big trouble. That's why I want them where no one will ever find them."

Carmen shrugged indifferently. "Okay, boss."

One by one he loaded them in the back of the company van that was in his charge. He squeezed them between the wet vac and a twenty-five gallon drum of cleaning solution.

"Make sure you get rid of them quickly," warned Enzo. He handed him a hundred dollar bill, which Carmen stuffed into the monogrammed breast pocket of his work uniform.

"Mañana."

"No, today, Carmen," he insisted. "The sooner the better."

Carmen didn't understand why he was in such a hurry to

get rid of them, but acquiesced. "Muy bien...today."

Enzo watched as he drove away, breathing a sigh of relief. "Doria," he said with disdain. "I've got to be careful with him."

After he left Rinaldi's, Carmen worked his way through the early morning traffic on the way to a cleaning job on East Ninety Sixth Street. Every time he checked in the rear view mirror, he caught a glimpse of one of the Pietàs in the back of the van. Each time he did, he became more confused as to why Enzo would want them thrown away. To him, they were perfectly good merchandise even if they weren't antiques. He was certain that he knew a number of people who would give him forty or fifty bucks apiece for them. The more traffic he hit, the more time he had to think about them. He finally decided that it would be a waste to dump them in the river. Anyway, he reasoned, Enzo had probably cheated him on some of the stolen antiques that he had sold him. "Enzo won't never know," he said out loud to himself, as he decided to save the three Christs and their Mothers from an ignominious watery grave.

One Piece Antiques was busy on Thursday, but failed to keep Zoe's mind off Melissa and her tumor. Each time the phone rang, she hoped it was Brad with the news that Melissa was free, clear and ultimately on her way home. It was not until almost closing that the call came.

"One Piece Antiques."

"She's okay," mumbled Brad. "They got it all."

Zoe jumped up from the desk and, in spite of the customers in the shop, began dancing around, bumping into objects and women as she did. "They got it all? Are you sure?"

"That's what they told me. Every bit of it."

"Are you going in to see her? I want to come."

"Not tonight," he said. "She's...she's out of it."

"But don't you want to see her?" Zoe asked enthusiastically.

"I'm going to wait till the morning," he slurred.

Zoe took the portable phone just outside the front door to continue her conversation. "Brad..."

"What?"

"Have you been drinking?"

"I'm just celebrating," he argued.

Zoe thought of her friend, dissected like a high school frog. "What did I tell you this morning, Brad? Be there for her, remember?"

"Tomorrow. Tonight, I'm going to...ah...let her rest."

Zoe filled with anger, knowing that Brad was more interested in drinking than sitting by Melissa's side as she woke up. "Let her rest?" she asked, recognizing his boozy excuse from experience. "You prick."

"Zoe..."

"Well, I'm going in now. Goodbye."

Zoe pressed the Off button on the portable phone, and for a brief moment thought about drinking herself. Then she went back in the store and quickly cleared out all but one of the remaining customers Next to the desk stood a women in her twenties, who seemed to be ignoring Zoe's need to close for the day.

"I'm sorry, but I have to close now. Family emergency," Zoe added.

"I want this cup," she said. The young woman held up the last member of Melissa's family of baby vessels that remained for sale. It was a sterling silver cup with a small dent to the lip. The name "Rose Angela" was etched with great flourish on the front of it.

Zoe was painfully aware of the sale of the seventeen other cups. Because they had been priced so inexpensively, most sold immediately. She also considered that Melissa, due to her successful operation, might regret selling off her entire collection.

"I can't let that one go. I'm sorry."

"What do you mean?" protested the woman.

As Zoe reached to take the cup from her hand, the woman pulled it toward her belly. It was then that Zoe noticed that she was well into a pregnancy.

"Oh...when are you due?" Zoe asked.

The woman beamed. "Four months. It's a girl."

"Congratulations."

As Zoe spoke, the pregnant woman rotated the cup in her hand until the name on it was visible to both of them. "Her name's going to be Rose Angela."

"What?" she asked, as if she didn't hear her correctly.

"Rose Angela," the woman said again. "After my grand-mother."

Zoe's mind flashed back to Christopher and the previous Brimfield. "The object finds you..." he had said to her as they sat on the edge of Route 20, sipping lemonade and watching people walk by with their newest treasures. Just as her Pietà had found her, Zoe thought. And how Melissa's baby cups had found her when she needed them most. And now, how her partner's last cup, inscribed "Rose Angela," had identified someone more in need of its magic than Melissa.

Zoe took a deep breath at the thought of such a grand plan. "Rose Angela," she said, smiling broadly at the woman. "Well, in that case, I'd say that cup's been waiting for you to take it home."

Melissa was in a post-operative state of consciousness, dozing in and out of reality as Zoe sat and held her hand.

"Where's Brad?" Melissa asked dreamily.

"At home. He wanted to come in with me but I talked him out of it. I told him I wanted to spend some time alone with my partner."

Melissa managed a smile.

"He'll be here first thing in the morning."

"I think everything's going to work out between us, Zoe."

Zoe squeezed her hand and prayed that Brad would come to his senses. "I'm sure it will."

For the next forty-five minutes, Zoe sat with her and did most of the talking. She told her about the sale of the last baby cup, and how that was surely a sign that they no longer needed to play a role in Melissa's life—that she was now free and clear to accept or reject Brad on her own terms, without reference to failed pregnancies or other one-sided marital expectations.

Zoe talked until Melissa gave in to her grogginess. Once she was sound asleep, Zoe left and found the bank of pay phones in the main lobby. The unpredictability of life, so poignantly demonstrated by Melissa's illness, made Zoe want to make the most of her own moments. She dialed Joanna's number.

After two rings, her daughter picked up. "Hello?"

"It's me."

"Mom," she sounded surprised. "Are you home? I just tried to call you."

"I'm in with Melissa."

"And?"

"She's going to be fine. At least that's what I've been told," she qualified. "Even if they find that the tumor was malignant, they feel confident they got all of it."

"Thank God," Joanna said with relief. "That one hit too close to home...I've been thinking about what I would do if that ever happened to you."

"I know what you're saying, Jo. It surfaced some feelings in me, too. Hey...what are you doing? Want to get together for a drink?"

"I'd love to. I need to talk to you about Ramon. That's why

I called."

"Is everything all right?"

Joanna hesitated before she spoke. "Yeah."

The two embraced warmly when they met up at the Black Rose, a bar located on the fringe of Faneuil Hall Marketplace. Although it was crowded, they found a table. Zoe immediately lit a cigarette.

"That's no way to act after just leaving a hospital," Joanna said. "You'd think the environment alone would scare you enough to stop."

"Everyone has to have at least one bad habit. That's the law," Zoe joked.

"I suppose."

Before they could continue, the waitress arrived to take their order. Joanna ordered a glass of white wine. Zoe asked for a Diet Coke. Rather than say anything while the waitress was still there, Joanna waited until she left to acknowledge her mother's choice of beverage.

"Diet Coke?"

"The new me," she smiled. "Now you can't accuse me of not listening to you, can you?"

Joanna looked at her mother with pride. "Enjoy your cigarette, Mom."

Zoe took a long drag. "So what's up with Ramon? Are we on again, or off again?"

"It's over," she said with little emotion.

Zoe regretted her flippant attitude. "How so?"

"All along, I've been waiting for him to decide what he wants to do. Then I realized that I hadn't asked myself the same question."

"Have you come up with an answer?"

"Yeah. He's not the one, Mom."

"Are you sure?"

"I am." Joanna looked at her intently. "Don't take this the wrong way," she said, "but I know that part of me was worried that I would end up alone like you. I was forcing myself into companionship and marriage. Now that Christopher's in your life, I don't feel that way anymore."

Her mother's heart went out to her. "Joanna, why would you think like that?"

She shrugged like a little girl. "I don't know, Mom. I guess because I never thought that Dad would die. I never imagined you as a widow. When it happened, it scared me."

Zoe reached over the table and took her by the hands. "You know, I spent much too much time worrying about being unfaithful to your father's spirit. And I was doing it for reasons that didn't make sense. Don't do that to yourself, Jo," she said lovingly. "Live your life, honey, not mine or anyone else's."

"I am, Mom." She smiled. "From now on."

On the second day of her hospital stay, a more comfortable and coherent Melissa called Zoe at the shop.

"One Piece Antiques."

Melissa did her best to disguise her voice. "Yes, I'm looking for Italian watercolors. Do you happen to have any in stock?"

"What?"

"Italian watercolors," she said again, as she broke into a giggle.

The familiar laugh gave her away. "Melissa," said Zoe, "what are you doing?"

"Just teasing you, that's all."

"You sound great for someone who just went through what you did."

"I'm sore as hell," she said, "but guess what?"

"What?"

"I'm the exception to the rule, Zoe." She laughed. "I may

be the only woman you'll ever know with a benign tumor."

"You got the pathology report already?"

"Three minutes ago. Can you believe it?"

"Thank God, Melissa. That is such good news!"

"I was sure it was going to come back the other way."

"What did Brad say?"

"I wanted to call you first, Zoe. Anyway," she said, "I might not tell him for awhile."

"What do you mean?"

"I've got to keep that sympathy going for as long as I can," she joked.

The two talked for a couple of minutes until Melissa was interrupted by someone who wanted to look at her incision. "Zoe," she said, "I've got a young doctor here who wants to look at my knife wound. I've got to go."

"Okay, Melissa."

"And Zoe..."

"What?"

"Thanks for being there for me."

"What are partners for?"

If hospitals could perform major surgery at a take-out window, they wouldn't hesitate to do so. In lieu of that, they make sure that no one, from newborn to elderly, overstays their welcome. Within four days, Melissa was released and sent home to begin her recuperation. For the first week she needed assistance around the house, and Brad took the week off from his septic hole business to be by her side. Nursing was a new and intimidating experience for him. If not for his love of Melissa, he could never have withstood the plasmatic, bandage and gauze environment. To his credit, he performed all his duties in a sober fashion.

With the loss of a working partner, Zoe's hours at the shop had become horrendous. She barely had time to stop by and see Melissa on the way home from work each night. When Zoe wasn't in the shop, she was home doing the books or out trying to find more inventory. She wondered how anyone, including Christopher, managed the business on their own.

After two weeks, Zoe was exhausted. Although Melissa had come back for a few hours each day, she was still invalid enough that she was of little help in the shop, leaving Zoe to do most of the work and all of the heavy lifting. Brimfield was only a week away, and it had become obvious to Zoe that Melissa would be unable to make the trip. Judging by her stint of running the shop solo, Zoe doubted if she could handle Brimfield by herself.

She had just finished pushing and rocking an oak icebox into a new space against the wall when Brad dropped Melissa off for the afternoon. The shop was empty of patrons.

"What did you do, Zoe?" asked Melissa, as she looked around the vacant shop, "scare all the customers away?"

"Very funny," she said as she wiped the sweat off her brow. "How do you like where I put the icebox?" she asked, expecting a compliment from the head decorator of the shop.

Melissa squinted. "It's too big for that wall." She pointed to the opposite side. "It should go over there next to the wicker set."

"You put it there, then," snapped Zoe.

Melissa was surprised at her reaction. "Hey, what's wrong?"

"I'm just tired, that's all. Doing it by myself has been a bitch."

Melissa felt guilt come over her. "I'm sorry, Zoe."

Zoe looked at her and realized how selfish she was being. Two weeks before, she was begging God for Melissa's good health, and now she was resentful that she couldn't pull her weight in the shop. She walked over and put her arms around her. "I'm the one who's sorry," she said. "I don't know what I was thinking of."

"I'll be better soon," Melissa promised. "But...I'm not going to be able to go to Brimfield next week."

"I've already figured that out. Melissa...I've been thinking..."

"What?"

"I want to pass on Brimfield this time. I don't think I can do it alone."

Melissa tried to imagine doing it by herself. The thought of it was depressing. "I don't blame you, Zoe. So don't do it. I know I couldn't," she added.

"Thanks, Melissa. I'll tell you what...I'll pay the shop the hundred and fifty bucks we've already paid for the space."

"Don't be ridiculous."

"Are you sure?"

"Of course, Zoe. And don't worry about it. We'll get back to Brimfield in the spring."

"There's one other thing," said Zoe timidly.

"What?"

"I still want to go to Brimfield to be with Christopher for a couple of days...if that's all right with you. The only problem is that I'd have to close the shop on Thursday and Friday. I could pick for us while I'm there."

"Zoe, don't you realize who you're talking to?" laughed Melissa.

Zoe was confused. "What do you mean?"

"You're talking to a woman who, two weeks ago, thought she'd be dead by now. Do you have any idea how my priorities have changed?"

Zoe blushed with embarrassment but didn't say anything.

"Go for the whole week if you want," she yelled. Melissa threw her tiny arms in the air. "I don't give a shit!" The volume of her voice and the flailing of her arms woke up her healing wound and made her wince with pain.

Zoe panicked. "Melissa, are you okay?"

As the pain subsided, a broad smile came over Melissa's face. "I couldn't be better."

14

The September Brimfield show happens during that almost indiscernible blink between summer and autumn in New England. Unlike the May show, which is always sunny, at least in terms of dealer anticipation, or the sweltering July show, hallmarked by legendary, china-breaking afternoon thunderstorms, the September show is best characterized by a sense of immediacy. For many dealers it is the last chance to shore up cash to hold them through the long winter. Although there are indoor shows during the cold months, none are laced with the same possibilities as Brimfield. For some dealers in September, no reasonable offer is refused.

Melissa was both surprised and delighted that Zoe had taken her up on her offer to extend her stay in Brimfield. Instead of just closing Thursday and Friday, Zoe planned to close on Tuesday and Wednesday as well—giving her more time to be with Christopher, and to experience Brimfield from the other side of the display table. In the two previous times that she had set up, selling had been her main preoccupation. She found it difficult to clear her mind enough to really enjoy the outrageousness that occurs when thousands of people come together to find that single object that they believe will forever change things for the better.

The drive up on Tuesday was a leisurely one—Zoe had waited for the rush hour traffic to subside before heading up Route 128 to the Massachusetts Turnpike. By the time she finally arrived in Brimfield, it was eleven o'clock, sunny and about seventy degrees. Route 20 was already deluged with a throng of people walking along the edge of the narrow, two lane road. In spite of dozens of police officers directing traffic and crossing pedestrians, the traffic itself was so thick that people could cross the road with no interruption to the flow.

She found a parking space in the rear of the New England Motel, where she would again make love among the cultural ruins for the next few days. After she parked, she walked west on Route 20 on her way to Dealer's Choice, the field where Christopher had set up for the day. Like many dealers, he would move from field to field during the course of the week, hoping for a fresh batch of customers at each newly opened location.

Although she was anxious to see him, Zoe walked slowly and browsed the booths set up on both sides of the street. She shopped the outskirts for over an hour, and didn't get to Dealer's Choice until most of the heavy buying was over. The crowd was down to a trickle, and the relaxed gait of the patrons indicated that the best bargains had been picked by those racing through when the field first opened.

Christopher was immersed in a book when she arrived at his booth, and didn't notice her standing there watching him. Zoe thought of the first time she saw him, sitting comfortably in a club chair and reading as if he were sitting in front of a fireplace at home.

"Do you like Italian art?" she asked, mimicking some of the

first words he ever spoke to her.

Christopher recognized her voice immediately but decided to play along. Without looking up from his book, he answered. "Only paintings of naked women."

Zoe walked over to where he was sitting. She took one of his hands from the edge of the book and boldly slid it under her blouse, holding it against her warm belly.

Christopher kept his attention on the page.

"Do you like real naked women?" she teased.

"Not as good as the painted ones."

Zoe removed his hand as if to scold him. "Maybe I should find someone who does."

With wrestler's speed, Christopher let go of the book and pinned his arms around her waist and yanked her toward him. Sitting in the chair, his head was at belly-level to her and he buried his face in it, making her screech in faux protest.

"Christopher...people are watching us!"

"That didn't bother you a minute ago," he laughed, pulling his head back and looking up at her. "Hi," he said sweetly.

"Hi,"

He stood up and kissed her. "I'm so glad you're here."

"Me, too."

Within minutes, they returned to normal Brimfield behavior and for the first time, Zoe got a good look at his booth. Unlike the last two Brimfields, his mix for the fall show was more focused, made up of almost all religious art and antiques.

"What did you do, rob a church?" she half-joked.

"It's the stuff I got in New York."

"Oh," she sounded relieved. "Beautiful stuff...how did you do this morning?"

"About twenty-five," he smiled.

"Twenty-five hundred? That's not so great."

"That's thousand, Zoe."

"You're kidding," she said. "How did you do that?"

"I pre-sold a lot of it last week on the phone. Plus," he laughed, "the new millennium's got a lot of people thinking about religion."

"That's unbelievable," she said, taking a new interest in the quality of his merchandise. As she had done before, she walked around his booth and looked at everything. Then she looked into the open back of his rented truck, parked just behind his display space. "Where's the Healy?" she asked, looking into the almost empty cargo area.

"Couldn't fit it this time. This stuff took up more space than I expected."

"That's too bad. I was looking forward to driving you down Route 20 again."

Christopher thought of his first hair-raising ride with her. "It's just as well it didn't fit."

As Zoe continued to poke around at the back of the truck, she noticed a painting inside it. It was the small oil painting of the Holy Family and a donkey. The finger-size rectangular plaque on the frame carried black lettering done by a calligrapher which read, *Flight Into Egypt*. Zoe was immediately taken by the delicate picture. "Where did you get this?" she asked with some urgency.

"It's part of the New York lot."

"I feel like I've seen this before."

"It's in every New Testament, Zoe."

"I know that. I mean...I think I felt this before."

He thought about mentioning his premonition about Brimfield the first time he looked at the painting, but decided it might spoil her stay. "I'm sure it's just your imagination," he assured her. "Or maybe you saw the same picture in a kid's bible or something. Who knows?"

"Are you going to sell it?"

He hesitated. "I'm not sure...that's why I didn't put it out."

"Don't," she said as she put it back in the truck.

"Why not?"

"I don't know Christopher. Just don't sell it."

Carmen Huerto was sitting in his van outside the town-house he was cleaning on Sixty First Street. It was his lunch break, and he was eating a ham and cheese sandwich and looking at the sports section of the newspaper. With all the foot traffic, he barely noticed the two men approach his vehicle.

"Carmen Huerto?"

"Yeah?" he said between bites.

While one man flashed the NYPD emblem, the other quickly opened the door and pulled him out. "You're under arrest. Grand larceny."

"What?"

Without answering him, they cuffed him. They read him his Miranda rights and stuffed him in the back of their car, parked in front of a hydrant just twenty feet away. As he continued to ask why he was being arrested, the car pulled out into traffic and headed for the station.

The interrogation room was hot, stuffy and municipal. While the detectives had the solid oak chairs, Carmen had to sit on a folding metal one that matched his brown jumpsuit. Although no stranger to the law, he was no frequent flyer either. Most of his record consisted of nickel and dime thefts, none of them worth the state's expense of long-term incarceration.

This time was different. The taller of the two detectives explained the situation. "We've been investigating a series of thefts of antiques on the Upper East Side. And guess what?" he smiled.

"What?"

"It seems that all of the thefts happened after the owners

had their carpets cleaned."

"So?"

"By Hassan's Rug Renew. The company you work for. Oddly enough," he added, "according to company records, all of them were your jobs."

"All that proves is that I cleaned a carpet at them places," Carmen argued. "It don't prove nothing else."

"We have fingerprints, Huerto."

He shrugged. "I was there."

"We found your prints in almost every room. On furniture. On objects." He paused. "In rooms without rugs."

Before Carmen had time to respond, two uniformed officers came into the room carrying two identical Pietàs. "We found these in the back of his van when we impounded it," one said.

"What are those, Carmen?" asked the detective.

Carmen put his head in his hands, and immediately regretted not throwing the bronzes in the East River as he had been paid to do. He had kept them in his van with the hope of selling them, but had only unloaded one of them to a flea market dealer in the Bronx.

"You know, if you help us on this, Carmen, it will be better for you."

"Si?" Not unexpected, Carmen thought of himself first. He had no allegiance to Enzo Rinaldi or, for that matter, to anyone else. He would do whatever was necessary to gain even a smidgen of leniency.

"What did you do with the stuff?" he asked. The detective pointed to the bronzes. "Are those part of it?"

Carmen shook his head. "No." Then he told them how the bronzes came into his hands.

After he finished the story of the reproductions, the detectives took him through a series of photographs furnished by the owners of some of the objects reported stolen. While he admitted that he was still in possession of some of them, Carmen also identified four items among the dozen or so pictures, that he had sold to Enzo Rinaldi, including the woodcut print by Albrecht Durer that Enzo had in turn sold to Christopher Doria.

The taller detective took the four photos from Carmen. "Does Rinaldi still have this stuff?"

Carmen shrugged. "Maybe...yo no sé."

Anytime the circus comes to town, the local residents try to sidebar the event and make a few bucks on their own. In the case of Brimfield, all the homeowners lucky enough to live near the fields turn their yards into parking lots. Some even sell barbecue along with parking spaces. As hard as it might be to imagine an urban parking lot offering grilled steak tips, it doesn't look the least bit out of place in Brimfield.

Residents aren't the only ones to share in the windfall. Each Brimfield, the Congregational Church dips into the hungry people pool and offers a comforting church supper in the basement of the classic white building. Since Zoe had never experienced its simplicity, Christopher decided to take her there for dinner. He had also invited Arthur Drake to join them for the evening of ham and beans. Like Christopher, Arthur also spent three weeks a year at Brimfield, and was a much sought after dealer there for the fine Americana that he offered.

Arthur left before dessert to meet a buyer from Pennsylvania, while Zoe and Christopher stayed for coffee, pie, and conversation. Although the hall was crowded and somewhat noisy, their table was isolated from most, and they were able to speak intimately and freely.

"Zoe..."

"Yes?"

"Do you remember when I asked you if you believed in fate?"

Zoe smiled. "It was the first night we made love...in your motel room down the street. Why?"

Christopher looked at her intensely. "I believe we were meant to be together, Zoe. I'm convinced of it. More than that, I want to be with you. For the rest of my life." He reached into his pocket and took out a rumpled paper bag and held it tightly in his hand. "Now that you know my family and faults, I feel like I can finally ask you this." His eyes asked the question even before he spoke. "Will you marry me?" he asked softly. "No," he interrupted himself, "will you be with me? And if marriage is part of it, then fine."

In the din of the room, Zoe wasn't sure that she heard the words correctly.

Before she could respond, he took a ring from the bag. "I bought this on the field for you today," he said, sliding it on her wedding finger. The ring was set in gold but there was no engagement diamond attached. Instead there was a black onyx stone with a delicate clear dome over it.

The same feeling of insecurity that Zoe experienced when Christopher slipped the camisole on her naked body, came over her as he put the ring on her finger. It was as if she were unworthy of such devotion—a wretched widow who had already had her day. Then she thought of the sad unopened nips of liquor at her last house call, half emptied by the march of time.

"It's beautiful, Christopher." She gently rubbed the side of it with her thumb.

"Zoe, I know how much Richard still means to you...that's why I thought this ring was so appropriate. As soon as I saw it, I knew I had to buy it." He hesitated. "It's not your average engagement ring," he said apologetically. "But I hope you'll understand why I bought it for you." He took hold of her left hand. "Look at it closely," he said. "It's a Victorian mourning ring."

She moved her hand slightly toward her face. Under the clear dome she could see a single lock of hair.

"That lock of hair is a memento of the death of a loved one. Zoe," he said with great sincerity, "I don't ever want you to forget Richard. And I promise I will never try to take his place."

Zoe felt overwhelmed with the presence of love. Richard was all around her, so much so that there was no need for him to speak. And Christopher held her hand as if he would never let go.

"Will you be with me, Zoe?"

"Yes." She looked down at the ring and then lovingly at him. "Yes, Christopher, I will."

By Wednesday afternoon, Christopher's name had surfaced in New York. Earlier in the day the police had picked up Enzo Rinaldi, known by his official criminal record as Ralph Rinaldi. In the same interrogation room, he cooperated fully to benefit himself, just like Carmen Huerto had the day before. He told them the story about the reproduction bronzes—where he got them, and how the original had been stolen from a summer home in Camden, Maine. He also told them the names of the dealers that he sold the other stolen pieces to, including the Albrecht Durer woodcut he sold to Christopher. Fortunately for Arthur Drake, the school girl sampler he had bought from Enzo had come from a source other that Carmen Huerto. Naturally, Enzo saw no reason to admit to any illegal activities of which the police were not aware.

By the end of the day, Enzo was free on bail and back on the street. Christopher, hand in hand with Zoe, was blissfully walking the pastures of Brimfield, totally in the dark about the trouble that was brewing.

Around ten-thirty on Thursday morning the Wiscasset Police pulled up in front of Relics. Before they had a chance to knock, one of the officers spotted a piece of paper taped to the inside door. On it was a computer-generated message that told potential customers that the shop would be closed for the week because of Brimfield. The note also apologized for any inconvenience. The two officers left, more disappointed than any customer would have been, and headed back to the station to turn over their duties to Brimfield's finest.

As the wheels of justice continued to turn, so did the merchandise at Brimfield. Christopher was set up on May's, a field that opened to the public at nine on Thursday morning. In the first couple of hours, with Zoe serving as cashier, he took in over eight thousand dollars. During the first lull in business, his cell phone rang.

"Hello?"

"Chris...it's Enzo."

The connection was not a good one. Christopher moved to the outside of his booth to try to get a better signal. "Hello?"

"It's Enzo, Chris. Can you hear me?"

"I can now. What's up?"

"I've got some bad news..."

Although Enzo had unloaded as much of the blame on Christopher as he could to the police, his allegiance to his criminal counterparts prompted him to contact Christopher—to tell him what had happened, as well as to warn him that the police were probably on their way. Even more of a motivation to get in touch with Christopher was the Albrecht Durer woodcut. If he hadn't already sold it, then Enzo wanted it back. Returning it to the authorities would make his situation easier.

Christopher listened without emotion. He had always believed he would be caught again, and he took an almost morbid satisfaction in knowing that his premonition about his trip to Brimfield had been correct. Immediately, he understood the significance of the *Flight Into Egypt*, the painting that initiated his foreboding while he was unpacking the religious lot from New York.

"I appreciate your calling me, Enzo," he said genuinely. "As far as the Durer is concerned, tell the police I sold it to Benjamin Divers. I just sent it to him. He'll have it in a day or two," he said, knowing full well that it was sitting in his inventory room at the motel.

"One other thing, Enzo," he said.

"What?"

"What about the sampler that Arthur bought?"

"Different source," he said. "They know nothing about it."

"Good. I'll let him know."

As soon as he got off the phone, he walked over to Zoe and put his arms around her.

"Who was that?" she asked.

"Fate."

"What are you talking about, Christopher?"

He picked up her left hand and touched the ring he had given her the night before. "Do you really want to be with me, Zoe? No matter what or where?"

"Of course," she said. "Christopher...what's wrong?"

He told her about what had happened and how the police would probably come for him on the field. He also told her, because it was his second offense, that imprisonment was almost guaranteed.

Zoe was devastated. She felt as angry as Melissa had when the discovery of her tumor collided with the long-awaited return of her ex-husband. She started to tremble. "You're going to jail?"

Christopher shook his head. "I don't want to, Zoe...I want to be with you. And I promise that I'll never do anything to jeopardize our relationship." He took her by the hand. "Come with me. I want to show you something."

They walked to the back of the truck and he jumped up into the bay. He grabbed the *Flight Into Egypt* painting. "Remember how you said you felt this painting, Zoe?"

"Yeah?"

"I did too," he said with excitement. "As soon as I saw it, I had a premonition about Brimfield. I knew something was going to happen here."

"Congratulations on your intuition, Christopher," she said nervously. "But how does that change anything?"

"Don't you see, Zoe?" He pointed to the picture.

"See what?"

"Herod's coming," he yelled. He pointed to the donkey. "And this is what we're supposed to do. That's why the picture meant something to both of us, Zoe. It's our chance to start a new life. Do you understand?"

The impact on Zoe was the same as the moment when she first saw the bronze Pietà. She accepted its message without question. "My God, Christopher," she uttered.

He put his arms tightly around her. "Zoe," he said softly, "I promise you an honest and good life."

Zoe looked up at his face and smiled. "I'm with you, Christopher."

Driven by the force of providence, the two of them immediately began to load the truck. They moved quickly and deliberately, in silence. While he worked, Christopher started making a list in his head of loose ends to tie up before they left.

"Hey, what are you doing?" asked the vendor set up next to them. "You can't pack up now. They won't let you."

Neither responded and within ten minutes, the only physical evidence that remained was the grass, now matted and flattened by the objects that had sat on it. Like the fugitives they were, they got into the cab of the truck and carefully began to make their way through the small but still obstructive crowd.

"Where are we going to go, Christopher?"

"I don't know...somewhere. Wherever we're supposed to go," he added with conviction.

Instead of turning right toward the gate, he took a left so he could stop at Arthur Drake's booth. When they arrived, Arthur had just finished up with a customer and was shocked to see his friend in the truck so early into the show.

"What's going on, Guido?"

"Enzo got nailed and turned them onto me."

Arthur turned pale.

"You're fine," Christopher assured him. "It's the bronzes and the Durer they know about."

"I'm sorry, Christopher," said Arthur. "Where are you going to go?"

"I don't know. I'll let you know when we get there."

"What can I do for you?" Arthur asked.

"As soon as we leave, get Zoe's stuff out of the room so no one will ever know that she was there with me."

"Okay."

"And Enzo wants the Durer back. I told him that I sold it to Divers and that the police could get it from him."

"You sold it to Divers?" he said in astonishment. "After what he did to you?"

"Of course not." Christopher smiled. "It's in the motel room, so grab it when you get Zoe's stuff. Then Fed-Ex it to Divers overnight from me. He doesn't know anything about what's happened and he's just greedy enough to keep it or sell it."

Arthur grinned widely at the thought of the police at Benjamin Diver's door. "You dog, Guido."

"I thought you'd like that."

"What about the rest of your inventory at the motel? Want me to get that?"

"Too risky, Arthur. Luckily, there's not much there, but I'll have to leave it." Christopher shook his head. "The same goes for the shop. I'm sure they'll be looking for me there."

"I wish I could help."

"It's okay, Arthur. That's why they call it starting over," he joked. Christopher turned to Zoe. "Zoe, give me the keys to your van."

"Sure." She took them out of the oversized canvas bag that her daughter had given her when she started in the business. She removed the van keys from the ring and handed them to him.

"Get her van back to Noble's Cove. It's parked in the lot behind the motel."

"The shop's name is on the side, Arthur," said Zoe.

"No problem. Anything else?"

"Yeah," said Christopher. "I'll get rid of the stuff in the truck, and I'll make sure you get your share out of it."

"I trust you," he smiled.

Christopher looked at Zoe and spoke with urgency. "We've got to go."

"Okay."

Christopher reached through the window and hugged Arthur.

"Are you going to be all right?" asked Arthur.

"Fine." Christopher paused. "And Arthur..."

He knew the topic by the tone of his voice. "Peter, right?"

Christopher nodded.

"Don't worry. I'll take care of him until I hear from you."

"I may need your help in relocating him at some point... once we get settled, anyway."

"I can supply anything from real paramedics to fake passports," he quipped.

"Thanks." Christopher sounded relieved.

Arthur walked to the other side of the cab and hugged Zoe. "He's a good man, Zoe."

She smiled. "He'll do."

Their truck slowly reentered the lane, peppered with pedestrians, and then turned right onto the gravel road that would take them to the exit and the safety of Route 20. As they crawled along, Christopher spotted two members of the Brimfield Police walking in tandem toward them. "There they are," he said, pointing them out to Zoe.

Zoe panicked. "Do they see us?"

Just as she asked, the two men took a right at the row where Christopher had been set up just fifteen minutes before.

"We're okay," he said, watching them disappear from sight.

As Christopher and Zoe pulled out into the bumper-to-bumper traffic of Route 20, they watched the thousands of people walk along with their treasures. One woman pulled a red wagon loaded with vintage metal toy cars, trucks, and motorcycles. Another used a two-wheeled shopping cart to carry her collection of antique parasols. There was a young man with a stuffed chimpanzee over his head, a Tarzan of a different jungle. And another with a full-size naked manikin of a woman that he held onto by breast and butt.

All of them found what they were looking for at Brimfield. Among the millions of items on display there, each person had encountered that elusive, tactile thing that each believed would make life more complete. Or at least that's what all those people wanted to believe. While most would love their objects forever, some would get them home and find an unforgivable scratch or dent that they hadn't noticed in the enthusiasm of their purchase. Others would become disinterested when they found an even better example of their obsession. Still others would be enraged to find out that what they bought was a forgery, with no recourse on the empty post-Brimfield acres.

But as always, one thing leads to another. Most objects are not the answers themselves, but merely clues on where to find them. For Zoe, that object was a reproduction bronze Pietà that shamelessly played on her devotion to her departed husband. But what she ended up with, where it lead her, was worth it in the end. She found another man whom she realized she could love as much and as wholly as Richard—something she never thought possible. Following the Pietà like crumbs through a forest, she had found Christopher at Brimfield. Just as she was, he too was flawed, but far from fake.

15

Melissa pulled into her booth space with as much hope as any dealer at Brimfield. And with good reason. She had her health back. She also had her husband back, who had managed to stay both sober and faithful for eight months. They had remarried on Valentine's Day, and Brad had already proven to be a better husband the second time around—acutely sensitive to her needs and how he could fill them. He had even agreed to do Brimfield with her, and was experiencing the same shock that she had on her first trip the previous May.

"Holy shit, 'Lis," he said as he got out of the van. "I can't believe you and Zoe did this by yourselves. This is goddam scary," he said, watching the crowds streaming along Route 20.

"It was pretty intimidating the first time," she laughed. "But I'm used to it now."

Brad looked at her with admiration. "I give you a lot of credit, 'Lis."

"I couldn't have done it without Zoe." Melissa gazed out at the sea of people. "It's not going to be the same without her," she said sadly.

Brad put his beefy arms around her "I'll do the best I can."

The shock of seeing Brimfield for the first time was nothing compared to the overwhelming trauma Brad suffered as the gates opened and hundreds of people converged on their booth.

"Hurry up, Brad," ordered Melissa. "Get the stuff out of the van."

"This is fucking crazy," he grunted as he single-handedly picked up a four-drawer pine bureau and then put it on the ground right outside the van.

"Put it out at the front of the booth," she directed him. "And watch your language," she said sternly, and then smiled. "One Piece Antiques is a class operation."

For the next hour, Brad got a workout that he had never experienced on the comfortable seat of his backhoe. As soon as the crowds subsided, he plopped himself down in the only painted country chair that hadn't sold. "I don't know how you do it, 'Lis. I'd much rather be digging shit holes."

Melissa was counting the cash. "I love it. Look at this," she said as she fanned the bills.

"How much?"

"Over two grand in cash," she said.

"Whoa!"

Melissa stuffed the money in her jeans. "I'm going to go off and pick for awhile, Brad."

"You're going to leave me here alone?" he asked with alarm.

She looked around the field. "The crowd's thinned out. You'll be fine."

"What if a customer comes? What should I do?"

Melissa looked at her ditch digger husband and smiled. "Sell them something, honey." She turned and walked out of the booth. "I'll be back in an hour or so."

"Don't get lost," he said sincerely.

"Don't you."

As she trudged through the aisles of booths in May's, she thought of her first Brimfield and how she had been afraid to stray too far from her own. Then she remembered how Zoe couldn't wait to venture out and pick the field, and how she had come back with the Pietà that started her on an even longer adventure. Melissa smiled to herself as she put her hand in her pocket to make sure the two thousand in cash was still there—to make sure that Zoe hadn't somehow snuck in her pocket and used the shop's money for some other icon of love.

With her thoughts of Zoe, she meandered around for an hour and even bought a few smalls for the shop. As she was paying for a painted, primitive document box, something familiar caught her eye in the next space. As soon as she finished the transaction, she went over and stood in front of the booth. "Oh my God," she said out loud. She walked into the booth and immediately picked up the object. It was a bronze Pietà, exactly like Zoe's. She rotated it in her hands and wondered if it could be hers.

"That's nice, isn't it?" offered the young dealer who owned it. "It was done by Bellini. Quite a good sculptor," he added. "The dealer price is fifteen hundred."

"Where did you get it?" she asked, without taking her eyes off of it.

"Sometimes you get lucky. I found it at a flea market in the Bronx of all places. The guy had no idea what he had," he laughed.

"I saw one just like it before."

"I doubt it. His work is pretty rare."

As Melissa continued to hold the bronze, her thoughts about Zoe intensified as if she were standing right beside her. She could feel her presence on the field. "I'll pass," she said as she put it down and grabbed her plastic bag of smalls.

"I can do a little better on the price," he said, as she briskly walked out of the booth.

"No thanks."

Trying not to run, Melissa quickly made her way back to her booth. When she was about forty feet from it, she noticed a couple coming toward her from the opposite direction. Before she was even close enough to recognize them, she instinctively knew it was Zoe and Christopher. She broke into a full run and yelled her name as loud as the intercom on the field. "Zoe!"

Along with everyone else in the general area, Zoe heard her name and spotted Melissa running toward her. She, too, began to run and the two women met and embraced almost right in front of Melissa's rented space.

"God, I've missed you," cried Melissa.

Zoe held her by the shoulders and extended her arms so she could see her. "Look at you, Melissa. You look great! You've put on weight," she said, as she stroked her full fore-arms. Then she gently cupped Melissa's cheeks. "And your face shines," she said. "No makeup?" she laughed as she looked closely at her eyes.

"I don't need it anymore, Zoe," she said as she looked toward Brad.

As Christopher joined them, Melissa threw her arms around his chest and laid her head against it. "Christopher, it's so good to see you."

"You too, Melissa. It's been a long time."

Brad was standing there looking rather left out. Zoe walked over and hugged him. "It's good to see you, Brad. I'm glad you two are still together."

"We're doing great."

"You must really love her if you agreed to do Brimfield with her," she laughed.

"I do, Zoe," he said sincerely.

Melissa was ecstatic over the homecoming. "So how's Rome?"

"It's as beautiful as I remembered it when Richard and I went there," said Zoe. Unconsciously, she rubbed her mourning ring as well as the wedding band next to it as she spoke.

"The Doria's of Rome," laughed Melissa.

Christopher put his arm around Zoe. "It's Christopher and Zoe Bellini now," he laughed. "We thought because of how we met that Bellini was the perfect name. Want to check our passports?"

"Bellini? You're not going to believe what I just saw." Melissa proceeded to tell them about the Bellini Pietà she saw for sale and asked if it was Zoe's.

"Mine's in our apartment in Rome," said Zoe. "Arthur sent it over after we got settled."

"It's probably just one that got away. I'm sure it will be making the rounds for years to come," Christopher said philosophically.

For the next hour, the two couples sat on the ground in the booth and exchanged stories. Christopher and Zoe talked enthusiastically about La Patina, the antique shop they had opened in Rome, and their antique web site on the Internet—enterprises that provided them with enough to live modestly. Between the store and the Internet, there was also enough income to take care of Christopher's brother, who, with Arthur's help, had been moved to a small rehabilitation center just outside of Rome.

"And how's Joanna?" asked Melissa. "Has she found anybody yet?"

"She's great. She came out here to have dinner with us last night." Zoe laughed. "She said she's seeing three different guys right now."

"Good for her."

"How's it working out with Elliot?" asked Zoe.

"Well, it's not like having a partner," she said regretfully. "But when you left, he was glad to rent half the space. So he has his stuff and I have mine. At least he's someone to help lift the heavy pieces. By the way, Zoe," she asked, "have you seen him? He's set up on the field."

"I thought we'd stop before we leave. We want to see Arthur Drake, too."

"Do you have time for lunch?" asked Melissa.

"Unfortunately not," said Christopher. "We got here yesterday and bought every good European antique we could find. Now we've got a plane to catch." He looked at Zoe. "We really do have to go," he said, punctuating his words by getting up from the ground.

"Okay," she said reluctantly.

Zoe and Melissa stood up at the same time and hugged each other tightly.

"I wish you were still my partner, Zoe," she said sadly.

Zoe's eyes misted up as she thought of all the hours they had spent together learning the business—the two of them huddled in the back of dingy auction halls, the wild goose chase house calls they had gone on, their scrounging through yard sales full of plastic furniture and discount store, household junk. Most of all, Zoe thought of how Melissa had been there for her at the time she needed a friend most. In the depths of the death of her husband, Melissa had invited her to become a partner in a small, inconsequential antique shop. Zoe was convinced that not only did that invitation save her life at the time, but was also responsible for the happiness she now had. "Melissa," she whispered lovingly. "I will always be your partner."

As the two walked out of the booth, Zoe turned around to see Melissa once more. In spite of the tears streaming down her face, she smiled. "See you here in July, Melissa."

Melissa nodded. "July, Zoe."

Brimfield is an epic place that indelibly touches everyone who has ever had the good fortune to experience it. Each year, there are newcomers who, in spite of being forewarned, are not prepared for all that Brimfield holds. Then there are the regulars— those who will be part of its fabric until they can no longer walk the endless aisles of objects of the heart. There is the one-legged man who searches out heavy cast iron cookware. The woman with a cardboard sign soliciting sewing spool cabinets. The man who only buys poker chips, playing cards, and gambling accessories. The man who walks quickly past the booths saying variations of the same sentence over and over again. "Any fireworks? Got any fireworks stuff?" And of course, there's Zoe and Christopher. They're the striking couple from Rome buying only European antiques, with an accent on the religious, the mystical. You'll recognize them by the love that seems to surround them as they walk the show. A love that oddly enough, they found at Brimfield. A love that is arguably, the greatest find ever to occur on that field of dreams.